Welcome to peaceful Marchbank, Scotland ... where people are suddenly being discovered with their throats slashed in a most inhuman manner.

DI Armistead and his faithful cohorts, Fabe Finnie and the incongruously beautiful DI Linda Ferris, are up to their elbows in superstitious Scots, suspected werewolves, and vice girls, as they try to unravel truth from hysteria in this latest of Liz Laighton's Marchbank series.

"A bewildering series of murders ... a great read"
- Maureen V. Ross

"Finally, a police procedural that is really different! Liz Laighton creates a world of her own in the rural community of Marchbank ...a healthy dose of gritty reality, leavened with wry humor"

MORE MARCHBANK MYSTERIES
FROM LIZ LAIGHTON:

A Killer Close at Hand

Hideous Gifts

The Moon and I

Liz Laighton

𝓜

Mimesis Publishing

**MYS
Pbk**

THE MOON AND I
Copyright © 2011 Liz Laighton
All rights reserved

This novel is a work of fiction. All characters appearing in this work are fictitious, and any resemblance to real persons, living or dead, is purely coincidental.

Published by Mimesis Publishing,
419 Lafayette Street, New York, NY 10003.

Typeset in Palatino and Broadway.
Designed by Annie Lamb and Ben Middleman.
Cover Art by Ruth Channing.

First Edition

ISBN 978-1-61364-761-5

THE MOON AND I

If I had put on any other shape than a wolf's she would not have seen me, for that is what is growing to be her own shape inside of her.

George MacDonald

Prologue

THE BREEZE from the spruces had died before dawn but the scent loitered: resin and mushrooms, sawdust and two-stroke oil and a deer carcase, much visited by foxes. She knew that carcase well enough. She lay quiet awhile, then lowered her head to clean between her fore-toes.

Her feet were healing. They'd carried her far from the place where she had lived, where fire had one day come and set her free. It was hard work being free. You had to hunt continually and live on field-mice. She could hear one now, high up on the scale of audible frequencies; but she'd eaten her fill.

The sun was growing stronger. The dawn-wind rose, blowing back to her from the places where men's houses stood rank on rank. It carried the small sounds that men make in the morning, and more smells. Flowers, cut grass, bacon, smoke; tar, paint, weedkiller, motor-cars; and dogs, many, many dogs, which made her lonely. Dogs smelled good, but when she tried to approach them they smelled of fear. She thought about howling to let her loneliness run out. But not here, not now: not with men so near.

As she worked on the other set of fore-toes her eyes closed to slits. Her tongue slowed down. It was time to sleep. This was a good place; she had thick brushwood at her back and the breeze would warn her if anything came. The breeze....

There was blood on the wind. She stopped licking and lay, chin on her forepaws, watching.

3

one

August

TRACY WISEMAN knew better than to have a favourite time of day.
All times were good. Secretly, though, she liked early mornings
best; so when she went to keep her appointment at half past
eight, she'd been up for nearly three hours.

The man she was meeting lived in a countrified corner of
town. He'd lately moved in and he wanted advice on interior
decorating. They were meeting at eight-thirty so that he'd have
time to get off afterwards to his work, so he said.

Tracy wondered at that, but not seriously. She hadn't told
Frank about this, it was true: he'd be sure to get the wrong idea.
But that was just Frank. He worried a lot. This was what she
did, interior design; it was a business appointment. People start
early these days, Tracy reasoned, how else can they fit things
in?

Never mind that the chap was living alone, never mind that
he'd have to show her all over the house. People worry too
much. We should trust one another.

St Margaret's Lane was waking up. Tracy could smell bacon
frying. She walked in the road, for this stretch of the lane had
no pavements; a newspaper-boy whirred up behind her on his
bicycle and slewed to a halt beside the next gate, stuffing the
paper into an enamelled green letterbox. He rode on, breaking
into tuneless song.

Tracy stepped over a puddle. The morning was fresh and
still, for it was August and most of the little birds were silent.

Sycamore leaves were a leathery green, and on some birches Tracy caught a hint of gold: all seasons are good.

His house was next.

No one answered the bell; she could hear it winding away somewhere within. She tried it again after a count of twenty: no footsteps, nothing. She listened.

Her client's house was large and made of brick. Like other houses in the lane it stood in ample grounds, with great old trees. Thick hawthorn hedges enclosed it. There's no light, Tracy thought. It's dark as a pocket in this garden.

She knocked for a change, then rattled the flap on the door. She lifted the flap and peeked in but saw only the glass-paned inner door some feet before her nose. They were pretty doors, varnished spruce, with brass fittings: but boring. She took hold of the handle.

The door wasn't locked. Tracy stood in the entry and contemplated the inner door with its secretive frosted glass. She should rap on this one too for awhile, she knew: but she opened it instead. The house was quiet.

'Mr Beames?' she called, up the carpeted stairs.

To her right, off the hallway, was an open door to some dim curtained room. The passage ahead of her, beyond the stairs, might lead to a kitchen or some sort of dining-room where Beames could be having breakfast. On the other hand he could be upstairs taking a shower: or maybe the lazy git was still in bed and missing this lovely day.

'Mr Bee-eames....'

She stepped in, leaving the two front doors wide open to the morning. Her business was with interiors, after all. She might as well get a feel for the place while she was here, and take some photographs.

Surprisingly light, this foyer, she thought, peering through her SLR. The low sun must have found some small crack in the greenery outside. Then, the previous owners or someone had been clever enough to use pale shades on the walls and ceiling. Tracy needed the light, because flash would be out of the question.

There: another bit of nonverbal thinking. Delicious to reason by instinct alone. But there must be a reason nevertheless. Why would it be out of the question?

Because of the picture. Of course. The gilt-framed monstrosity there on the wall. The glass was reflective.

So Beames had just moved here, but already he had pictures up. Could he really be into such stuff, she wondered, with bracken and sheep and what looked like a thoroughly hydrophobic dog? Surely not.

Back in the doorway, against the light, something moved: a robin. It hopped along the step just outside, its head cocked, then stopped and thrust its beak into some invisible crevice.

'Good morning birdie boo,' said Tracy.

The bird tried the crevice again, pulled out a wriggly black thing, and swallowed, wriggling itself a little, with its head tipped back. Then it hopped out of sight round the door-frame. Tracy turned back to her hallway with a sigh, and began to photograph aspects of the interior.

Beyond the stairs the passage did, in fact, lead to a dining-room. It also made a right-angle bend towards what must be the kitchen. Once more Tracy called for Mr Beames; she knocked on the open door of the dining-room, too, but no one answered.

Then she heard a sound behind her and swung round. The hallway was deserted. There was the open door, the blank front step. But something was on the stairs.

It was the robin.

'Get out of this,' she said in alarm. 'You silly bird.'

But as she rounded the bottom of the staircase the robin took wing. It flitted upwards and out of sight. 'Damn and bugger it,' Tracy said.

She looked up the staircase. The bloody bird had vanished. 'Mr Beames!' she called. 'Hey, is anybody there!'

The hell with him. She went up two steps at a time, her camera bouncing about like a stone. There was a landing, a hallway, bedroom doors or whatever and more stairs climbing away to her right. But thank heavens, the bloody robin had perched on some nondescript lump of furniture opposite the landing and was watching her with its head on one side.

'Now now,' said Tracy, advancing. Birdie took off and whizzed past her ear. Don't go up, you sod, she thought, moving towards the upper stairs. But it didn't go up. There was a window at the end of the passage and the bird flew straight against the glass, with a bump that set Tracy's teeth on edge.

Got ya now, she thought, seeing it sit up safe and whole on the sill. She reached with both hands cupped but the creature was too quick. It brushed her hand and zipped down the hall towards the bedrooms.

Quite sure now that there was no one home, Tracy hurried along the passage. One door stood ajar and she pushed it to look in: a bathroom. The bird wasn't there. She withdrew and prowled on.

At the end of the passage was another open door, and beyond it, an open window. So that's that, she thought, he's got out. Thank....

Goodness, where's Beames, with his flaming window wide open?

She'd paused with her hand on the lumpish object: a washstand, out of place and grotesque, with polished mahogany knobs on its corners. She had hold of one of these knobs and she found she was squeezing it rhythmically. She let go, and walked towards the open door.

There were sounds from the room, very faint: tiny clicks, whispers, scuffling. Tracy tried to say 'Mr Beames' again but instead she swallowed. All she could see of the room from here was the window with a chair beneath, and some sort of wardrobe to one side. The door hid everything else.

All at once, from somewhere out of sight, the robin sang its brief sweet song and then fell silent. There were no more sounds: nothing animal, nothing human. Tracy stepped into the room.

The robin was on the bed. He'd been there only a minute, certainly not three; but already his feet had overprinted the pale blue coverlet with red, three delicate toes forward and one back, like asterisks pulled long. He'd hopped through an enormous pool of blood which lay, unabsorbed, in the hollow made by a naked man half on and half off the pillows. The man's head was thrown back, his eyes and mouth were open;

his throat gaped with a vast and complex wound. The robin had been probing, tempted by something that glittered. Now he flew to the window and fell out of sight into the air.

Tracy thought, I'm supposed to call someone now. And I will, I will.

When the robin returned and alighted on the sill, Tracy went downstairs. She took out her phone.

'Frank,' she said, 'Frankie.' Her throat was tight all of a sudden but she went on, 'You know how your sister loves murders.'

* * *

'Crank it up a bit for God's sake, Guin,' Frank Catto said. 'She could be in danger.'

'The guy's dead,' said his sister. She glanced at the dashboard, then back to the road. 'I can't help this traffic.'

'Could be a psycho in the house. In the garden. You know that neighbourhood.'

'I do,' Guin said. 'It has very few psychos. And Fabe's on his way. So –'

'Fabe,' said Frank. 'Thank God I'll be getting to her before he does.'

Funny, Guin thought. I never thought before about a psycho lurking. 'It's OK Frankie,' she said. 'It'll be OK.'

'Tracy's had enough shit from the polis,' said Frank. He was leaning forward, hotching about, willing her to go faster. He'd been speaking to himself.

It's strange, Guin thought, swinging the pickup at last into St Margaret's Lane. There was really a murderer living here, only a year ago. A killer lived here in the house where we used to play. Then Fabe's boss was attacked and nearly died. Why don't I think about things like these? Am I crazy?

'Come on, come on,' said Frank. He was ready to climb out of the cab at twenty-five miles an hour. 'Tracy....'

Tracy was standing in the road. She waved, and skipped to the passenger door as the pickup halted. Frank tumbled into her arms. Guin drove on a few feet, pulled over, got out. She looked up at the hawthorn hedge.

8

'Gloomy old place.'

'Gloomy old neighbourhood,' said her brother. 'I hate it.'

'I don't,' said Tracy, 'I love these old trees. Oh Frankie, it's so, so good to see you.'

Like Guin, Detective Sergeant Fabe Finnie never thought about the psycho lurking. He was a big guy, tall, bony, a bit hatchety about the face and with eyes of a disturbing blue. Up to now the psychos, if that's what they were, had kept out of his way.

Fabe was ahead of the squad of mixed experts, the ambulance, pathologist, and SOCO team. Even his colleagues DI Armistead and DC Linda Ferris were out on another call. He was alone in the blue-and-lime-green patrol car and he grinned to himself: fly, fly, to the side of that fair maiden, Guin's useless brother's girlfriend, for she is in distress.

Except she's not, he realised as Tracy came in sight: she's not in distress, she's in love. He knew all about being in love: it transcended mere corpses. Tracy and Frank were holding hands now, and there, sniffing round the gateposts, for all the world like her own big dog which for once she'd left at home, there was his Guinevere.

She straightened up. She'd seen him. He slowed to a stop, put the window down. She had a caterpillar on her nose. She was smiling at him.

DI Armistead and DC Ferris were in Armistead's car, sitting at some of Hornbridge's rare traffic lights, when they got the call.

'Hell's teeth,' Armie said. 'Marchbank again.'

'St Margaret's Lane again,' said Linda.

'What did you make of that girl back there, Linda?'

'She's telling the truth.'

The lights changed. Armie took the road out of town. 'She might be too,' he said. 'The truth… or bits of it.'

'She looked awful,' said Linda. 'She's actually very pretty, you know? I mean I've seen her looking better.'

Beauty, Armie thought: how fragile it is. Linda Ferris herself was beautiful and looking at her usually cheered him up, but not now, with the sight of the beat-up vice girl in his mind.

'Put her in hospital,' he said, 'I hope he's proud of himself.'

'You don't mean the boyfriend.'

'I mean whoever. But....' He slowed, pulled in behind a tractor hauling a trailer loaded with grain. 'Can't see a bloody thing here. Bloody harvest.' He nosed out and stomped on the throttle, surging past the tractor. 'Sorry. See me, I like to live dangerously.... So. This girl, she's banged up in the hospital, she didn't call us in, they did. See what I'm saying?'

'Nnn.... Not exactly, no.'

'If she'd filed a complaint and said it wasn't the boyfriend, I'd say it wasn't the boyfriend. But she hasn't filed a complaint, you see, this is the thing.'

They drove for awhile in silence. Linda looked out the window at the beginnings of Marchbank, the scattered bungalows, the new estate. Presently Armie shifted his gears ferociously and said, 'Good thumping. How I hate that expression.'

'Who said good thumping?' Linda said.

'The guy who thumped her. Or he will say it when we find him. They all do, hadn't you noticed?'

They were through the centre of Marchbank. There was St Margaret's Church on its eminence, and the leafy lane was coming up.

* * *

The pool of blood, the naked corpse, Fabe noted without emotion. It wasn't until he looked in the dead man's address book that he felt faint.

'Armie,' he said, sinking into the chair that stood before the open window.

'Careful,' said his boss absently, peering under the bed, 'mind the forensic.... What's wrong?'

'It's this, the little black book.'

'Fabe,' Armie said, 'what are you doing? I don't know what I'm going to tell the SOC people. Fingerprints –'

'Bugger fingerprints, Armie, look.'

Armie took the book from him, shielding the imagined fingerprints with a handkerchief. It was in fact blue: a tiny book stuffed with names and telephone numbers and in many cases, addresses too. But the names were those of women.

'Tracy Wiseman,' said Armie. 'I see what you're saying, aye.'

'Turn back.'

'Well, if it… ah. I see what you're saying.'

'What's he doing with her? Why's she in there?'

'Misspelled it,' said Armie.

'That's no comfort.'

Gwen Catto, it said on the page before the one where Tracy's name appeared. Catto and Sons Motor Cycles Ltd, The Hornway. Tel 700333…. 'Hasn't got her home number,' Armie said, 'that's one comfort. And the fellow's dead.'

'If this is his!'

'Calm down Fabe. That's an order. And keep your paws off things – here's SOCO now, thank God, whatever kept 'em? And the doctor.'

Dr Greig, at the head of the stairs, held up his hand, and the white-suited figures behind him paused. 'Won't be a sec,' he told them. 'Armie. Lovely morning. Fabe! Had a shock?'

'Guin's all right, Fabe, you've seen her with your own eyes,' Armie said. 'You go downstairs, give these guys some room.'

'Why's she in his book?' Fabe said plaintively as he went out. But he left the little book with Armie.

'Dead,' said the doctor. 'Official. Oh look, did you see these?'

Armie bent over the pillow. Greig held the head gently, grasping the hair: both men could see a glitter on the pillowcase, a slender shard of glass.

'And here, look,' said the doctor. There was glass in the hair. 'Here, smacked on the head. With a bottle? Decanter?'

'Why not?' said Armie. 'Why not bottle? It's simpler. Except there's no broken bottle around. So – cause of death. The blow didn't kill him, did it.'

'No. The wound killed him. He's been cut while alive.'

'Knocked out?'

'Quite likely, at least, for a moment.'

'A long moment,' Armie said. 'Weapon the bottle? The hypothetical bottle.'

'Aye,' said the doctor, 'if it's simpler.'

Late that morning, at Hornbridge police station, the detectives studied the little blue book. It seemed stuffed with possibilities. But the first two pages were missing, sliced out.

'This book's a gift,' Linda said. 'We interview these women, we must get something.'

'Right! We'll interview the women.' Armie got up from the corner of his desk where he'd been sitting. 'But…. That wound. Was that a woman?'

'What do you mean was that a woman?' Fabe said. 'Was that a human being, that's what you ought to ask. Though obviously it was.'

'Linda?' said Armie. 'What do you say? Gouge a guy's throat out – you happy with that?'

'I am a woman, Armie,' said Linda, 'but I've never actually wanted to kill anyone. So I don't know. You're not being logical.'

'OK,' said Armie, 'I'm not, you're right. And as you say, we must get something from the women. Read 'em out to me would you? I'm going to draw up a table.' He went to the whiteboard. 'Start with the last one.'

'Arlene Third,' said Linda. 'I know her. She's a cow.'

'The night-club owner,' said Fabe.

'Tracy Wiseman, did her this morning. Zoe D. A mobile number. Zoe D, that's our little tart!'

'What do you mean your little tart?' Fabe said.

Armie was writing: night clubs, tart; he rubbed out 'tart' and put 'sex worker' instead. 'We saw her this morning. Got beaten up. Zoe Davis, quite a coincidence, if it's her.'

'Marianne Donald,' Linda went on, 'Springholm, Horn Crescent --'

'Barmaid,' Fabe said. 'Barmaid at the Crown.'

'Nikki Cowie. Oo. I know Nikki Cowie, she's a technician at the school,' Linda said. 'Ena Millar, 17 Newlands….'

'Slow down,' Armie said. 'Newlands, OK. That's Ena the clerk at the post office, isn't it.'

'Brenda Ritchie. Ritchie. There's a teacher named Ritchie, aye this is the one…. Ann Ferguson, Beechfield, Cot-town, Hornbridge.'

'Don't know her,' Armie said.

There were eighteen women. The first one in the book, after the missing pages, had an Edinburgh phone number. The rest were local: Marchbank or Hornbridge, except for two, one at Whixton and one out on the Kirkton road.

'Edinburgh,' Armie said. 'That's where he's come from.'

'Where his bank statements came from,' said Fabe. The SOC men had been sending boxes of evidence back from the murder house all morning.

'Right, Portobello wasn't it?' said Armie. 'Right. Suppose the missing entries will be Edinburgh too. Not that that'll bring 'em back to life.'

But they'd get in touch with Edinburgh later. Meantime they parcelled out the local names for interviews. Armie would do Marchbank because Linda didn't get on with Mrs Third, and he'd take in Kirkton and Whixton. Linda and Fabe would split Hornbridge. 'Meet you here,' Armie said. He flung open the door, dived through it and ploughed into Detective Superintendent Marshall. 'Bob,' he said, 'hell's teeth, why didn't you knock?'

'Come in my office a minute Armie.'

'Sorry Bob. Got to do Marchbank.'

'Delegate, delegate!' Bob said. 'You've two fine officers here.'

'See you in a bit,' Linda called as she trotted down the corridor.

'I'm off, Armie,' Fabe said. 'Morning, chief.'

'Still got to do Marchbank,' Armie muttered as he followed Bob Marshall into his office.

They sat. 'Listen, Armie.... Do what in Marchbank? Sorry, I only just got in.'

'Did they really not tell you? A murder. Guy with his throat cut in St Margaret's Lane.'

'Oh I see,' Bob said, 'that's why everyone has that sparkle this morning.'

'I have to interview seven women from his little black book. Seven women, Bob, I really ought to get moving....'

'Sit down. Sit. This won't take long. Or at least I certainly hope not.' Bob had his back to the window, Armie was facing the light. Interrogatory mode, thought Armie, what's up with him? 'Ronnie Goudie,' Bob said.

Hell's bloody teeth. 'Haven't seen him in a long time,' said Armie, turning pale.

'Tell me about your relationship with him.'

'Haven't one.'

'Your dealings with him then. Come on,' Bob said, 'I thought you were in a hurry.'

'I am in a hurry. Bob, don't even try to bully me. I don't know what you think you know about Goudie and I don't care. Just say what you have to say.'

'Take it easy. I'm not bullying anybody. You've gone on the defensive and you've no reason. Tell me….'

'There's nothing to tell,' Armie said, 'I nicked him after an armed robbery in the summer of eighty-five, he got twelve years. A bad bastard, a walking talking living shite.'

'An armed robbery. A fatal shooting,' said Bob. 'For which he never served a single day. Seen him lately have you?'

'I haven't seen him since they put him inside and I don't want to see him. Come on Bob, what are you trying to say?' Armie was on his feet. 'You're not after information, you're after my reaction and I resent that. I –'

'Out,' Bob said. 'Out, Armie, go and do Marchbank.'

'You think I –'

'You heard me. Go on, you've a murder on the go. Forget Goudie. Forget I spoke.'

'I'm not going to forget you spoke.'

'I can't understand why you're taking it like this,' Bob said. Armie left, shaking. After the door had closed behind him Bob realised that he was shaking too.

* * *

Arlene Third got up early, a little after ten. She had to go to Hornbridge to hassle the licensing people. Apparently, night clubs were among the many things that the local council didn't entirely understand or approve of.

She was nearly dressed when the doorbell clanged. The Thirds' doorbell was a large brass one which startled the rooks from the trees. The Thirds lived on the outskirts of town, in a converted steading: Nellfield House, it was called. It was almost in the country. The only human neighbours were Debbie and Geoff across the way in Nellfield Mains. They weren't around to ring doorbells at this hour.

'Ask not for whom the bell tolls,' Arlene muttered. She glanced in the hall mirror. Her dark red hair stuck up in back but that was all the go these days. 'It tolls for thee,' she said with finality, opening the door.

There was a cop on the doorstep: short for a cop, but he had that plain-clothes uniform of frayed tweed jacket and world-weary expression. He was an oldish specimen. His curls were grey.

'Hello Inspector,' she said. 'To what do I owe the pleasure?'

'Mrs Third?' said Armie. 'DI George Armistead, Hornbridge CID....'

'Ah.'

'I wonder if you can help me. I'm investigating a murder.'

'Really! Come in,' said Arlene. 'Coffee? A murder.' She led him to a big dining-kitchen where, on a handsome solid-fuel stove, a kettle simmered. 'Anyone I know?'

'I think so.' Armie watched as she loaded coffee into the cafetiere. 'Your name is in his address-book....'

She poured the water and set the kettle down. 'I know an awful lot of people. Anyone I like?'

'We think his name was Beames. Neil Beames,' Armie said.

Slowly she pushed down the plunger. He couldn't really see her face. 'Beames? I do meet a lot of people, Inspector. I mean I run three night clubs. Not run, I mean I have managers running two of them, I run one myself, I'm always in and out of them. So... what's he like? Neil Beames? Besides dead.'

He handed her the dead guy's driving license. 'His hair's shorter now,' he said. 'How'd he get your number? Do you remember giving it to anyone? I mean would you do that, tell someone your home number?'

'I might.' She considered the picture. 'But I didn't. Nice looking fellow. And only thirty-four, isn't life a bitch. Or rather death.'

'His address book,' Armie said. 'It's quite an exhibit.'

From his jacket pocket he took out the list of seventeen women's names, along with his spectacles, which he put on.

Arlene moved round the table, and peered over his shoulder. 'My God!' she said. 'It's half of Hornbridge you've got there. Or rather Marchbank.... He got around, didn't he? This one,' she said, pointing, 'she lives at Whixton. This one's on the game, you know? In Hornbridge.... He did get around. Funny I don't remember him.'

'You actually know all these women,' Armie said.

'Not all, no no. Just some. By sight or whatever. It's a close community round here. You from the city, are you?'

'Originally,' Armie said.

'Hmmm! Well, you know how it is in Hornsdale, you kick one of 'em and they all rattle.' Armie chuckled. 'So,' she went on. 'I'm in this little black book of his. And somebody killed him. Why?'

'I wish I knew.'

'Any ideas?'

'A lover,' said Armie, 'he was found in bed, naked, with his throat cut.'

'Classic stuff!' Arlene sat down again, on the other side of the table. 'And we're all suspects in his little black book.'

* * *

They have alibis, thought Armie later, as he drove from Whixton back towards Hornbridge. They have alibis and they weren't all sleeping with him. They weren't any of them sleeping with him, or probably not.

The killer didn't have to be one of the women. Suppose Beames was in bed with a woman, her husband or lover might be in the frame. There were obviously men they'd need to talk to. Or maybe Beames had been in bed with a man. Or maybe....

Armie was famished; his interviews had overrun lunchtime. He wondered what Susie was doing, if she'd mind if he just dropped in. His wife – thank God she too hadn't turned up in the book! – his wife was the manager of a Hornbridge bank. She ate lunch late most days. Unfortunately she usually packed only enough sandwiches for one.

But the women in the book, he thought as he slowed down to look for a parking space: the women in the book were all under forty, or just forty, the ones he'd met. Chances were that

Susie was over the limit at fifty-three. Then, Beames didn't bank with Susie, but at a rival's in Marchbank. They knew that from those bank statements SOCO had found: and naturally, two young female tellers had gone straight into his book.

'Suze,' he said, peeking round her office door. 'You busy?'

'On the phone, Geordie, hang on a minute.' He slunk to a seat beside her desk, and waited, thinking after all, Arlene had a point: it's simplest to start with the women. Then Susie put down the phone, and said, 'I have some not so wonderful news for you, honey. I'm sorry.'

'What? Why?'

'Ronnie Goudie.'

'Hell's teeth, not again.'

'Not again, how not again? Did you know he was here, then?'

'Here. He's here? No I didn't know he was here,' Armie said. 'Hell's teeth. My chickens have come home to roost.'

'Geordie, are you OK? You look terrible. Have you had any lunch? Here. Have a sandwich. I'll get you some chocolate. Hang on....'

'I'm fine,' Armie said, taking the sandwich, 'honest. Thanks, Suze. Where'd you see Ronnie, in here?'

'He came in,' Susie said. 'He's opened an account here. I don't think he knows who I am, I didn't let on to him.'

'He knows who you are,' Armie said.

'He's probably straight now. He's changed.... He's totally pleasant and respectable on the surface.'

'Oh aye. He'll have changed. But not much, I don't think. But it's crazy, this morning – oh, did I say? There's a murder case.'

'Someone told me. Two or three people did. They heard it on the radio earlier.'

'Well that'll be Bob. I mean telling the world. He never asked me how I wanted it played. How much did they know?'

'I don't know, not a lot,' Susie said. 'One guy dead in Marchbank – stabbed, was he?'

'Throat cut,' said Armie. 'A gory story. There isn't much to say yet. No, but Bob.... He asked me this morning just before I came out, what dealings I'd had with Goudie. And had I seen him lately. I mean what's that about? But it must be....'

'He must know Ronnie's here,' said Susie, 'you'd think he'd have said so.'

'Well he didn't.'

'So is this something Ronnie's done, this murder?'

'Good thinking, Suze.' Armie sat back, clasping his cocoa mug in both hands and gazing into her eyes. 'Good thinking.... I could sit here all day. I feel lots better.'

'You could not sit here all day, I have work to do. Think you'll be OK now? I mean time's ticking on.'

* * *

Frank Catto, senior, was happy for his son. It was fine to see the lad in love at last, and Tracy was a nice girl: a bit weird, a bit like the boy's mother actually, but it wouldn't do to dwell on that. No: on the whole it was fine to see young people happy and in love. But young Frank never did any work these days. He'd rather be dreaming.

This morning had been particularly trying. Both the kids, full partners in Frank senior's business, had rushed off at ten minutes to nine and left him to manage all alone. No, not quite: he'd had Martok, their Alsatian dog. Martok was more use around the place than Frankie nowadays. But the dog and his boy were back at work now: lunch was over and they'd vanished into their workshop, and Frank could hear spanners clinking and falling to the floor. Guin was in the showroom with him, trying to untangle the book-keeping.

Tracy had gone shopping.

'She's a cool one,' said Big Frank, 'Tracy.'

'Mmm,' said Guin.

'Did she seem at all upset to you? You'd think it'd turn her up, a thing like that.'

'It made a deep impression on her. I mean I think she was mostly awed. She doesn't give much away.'

'Awed,' Frank said. 'I should think so too. So, Guin. You OK?'

'I'm fine.'

'Armistead asked you a shitload of questions.'

'He has to ask questions. He's a detective.'

'Isn't he scraping the barrel a bit? So you're in this guy's address book, big deal.'

'It's a link.'

'But Armistead knows you,' said her father. 'He ought to be protecting you, not asking you questions. I thought you two were pals.'

She hadn't told Armie everything yet. There'd be time for that.

He hadn't asked a shitload of questions either: no 'Where were you last night' or 'were you having an affair', or any of that nonsense. He had asked how she came to be in the book, and whether or not she and Beames had any mutual acquaintances. He'd asked if she'd ever seen Beames around the town.

But she'd only seen Beames in the showroom. Both she and her father remembered his visit. To be sure, they'd needed their memories jogged, but Beames had certainly been looking at bikes in June or early July. It had to be after the third week of June – they knew that much.

'The Duke came in then. This Ducati, he sort of admired it. You know, just fantasising.' Frank Catto had seen plenty of that.

'Just window-shopping,' Armie had said. 'Window-shopping for women.'

'He must've heard Dad call me Guin and thought it was Gwen. And he never asked for my number.'

'If he had,' Armie had asked her, 'would you have given it him? I'm only asking.'

'No I wouldn't. Next question.'

But he hadn't asked anything more: nothing about Tracy, which was just as well. Guin herself would've liked to know why Tracy had taken the film from her camera that morning, and slipped it into Frankie's pocket.

two

The Romantics

THE DETECTIVES' base at Hornbridge police station was a large upstairs room. Its high steel-framed windows looked out, this August day, on sun-washed concrete striped by lengthening blue shadows. Armie, standing at the window, noted with a part of his mind that the cars that turned into their street crawled past the cop shop, then, rounding the corner, zipped up to forty.

With other parts of his mind, he thought about Ronnie Goudie.

'Armie,' said Linda from somewhere behind him.

'Mmm?'

'I said Fabe rang while you were in the loo. He says – you are listening now, aren't you?'

He turned from the window. 'Sorry hen. Things on my mind.'

'He says he's bringing back more boxes from the house, that's why he's late.'

'See these stack-a-boxes,' Armie said, 'natty, aren't they? Wattie got them, his brother's bought a containerload. Let's look at these women again.'

He lifted two of the boxes from his desk, and sitting down on it, took the address book from his pocket and flipped the tiny pages. Backwards from Wiseman, the final entry: back towards Edinburgh.

For the Edinburgh woman, Jennifer W, there was only a phone number. They'd tried ringing it earlier. It was out of service.

Armie passed the book to Linda. 'No point in ringing little Zoe just yet. You went to see her boyfriend, am I right?'

'I did,' said Linda. 'Allie Hendry. He was home in bed. In Zoe's bed, and he didn't even know she'd been attacked. So he said. He's a slob. But quite an imposing figure.'

'In what way?'

'He's huge. Just massive. I don't mean fat, I mean big, you know? But sort of a gentle giant type. Non-violent.'

'How d'you make that out?' said Armie. 'You offer to fight him?'

'I can tell.'

'You look at his knuckles, all that?'

'Course I did. They were fine, not that that'd prove anything.... No, he just comes across as the kind of a guy who's aware of his size. Like he has to be extra careful or he'll squash people. He was pissed off about Zoe, which is bloody stupid when he's got her out on the street in the first place.'

'And you say he's big,' said Armie. 'I have a thought. Suppose a new boy comes to town.... A guy who runs various operations – in wherever it is he lives. He's got people working for him, runs some whores, and he comes here to try and extend his territory.'

'It's not much of a career move,' Linda said. 'I mean I don't see why she wasn't smacked up by some client who turned weird on her.'

'But just suppose for the sake of argument. Suppose it's this new guy, OK?'

'OK.'

'So. When he gets here, what does he find? We've got a few guys running some girls, they're small time though, a shower of amateurs. Our new boy's a pro. He'll have no bother shutting them down and taking over. What's to stop him?'

'Not the girls,' Linda said. 'The guys might give him trouble.'

'They might, and then he'll threaten the girls. And he'll threaten the guys, which is much more efficient. In fact he'll just beat up the guys and tell them, Thanks for being so reasonable! But your friend Hendry he might not beat up. He's so big. He'll bottle out, and beat up the girl instead....'

21

'And where are all the guys that he did beat up?' Linda said. 'Just hiding?'

'Exactly,' said Armie. 'So what do we do?'

'Look for duffed-up pimps?'

'Right! To test the theory, we look for duffed-up pimps. And if we find some....'

'Do you know these amateur pimps?' said Linda.

'Not as such. I was counting on you. You know everything that goes on in town.'

'No I don't,' she said, 'I just know more than you, it's not hard. I'll get something from the girls.... but surely this murder....'

'You're right. You're right.' He stood up and lifted a stack-a-box onto his desk. 'So let's have a look at these goodies here.'

* * *

Through the old part of Hornbridge ran the river Horn. The market cross stood near it by a venerable bridge. Here, on Friday mornings, stallholders still came, and tried to flog produce and cheap record albums to a knowing public.

But this was Wednesday. The market square was empty save for some sparrows, and a starling who strode across the cobbles like a spell-bound prince. Tracy stepped carefully round the birds, past the cross, carrying fat bags stuffed with curtains from the charity shop. She pondered: not on death alone, but on police officers faced with death.

She knew she'd responded too coolly to the discovery of the corpse. Everybody'd think so. Why hadn't she been throwing up, why hadn't she fainted? Simple. The guy was dead, his suffering, if he'd suffered, was over: the situation didn't call for excitement, but for cops.

Tracy walked to the riverside, and sat down on a bench. On the opposite bank, where a cinder-track ran, some kids slouched past with a collie dog. People crossed the bridge above on bicycles, shoulders working, heads down. The sun still shone: the promise of the clear morning had held good. Even the polis couldn't take that away.

Tracy didn't like coppers at all, but she had no bone to pick with Armistead and Co. She even knew Finnie, Guin's boyfriend, a little: he was tolerable in small doses. In any case it wasn't these detectives who'd given her a hard time last summer, when she'd got community service for stomping a crop of genetically modified oilseed rape near Whixton.

Not far from the market was a small public garden that Tracy and other wrongdoers had made. She and Frankie had actually met on that job: but she wasn't going to thank the polis for bringing them together.

Armistead had questioned her that morning at the house.

'You say you met him on Monday, Miss Wiseman,' he'd said. 'For the first time?' So she'd said of course, for the first time, I met him on Monday. I didn't know him.

'And you're sure this is him. You can recognise him.' With his clothes off, right, she'd snapped back, I get it. I actually looked at his face, you know?

'OK, Miss Wiseman. You're certain it's him. And on Monday you met him.... Where was this?' If you must know, she'd told him, the furniture store. Masson's in Marchbank. I actually went in there to ask for a job.

'I thought you worked for yourself,' the detective had said. Well, yes, she'd explained, but it's not like I'm all that busy. But the thing is I do it professionally and these creeps in the store – I don't know why I'm telling you that.

'I can guess,' said the cop, 'they've got no idea about interior design and you do. Am I right? They're hacks. I'm just guessing here.' Damn sharp guess, she'd thought sourly. 'Anyway this was where you met Beames... in the store? Did he speak to you first?' Yes he did, do you think I go round combing the soft-furnishing departments for middle-aged men to pick up? 'I don't think,' the Inspector had said, 'I find out.' Oh. Well you just found out that I don't go around – 'Right, Miss Wiseman, I'm sorry. I think Mr Beames might've been like that though. He collected women. Apparently. I'm just trying to find out.'

Then there was Ferris, the sexy blonde. Fabe Finnie had left her outside by the gate to stay with Tracy: 'Just look after her will you Linda, Armie'll be down in a bit,' at which Ferris had snarled, 'Since when are you telling me who I can talk to?' But when Finnie was gone she'd said, 'Just trying to protect poor me from looking at horrid corpses. Oo. Sorry Miss Wiseman, it must've been a shock.' I'm fine, Tracy had told her. Really.

She wondered now, as she rose to make her way to the Marchbank bus, what it would be like to be Ferris: a detective trapped in the body of a beautiful girl, like something in some godawful B-movie.

* * *

'So,' Bob Marshall said. He leaned back in his chair; Fabe, Armie and Linda, squashed into his office on a chair and two stools, thought how stuffy the room was getting. It was late afternoon. 'So! Neil Beames. He came here from the city. Edinburgh.... So you've been on to CID there. What's the story?'

'They had nothing on him,' said Armie. 'He's clean.'

'His job?'

'He worked for himself,' Linda said. 'A computer consultant.'

'That's a racket for you,' said Bob. 'All bloody cowboys. Now this woman, the one with the Edinburgh number.'

'They haven't got back to us yet on her,' Linda said, 'but they are – is that our phone?'

The ringing stopped before she got to the door, and Bob's phone rang instead. 'Detective Chief Superintendent Marshall.... Dunc! Good to hear you too! Have you.... Christ. Is it really? Oh no, this is definitely – Oh, that's rare. Weren't there others? Other suspected – oh.... DNA? Course you will, soon as we get 'em, I'll tell the lab to send 'em on up to you.... Aye well come down yourself, Gemma'd love to see you. OK Dunc, catch ya later. Bye.' He put down the phone. The detectives eyed him like terriers round a rat hole. 'Your man Beames,' he said. 'Fancy him for a killer?'

'Absolutely,' said Armie.

'Jennifer W,' said Bob. 'From your address book? OK, she's Jenny Wells. The Portobello killings.'

'Oo!' said Linda. 'God! I can't believe I missed that.'

'Jenny Wells!' Armie shook his head. 'Why didn't I think of that. I am thick... but you two aren't. Why didn't you see it?' But of course, Armie thought, it's not as if we sit around

24

reading the papers. 'There are others, aren't there. He's killed a few.'

'Six,' Linda said.

'Suspected,' Bob said. The fax machine on his desk came to life and began to grind out its paper tongue. 'Look, read all about it.'

Linda grabbed the leading edge of the fax; the pages rolled out, sagging to the floor. 'June seventeenth. Jenny Wells, twenty-eight, divorced, in catering – strangled. And they'd had sex. The forensic…. Oh that's very helpful.'

'No DNA,' said Fabe, reading the third sheet sideways.

'No? said Armie.

'Not a second person's, not conclusively,' said Fabe. He tore off the paper. 'Look, it's a forensic desert.'

'But there are these other… six women,' said Armie. 'So how are they linked?'

'The MO's similar,' Bob said, 'and there was DNA in at least two cases. And those two match. So we're looking at a serial killer. You never know, you may have got lucky, Armie.'

The detectives were back in their high room. Outside it was dark: the uncurtained windows reflected Armie bobbing about at the whiteboard, fiddling with the lists of names and staining his knuckles with pink ink. 'They don't fit anymore,' he complained. 'We have too much data. Why don't we have more space?'

'Write smaller,' said Fabe. 'I don't like this. This guy had a list of women he meant to kill. He was planning to kill them.'

'How do you actually know that, Fabe?' said Linda. 'I mean think about it a minute.'

'If he was the murderer you should be happy,' said Armie, writing smaller. 'Cause then Guin's out of danger. If he wasn't….'

'I should give her a ring,' Fabe said. 'Back in a minute, OK?'

'So you should,' said Armie, sitting down on his desk. The door closed behind Fabe and Armie added, 'A wedding ring. Look at that moon out there. It's putting the street lamps to shame.'

'You're the worst romantic,' said Linda.

'Go and look, go on. Is it full? It looks full.'

'No,' said Linda, dutifully peering out: sure enough, it was over the rooftops. 'I think it was full last night.'

'Beames had his throat torn out,' said Armie, 'when the moon was full.'

'What's that supposed to mean?'

'That I'm a romantic.'

'I thought you were meant to be scientific.'

'I try.'

'Do you believe in werewolves?' said Linda.

Armie got up and went to the window. 'I don't believe. I find out,' he said.

* * *

At nine that evening Arlene Third put on a snappy little patent-leather jacket and kissed her husband on the cheek. 'I'm off,' she said, 'don't be lonely, darling.'

'Be good!' Sandy Third said. He went to the door, and as she walked away down the path he waved to her. At that moment she looked over her shoulder and waved back, her jacket flickering faintly in the moonlight.

He closed the door. He heard the Toyota start up, crunch past on the gravel and roll out of hearing. Except for the tick of a clock and the muffled chiming of bottles as the refrigerator pump shut off, the house was silent. Sandy stepped to a window to the right of the door and leaned over slightly to peer obliquely through it. A light showed in the house across the drive.

He ran a hand through what remained of his hair, wandered into his study and sat down in an armchair. On a table at his elbow was a telephone. He stared at it. Minutes passed.

All at once he picked up the receiver and pressed a key. He listened to the ring.

Debbie Chalmers put down her book with a smack on the kitchen table. She'd been expecting this, she'd heard the car leave. Wednesday night was one of Arlene's obsessions: she'd go to her club, the Odd Spot, and chivvy her employees round and round until four-thirty Thursday morning.

The phone rang four times before Debbie left the table and walked over to the extension by the kitchen door. 'Debbie Chalmers,' she said brightly.

'Hi.'

'Hi, hi.'

'Want to come over?'

'Sandy, I told you, I'm packing it in.'

'I could come over to you if you'd rather.'

'I know you heard me. I'm packing this in, Sandy, I mean it.'

'You said that that other time.'

'Did I really?' said Debbie. 'I probably meant it too. Look, come over here. I'll make us a drink. I wanted to go out tonight,' she lied, 'and not with you.'

'Obviously not with me. I'm not stupid....'

'You're very pigheaded for someone who isn't stupid.'

* * *

Around ten, the detectives decided to call it a night. They'd gone through their interviews, collated the lot, re-written the whole of Armie's tables five times. Greig was nearly certain that Beames had been killed sometime after three, but probably nearer five a.m. Several of the women had no alibis for that time.

With this blitz on the women, they hadn't time for the boxes of evidence that had finally stopped rolling in after dark. But the boxes weren't going to scamper away, whereas you never could tell with women. Besides, thought Armie, there's a lot to be said for tackling one thing at a time.

Now he headed for home. Fabe drove towards Guin's flat. Linda went round by the hospital to check up on Zoe. Fabe had questioned Zoe around one o'clock, and found her subdued and groggy with painkillers. But now she was gone: she'd signed herself out.

Linda cruised briefly through Hornbridge's idea of a red-light district. This was centred on Polwarth Avenue, a dual carriageway with a strip of grass down the middle and, at intervals, trees. It gave excellent cover, and the tall brick houses that lined both carriageways were full of possibilities and cheap rooms. The Goat Hotel stood on Polwarth Parade at the townward end, along with a run-down curry house and a chip shop. At the farther end was a junction with the so-called Parkway, which would get you on the road to Marchbank.

Zoe was walking along the Avenue on the centre strip. She didn't hurry. A street lamp shone on her face, turning her skin yellow and her bruises and stitches black. She had on a little skirt with a flounce, platform sandals, and a top that was mostly fringes.

Linda pulled over. Zoe eyed the ratty old car and then drew away. Linda rolled down the window.

'Zoe,' she called. 'Wait a sec.'

'I don't want to talk to you,' Zoe said, stepping into the shadows. 'I talked to you already.'

'Wait a sec, what are you doing out? You should be in hospital.'

'I told your ugly pal before, I never went with that weird guy.'

'It's not that, Zoe, it's – you could be in danger. Whoever. ...'

'I'm not. Bugger off.' She was moving on behind the trees, in the gloom. Linda, rolling alongside, couldn't keep her in view. She stopped and peered out the window: no Zoe. The centre strip was deserted.

'Like she vanished,' said Linda fifteen minutes later in her boyfriend's favourite pub, the Crown in Marchbank.

'Maybe she shinned up a tree,' said Grassy Knowles.

Grassy had his elbows on the table, his large hard hands curled round a half-pint mug. He'd been nursing his drink for an hour, gassing with his pals and waiting for Linda; he only had a half most evenings anyway. It was closing time now, but the management at the Crown were easygoing.

'Anyway,' he said, 'you're off duty, why not give yourself a break? She won't thank you for chasing her around all night.'

The pub was emptying out. Grassy's friends by ones and twos shouted their goodnights, and bike engines could be heard starting up outside. Grassy leaned back, his leather jacket creaking slightly. 'Have to go soon,' he said. 'Or get thrown out.'

'I'm sorry. I'm helluva late,' said Linda. 'It's this murder.'

'You must be knackered.'

'And this girl, I needed to see her. I'm worried about her. Someone's after her.'

Grassy drained his mug and stood up. 'You all set then? Let's go.' He bent and retrieved his helmet from under the table. 'Someone after her? But she didn't say who.'

'She doesn't know the guy.'

'So let's tail her. I'll pick up your helmet from home and we'll sit on her tail, she won't know you.'

'It's tempting. But you know… I've just realised how tired I am….'

She phoned the station, asked the people on duty to send a car along the Avenue once or twice. She knew it was feeble, but so would a crawl round the neighbourhood be. Zoe didn't want to be found. She'd be staying out of sight.

* * *

Guin's flat: it felt like home, too much so, Fabe admitted to himself. Still she hadn't given him his own key. He stood in the street chucking pebbles at the window, trying not to hit those of the downstairs neighbours.

She opened the door wearing track pants and an oil-stained sweatshirt. 'I was about to go to bed,' she whispered, heading for the stairs.

'In that?'

'Why not? Have you got the killer?' She let them into the flat and shut the door. 'Is it a woman?' she said in normal tones.

'We don't know who it is. What we do know… oh look… garlic bread, aren't you a princess.'

'I – wait a minute, let me warm it up. Aw, too late.' She put on the kettle instead. 'You did say he was a murderer himself.'

'Mmmm any butter? Mmm…. Aye. No. No, we haven't got actual proof yet… pretty sure though… mm… be him.'

'So he killed a woman, and a woman killed him. Or not. You don't suspect Tracy.' Fabe munched a while. 'You don't,' she repeated, 'do you.'

'We don't suspect you.'

'Oh what a relief. I've been working on my alibi all day.'

'You don't have one, we just don't suspect you. Don't push your luck.'

'You don't suspect Tracy.'

Communing with his garlic bread, Fabe looked her in the eyes. She looked back. Presently he said, 'You keep saying that.'

'I'd like to believe it.'

'She hasn't an alibi either, has she. She wasn't with your brother.'

'I know.'

'She says she went out for a walk in the moonlight,' Fabe said. 'Moonlight? In Mill Circle? Brand new street lights all over the place. Went to bed around one or one-thirty, that's what she told Armie. When Beames was killed she'd be sleeping.'

'I wish she and Frank would just move in together,' Guin said.

'You do?'

'Course I do.'

'But not us.'

'Well I didn't mean us. I meant they should.' Look at you, she thought. You're a wonderful man. This isn't a wonderful flat, is it. I ought to just do it. Why don't I just do it? 'At least then we'd know where the hell she was.'

Fabe grinned. 'Bet we wouldn't.'

'No. No, she does funny things.' Guin poured his tea, sat down opposite him and watched as he slipped into civilian ease. 'She was totally into that eclipse of the sun. Remember?'

'I don't think that's weird,' said Fabe. 'Lots of people went north to see that.'

'Lots of people didn't pester their boyfriends to go north with them and copulate on a beach as the thing reached totality. With druids in attendance to pronounce them man and wife.'

'I think he should've gone through with that,' said Fabe.

They liked to sit, wrapped up in each other, never hurrying things, sometimes not even speaking. Fabe liked the smell of her hair. She liked the shapes of his bones. They weren't rushing off to bed.

It was better not to talk when there were bits of their lives, like this business of Tracy, that they couldn't share without reserve. It had happened before. For a time they'd work privately and confer only if they were stuck. Eventually, though, as things became clearer, one or the other would pull out the cork and suddenly they'd both be spouting ideas. But not now: this was the quiet time.

He marvelled again at how strong she was. She'd told him once that it was an illusion: you coped with your troubles and everyone said, She's so tough, thank God that at least we shan't have to worry about her, and it was a totally circular argument. But she was tough. Face facts, lady.

Guin's mother had buggered off when she was twelve, this was the thing. Guin had brought up her little brother and sister. Her dad had told those two, just for something to say, that their mum had run off with the gypsies.

There weren't any gypsies in those parts, so it sounded a bit like a fairy tale.

Then when they were all grown up, her sister had been murdered. Fabe had blown in on that ill wind. So they'd fallen in love; solved the murder too. Fabe had never met that sister of hers that everyone was so crazy about. But he knew that if he'd met her, he'd have fallen for Guin all the same.

three

Rubbish

ON THURSDAY morning Tracy got up at six, and stood for a long time looking out the bathroom window. The new brick houses opposite glowed pink in the dawn. Some of their windows flared red, fiery while the low sun touched them. Others she could see into.

Tracy's small flat was in a new residential development called Millburn Park. You could get a place here with no deposit, just sign up for a mortgage and take nine-tenths of forever to pay it off. There were tall, narrow semis for starting families in; for young salaried single folk there was a sprinkling of maisonettes and flats. Tracy leased her place. Her landlady had taken out a mortgage on it, then landed a better job and moved to Hornbridge.

Tracy put on some clothes and went back to the bathroom window. The world was waking up: it was neighbour-watching time. But only one neighbour interested her, the man in the ground-floor maisonette that backed onto the lawn below. He was thirty or so, tall and thin, with dark hair and a face suggesting permanent bellyache. His name was Ian Barclay; he was a police sergeant.

The blinds on Barclay's bedroom window were drawn, but Tracy could see down into the kitchen. There was the fridge, a worktop and some cupboards. On the outer windowledge a black cat walked to and fro, looking in.

How like him that cat is, thought Tracy: long, dark and miserable. He could've put a flap in the door for it. Perhaps he doesn't feel settled here.

The cat jumped to the ground and ran to the door. A light went on in the kitchen. Whoever was in there didn't bother to let in the cat: instead he strode about the room, and opened and closed the fridge. Someone smallish: it wasn't Barclay. It wasn't a he, either, she saw now, but a woman with long dark hair. She was wearing Barclay's tartan bathrobe.

The cat stood on its hind legs, and put its paws to the doorknob. The woman paused. Then she flung something down on the worktop and vanished from view. The cat jumped back up on the sill.

The thing was, Ian Barclay headed the Hornbridge car crime unit. The previous summer, he'd arrested Frankie for dealing in stolen bikes. Frankie wasn't bitter, he'd known it was risky, but all the same it was weird how the polis had thrown the book at him when the whole scam had been his pal's idea. It was more than weird, it was unfair.

One day, while they worked on their public garden, Frank had pointed out this guy as he passed by on the street. Barclay, his evil genius. It was the same guy she saw all the time, the gloomy bloke living across from her in Mill Circle.

He'd seemed to be living alone. But Guin, who hung out at the cop shop, had told her that he was married. He didn't act like it. This dark girl was the latest in a long parade of girls, no two the same.

It's astonishing what you get to know about your neighbours, Tracy thought. And knowledge is power.

* * *

At six in the morning, with the utmost care, Arlene Third drove in past her neighbours' door. They were an open book, those two.

It wasn't one she wanted to read, though. Debbie and Geoff were a lovely couple, but unbelievably boring. It was true that they lived in a house a lot like hers and Sandy's; they also owned a similar sort of car. But that was superficial stuff. Arlene was a bohemian, and they were straights.

Mind you, old Sandy was pretty straight as well.

Sandy was a car dealer. He'd built up his trade, bought up several rivals, and now had a little local empire. His early ambition had taken its toll: he'd lost most of his hair. But he was more laid back these days. He was heading for a comfortable middle age.

Arlene closed the car door silently. She crossed the gravel, light-footed, and gently opened the front door, the fingers of her free hand on the bell in case it dared to sound. Once inside she relaxed. The Chalmerses might awaken if a mouse farted, but dear Sandy would sleep through anything. She smiled, and went to the kitchen for a belt of White Horse before bed.

Where were you last night, she thought, still smiling, sitting down at the table where she'd entertained DI Armistead the day before. She raised her glass in silent tribute to the detective and his quest. Where was I on the night, no the early morning of the thirteenth inst. Well for once I was home. My husband, Sandy... who's a very deep sleeper but you don't need to know that... will vouch for me.

And I for him.

* * *

Around six that morning, Armie had been dreaming about women. It had taken him ages to get to sleep, his head was buzzing like a wasps' nest, and when he'd finally drifted off the women in the case assumed new shapes to match the atrocity of the murder.

But then he'd waked up because Susie was stirring. He waked gratefully. With any luck he'd soon forget the wolf-eyed females of his dreams.

'Suze,' he said. She opened her eyes. To his relief, they were much as usual, complete with whites and round pupils. 'Getting up?'

'No.'

'I am. Want coffee?'

'No.'

'You getting up later?'

'Seven.' The eyes closed.

He didn't make coffee. He stuck a scone in his pocket, left her a note and went out into the near-silence of the suburban morning. His sleeve brushed against the buddleia that bloomed beside the drive: quite a dew-fall last night, he noted, looking up at a brightening sky. He shook the drops from his cuff and got in the car.

Ronnie Goudie. At least he hadn't dreamed about him. Or rather he didn't remember dreaming of Ronnie, which was mercy enough. The murder had taken over, as it should, because Ronnie was personal, although nonetheless worth watching.

Armie hadn't seen Ronnie Goudie for so long that he wondered now if he'd recognise him. Of course he would, if the man confronted him: Susie had known him at once, after all. But seen in the street, hurrying, walking away, he might look like anyone else.

He wasn't going to check out everyone he saw just in case they were bloody Ronnie Goudie.

Armie's Vauxhall whuffled through the streets, following the river, and reaching the market it turned for the town centre. Hardly anyone was stirring; but out of the corner of his eye

34

Armie saw someone loitering by the market cross, with a black lurcher dog at his feet... or her feet.

I should go back, he thought, take a look. He took a side turning and swung through the market: yes, a man, not old, not especially tall, a dark man in a brown leather jacket with side-vents and silver buttons, and high boots. A gypsy.

There are no gypsies around here, Armie thought. The lurcher looked up as he passed; he caught its eye and smiled involuntarily. After all, he thought, what harm can they do, compared with our local beauties?

The youngsters weren't in yet. In the high room Armie stepped to the window, gazed down at the street, but found no inspiration in the view. He sighed and went over to the whiteboard.

Apparently, a curse lay on it. No matter how the data were arranged, they made no sense. You'd think they'd form some sort of pattern by this time.

He sat on his desk. The killer, he thought, had struck with a bottle, then used it to stab. The bottle had broken: an empty one, then, for no drink was spilled; and a stout one to strike so hard. The lab had suggested a quality beer, because beer demands heavier glass than do still drinks like whisky.

Their victim hadn't been drinking beer, or anything else, that night. More detailed toxicology stuff would come, but drink smells; even beer smells a little, even with the window wide open and all that blood in the room. With the bottle gone there'd been nothing to smell. Who had drunk that beer, and where was that bottle now?

When Linda had looked at the murder scene after finally forcing her way through the SOC men, she'd noticed that one of the pillows had no pillowcase on. This was the one that wasn't under the dead man's head. She thought that the killer had taken the broken glass away in the pillowcase. Only a couple of shards had got left behind.

'With any luck,' Linda had said, 'she's sliced her finger open and bled all over the bed.'

If she had, they'd find her DNA, not that they'd know they had. In any case it'd be days before the DNA was done.

As to who drank the beer, Beames himself might have done so. He just hadn't done so the night before his death. He could've drunk it anytime, and having no one to tidy up for he'd left the bottle sitting by his bed. When the time came it had offered itself to hand.

Armie had had cases where there weren't any suspects at all. In this one there seemed to be millions. There were the women from the little book. There were men attached to these women. There were women, and attached men, from Beames's past in Portobello or wherever. One of those women was dead: who might wish to avenge her?

Then there were all these stack-a-boxes. Beames hadn't lived in that house long, he didn't have mountains of stuff, but any of this miscellany might prove important and there seemed no way to tell which bits to look at twice. Beames kept EPOS slips, the things from credit-card transactions. He stuck them in with his bank statements in a desk drawer in his front room. But there weren't very many. His wants had seemingly been few since moving to St Margaret's Lane.

He hadn't kept beer bottles, at least, not lately. They knew he bought bottled beer sometimes though. One of those slips had been folded round an itemised receipt that mentioned Newcastle Brown Ale four times. It had come from the Asda in Hornbridge and, Armie noticed, the ale had been on offer two-for-one at the time, July the eleventh at 1750hrs.

Newcastle Brown comes in clear glass, he thought: clear glass to cloud the wits. The bottle that struck Beames down was of clear glass. That's if we're right, if it was a bottle at all.

Maybe he should go back to the murder house... at least he'd be doing something. Had he seen all the evidence yet? That was the thing.

One more look in this box, the one on Fabe's desk. What was in here? He'd forgotten: some rubbish. He'd check it and then he could go.

* * *

At seven forty-five Debbie Chalmers pedalled into the Safeways car park, hopped off her bike and trotted to a halt beside a row of bicycle chaining-points. She locked the bike to one of them just in case, and taking her coverall from the carrier she hurried inside. Her shift was starting.

'If you want to work in a supermarket,' Arlene had once said, 'why don't you get Geoff to just buy you one? He's making enough.'

But that wasn't the point. Arlene ought to know: her too-hip lifestyle was her version of the same thing. Their husbands were earning, they didn't have kids, they needed a little something of their own to do.

Debbie had once been a teacher of games. It had seemed like the right career when she was young. But after her marriage, when she hadn't worked at anything for a time, she'd thought about her old job and it turned her right off. It was the responsibility, mainly. Also there was something about kids that made her sad.

But supermarket checkouts don't plant the world on your shoulders.

The Safeways in Marchbank was handy for her, but actually Debbie had taken a job at the Hornbridge Asda for awhile before this one fell vacant. To get to the Asda she'd had to use the car: the bus schedule was hopeless. So she'd spent a lot of her earnings on petrol. It made Arlene laugh. Many things did.

Arlene herself seldom shopped at the Safeways when Debbie was there. She didn't get up that early. Occasionally she'd swagger in before going home to bed, but happily, not often. Arlene wasn't really a woman's woman, Debbie reflected, wondering as she unlocked her till why in hell she was thinking about her this morning.

Oh of course – Sandy! That'd be why.

* * *

Fabe looked over Armie's shoulder. He sighed. 'I went through that box. It's rubbish.'

'No.'

'What do you mean no? It's come from the bin. At least the bloody man had the sense to rinse out his tins or this'd be mingin'.'

'Look at the bag, Fabe man.'

'It's a Safeways bag. He's used it for the rubbish.'

'He has, that's right. He's used it to line the bin.'

'So?'

'He never took out the ticket first. The slip. Look here.'

It was mingin, rinsed tins or no rinsed tins. Beames had been chucking wet coffee-grounds and dead lemon-slices in there. That's probably why he'd lined the bin with a plastic bag. Unfortunately plastic carrier bags aren't watertight: foul fluids oozed from the corners.

'Take that bloody thing off my desk,' said Fabe.

Armie put the bag back in the stack-a-box and lovingly displayed the soggy little square of paper, the transaction slip he'd found stuck inside the bottom of the bag.

'It isn't his,' he said.

'What isn't, the slip? The rubbish? What?'

'The account. Look, it's a debit card, the number's printed on. The last four digits. Only they're not – see these other ones? From his desk drawer? They've got a different number.'

'He'd just transferred his account,' said Fabe. 'It's probably not –'

'No. This is dated the tenth, it's last Sunday. I can't think he'd still use the old Switch card. I called Susie; she says not.'

'OK,' Fabe said, 'but this doesn't tell us…. You can't tell whose card it is. With the kind that you sign –'

'With this kind you've signed a slip for the store but they keep it and give you this one instead. They keep it, Fabe. And the transaction's traceable anyway. Get on the phone – no I'll do it.'

'I'll do it Armie, don't hop round the place like a flea. Do some thinking. What does it mean?' Fabe looked up the supermarket's number in the phone book. 'Does it mean anything?'

'It ought to. Why should he buy…. I wish he'd left in the till slip as well,' said Armie. 'What did he buy? But anyway, why buy eleven pounds thirty-four pence worth of groceries with somebody else's card?'

'Good morning,' Fabe said into the phone. 'It's DS Finnie of Hornbridge CID. I'm wanting a favour….'

In the motorcycle showroom, lingering over coffee, Guin looked up at the posters on the walls. They sagged, and from underneath the lower corners spiders' dung rained down on whatever merchandise lay beneath. Those adverts are history, she thought: why can't Kawasaki send us new ones?

Guin wondered if she ought to ring up the Majestic in Hornbridge for posters for the latest film. Not that they'll be showing the latest for awhile, she reflected as she reached for the phone.

It rang under her hand and she jumped. It was Fabe. 'We got something,' he said. 'I have to stay at the station, I can't say when I'll be done.'

'You got something,' Guin said, 'what?'

'Armie found this supermarket slip. In Beames's rubbish.'

'Oh.'

'It isn't his. The account, the debit card. It's this guy from Edinburgh, they've traced him....'

'He's the killer?'

'He could be. He's connected with the Edinburgh killings.'

'But Fabe, it's one of the women.'

'Who says it is, though?'

'I do.'

'Don't get tunnel vision. And you know, we won't actually know much without the results from the lab. I mean, that we could do with, all right. But meanwhile... I'm sorry... I'll see you as soon as we're done.'

'But you shouldn't be done. I mean this isn't finished. It's one of the women,' Guin said.

* * *

'Well this is a development,' Bob Marshall said.

He'd crammed the detectives into his office once again. It was getting near lunchtime; in the small space the growls of stomachs sounded eerily close. Linda kept thinking irrationally of salad sandwiches.

'Scuse me,' she said, 'only I was out in the fresh air all morning looking for duffed-up pimps.'

'You got it wrong then,' said Fabe. 'All pimps hate fresh air.'

'I said this is a development,' said Bob. 'Dunc Brown's coming down.'

Armie sighed. 'OK, it could be. It could be the end... I mean, this could be the guy... but the lab, we need the results from the lab.'

'Run this past me again,' said Fabe. 'There are two murdered women.'

'Three,' said Armie.

'Two,' said Bob. 'Only two that we know were killed by the same guy. The DNA matches – DNA recovered from the bodies.'

'Are we talking semen?' Fabe said.

'No. Thought I told you, he isn't that stupid, whatever else he is.'

'But there's material.'

'Aye,' Bob said. 'Epidermal cells, Dunc says.'

'OK,' said Fabe. 'Two victims, one killer. So one of these women, her ex-husband... the transaction slip Armie found in the bag was his.'

'Right,' said Bob. 'Now this ex-husband. Dunc talked to him after the wife turned up dead. He was gutted, apparently.'

'Not surprising,' said Armie. 'Poor guy.' He gazed at the whiteboard, newly splashed with names in green. 'Roderick Andrew... Lucy Andrew. Strangled in bed.'

'So this was revenge,' Fabe said. 'For Lucy. He came here to kill this Beames.'

'With the ale,' said Armie. 'Don't forget the ale.' The Safeways records for August the tenth had Andrew, or his Switch card, down for six bottles of Newcastle Brown.

'So Andrew had solved the murder,' Linda said. 'How'd he do that? And how'd he find Beames down here?'

'Questions, questions,' said Bob.

But when DCI Brown showed up he had answers.

After lunch, the detectives assembled in their base and roosted at their desks. Bob took a chair; Mira Chandra, from uniform, borrowed a stool. Brown addressed them all from an imaginary platform by the whiteboard.

'Rod Andrew and Neil Beames,' Brown said. He tapped the board, where these names were now blazoned in magenta ink. 'Rod Andrew and Neil Beames are old friends. They worked together in the nineties, and when Beames went into business for himself he gave Andrew little jobs.... Quite a lot of little jobs. They saw each other socially. Even recently, even though Beames hadn't employed Andrew for over a year. They met regularly – up until last April. Lucy Andrew,' he tapped the board, 'died in March. Neil Beames moved away from the city in June.'

'You say they didn't socialise after April,' Armie said. 'Did they fall out?'

'Not according to Andrew, no. Andrew was depressed after his wife died. Or ex-wife rather... he blamed himself for not being there. She'd divorced him, but people aren't logical, are they? Now – I questioned Andrew after the murder, I actually thought he might've done it. But the DNA put him out of the picture. And the other wifies, he didn't look like having anything to do with them.'

'But you think Beames did,' Armie said.

'Well that's going to be clearer when we get your results from the lab. But I do, aye.' Brown smacked the whiteboard, producing a Turnerish sunset effect. 'I mean look at all these women.'

'How'd he find him down here then?' said Armie. 'They must've been keeping in touch.'

'They might, they might not,' said Brown. 'I mean people find you. He claims they'd kept in touch right enough.'

'I take it you never suspected Beames before,' Bob said.

'Didn't know he existed. No.... So I'm a bit keen to see these results. We could hurry 'em up.'

'Mills of science grind slowly,' said Bob.

'Is Andrew under arrest?' said Armie, wondering why Brown hadn't arranged for them to see him; the mills of interrogation could've used some grist.

'Got bail,' said Brown.

'Ah weel,' said Bob. 'You'll be staying the night. Gemma's looking forward to seeing you.'

'Well that's fine,' said Brown, 'aye, thanks and all that.... I'll maybe take a wee peek at all this evidence of yours.'

'What a dick,' Linda said on the way down the stairs. 'Like it's all done and dusted.'

'I notice you couldn't wait to get out of the room,' said Mira.

'Hope it was obvious.'

'But you've got your prostitute case,' said Mira. 'You've made progress on that.'

'Aye I have, but I hate to see Armie get shafted that way.' And Linda intoned, 'O DCI Brown, you bloody moron, I pray you teach me of thy wisdom, great sage.'

four

Wild Time

THE CLEARINGS in the spruce wood were hot in the afternoons. The metal cans smelled sharp: men had been bringing them that day, standing them in the sunlight. They'd brought machines too, even clothes. In some clearings where the ground was overlaid with stones, a smell of men had ousted the other airs.

As the sun grew low she abandoned her refuge and made her way down to the water. She drank, then stood looking south, stock still but for her ears: these she moved east, then west. Thick fuzz grew in her ears but they heard plenty. West was the way, against the run of the water.

Darkness fell. She followed the deer-track at the foot of the wood. Soon the trees gave way to open ground, a tussocky breezy land where sheep lay bunched up, their lambs nearly grown, torpid and smelling of grease. Against the fences and dykes the nettles stood tall and gave her cover as she trotted, trotted, the river on her southward flank.

The moon rose late: it glinted on the water, casting her shadow before her. The way climbed. The river chattered louder and bent round to the north: her shadow swung with it, for the moon hung low. From time to time she paused to drink among the boulders. There was no time to feed.

The way climbed. No more nettles: lichen, musk on the ferns, the cry of a buzzard in the growing light. Pines grew in crevices among the stones, and on the track, away from the leaping stream, fine grasses hung like hair.

Men had been here; not for many hours, but they'd come again. She bounded onward.

* * *

It was coffee time at Frank Catto and Sons. In the workshop young Frank sat at floor level in an old leather bucket seat, with Martok beside him. Tracy sat on a grease-tin.

It had been a week since she'd found that guy, seen all that blood and the rest of it. Frank kept having to stop himself asking if she was OK. She's obviously OK, he thought, though God alone knows how she does it. And after all they got the killer. Let's move on to better things.

'I really ought to get a car,' she was saying. 'Or a bike.'

'I was hoping you'd say bike,' said Frank. 'It's what we do.'

'But I couldn't take a doggie biking.' She reached over to stroke Martok's ears. 'Like you always have your pickup. It's better.'

'Costs the earth to run,' Frank said.

'Can I borrow it? Today?'

Frank wasn't sure if the firm's insurance would stretch to Tracy but he didn't care. 'You taking Martok?'

'I hadn't thought. I mean I could. I want to go up to the forest.'

'You mean the forestry, Fairyhill?'

'No,' said Tracy, 'up Horncross Forest. Actually… you know they've started felling Fairyhill, it's hellish.'

She put the lid on the biscuit tin and drained her mug. At this Martok rose and shook himself, showering them with swarf and grit; then he stuck his nose in Tracy's eye. 'I think he's trying to tell me something,' she said.

'Guin usually takes him after work,' said Frank. 'But if you're going.... What's the deal with Horncross? Anything?'

'I just feel like being there. I'll wait if you like, we could all go.'

'No time. I finish too late.'

'Doesn't matter, I can see in the dark.'

'We'll go Sunday,' said Frank. 'No, Saturday, I can pack in at noon. No big jobs on.' He got to his feet and put his mug in the sink. 'You'll need diesel if you're going now.'

He'd heard people say that Tracy was a rotten driver. They had no idea: she was an artist, so they thought she was impractical, whereas the opposite was true. In any case she could scarcely practise her driving, could she, with no wheels.

He watched as the pickup pulled away in the direction of the River Park. It wasn't the best way to Horncross but it was the way to take, if you didn't want Dad to see you.

Can't decide, Tracy thought, as she wrestled with the steering, if it's freedom or a bind. I mean here I am sitting up above the plebs, rolling along as free as air. Except I need fuel, Frank said; and then there's having to actually drive this bloody thing, you can't relax for a moment.

You've no sooner shifted up, than you have to shift down. You get going and they make you stop. You roll grandly down the left-hand carriageway only to find that some cretin has parked a damn great Luton in the way. So you have to get round it. Signal one way, signal the other way, then creep along at a pace you could've walked at.

Besides, the windshield's that grimy it totally spoils the view.

From the seat beside her Martok watched the passing scene, tongue lolling out. He seemed hot, perhaps because he was going somewhere different, with someone different: it wasn't a hot day. It was perfect for walking, walking in the forest. Tracy decided it was freedom after all.

* * *

'Someone to see you,' Mira said, opening the door of the detectives' base. Armie looked up. There stood Guin, helmet in hand: so, he thought, the old scooter's not dead yet.

'Thanks Mira,' he called as the constable withdrew. 'To see me? What a nice surprise.'

Guin looked round the big room, glanced at Bob Marshall's office door, and crossed to the seat that Armie had cleared for her. 'It's probably kind of stupid.'

'Oh really? What is?'

She wondered if she was just stirring the shit. 'You know the Beames thing. Like you've got the guy who did it, I know that.'

'You have doubts,' said Armie.

'Well I do have doubts. I know it sounds flaky but I've just got a feeling. Don't you ever suspect other people?'

'I did.'

'I mean, women. At the start you had all those women.'

'We had Tracy Wiseman,' said Armie. 'We had you....'

'Did you think I could rip someone's throat out?'

'Why not?'

'But you don't think I did.'

'No, I know that you didn't.' It came to him now that if Guin had been guilty, she'd have told him somehow. At least, that was what he imagined. 'I know that you didn't, I don't know that Tracy didn't.'

'Except you do now, you've got Andrew.'

'Aye we have,' said Armie, 'but I mean in principal.' He too glanced over at Bob's office door; Bob was out, wasn't he? 'What's this niggle of yours? This doubt?'

'It's....' How could she put it? 'There's sex involved. I mean someone was there. Beames had....'

'He hadn't had sex,' said Armie, 'didn't you know that? I'm sorry, I don't know what Fabe tells you, do I. I've put my foot in it.'

'No, he did tell me. I know about that. In fact he thinks.... It's a big part of why he thinks Andrew did it. But I don't.... Beames, OK, he didn't have sex. But he had to have, like, the intention of sex. To be naked.'

'A lot of guys sleep with no clothes on, Guin.'

'Away and teach your grandmother to suck eggs.' She caught his eye, they both grinned. 'I think he had someone there that night,' she went on, 'and that someone was going to go to bed with him. And unless Rod Andrew is his lover – well why not. But you know, I think it's a woman.'

'OK, there's a woman. They're going to bed. For some reason they don't have sex, and Andrew turns up and he kills him.'

'No.'

'Tell me why not,' Armie said. And while you're about it, he thought, you can tell me why I care why you think why not. I know why, I want you to be right, damn it.

'The bottle,' she said, 'the weapon. Impulse.'

'I told them that.'

'Told who?'

Hell, he'd dropped one more of his unfailing brick supply. 'I blurted that out, OK. So you won't think I'm stupid. Cause I value your good opinion…. Of course it was impulse! The party line is that Andrew's guilty. I don't buy it.'

'You don't?'

'No.'

'Then you think it's a woman?'

'I think it – OK. If Andrew killed on impulse, then, fine, it could be him. We're hanging the Andrew guilty-or-not-guilty debate on the supposition that he came for revenge. Premeditation, all that. And there he is, armed to the teeth with bottles of Newkie – six of 'em lest the first one fails. I mean Jesus Christ on stalks, Guin. I really can't see it.'

The phone on his desk rang. It was Mira. 'Inspector,' she said, 'Chief Superintendent Marshall's come in.'

'Thanks Mira.' Armie made a rueful face. 'You're a star.'

* * *

Trees, trees: each one was unique. Tracy thought about the word unique, how ugly it was and yet how apt. The pines in Horncross Forest were individuals, not only in fact, but in appearance, for they'd grown to suit their surroundings: here twisting round rocks, there leaning from the wind. In addition

46

there seemed to be lots that had borne some hurt in their youth, and afterwards flourished wildly in defiance.

The pines had thick foliage like fur. It formed dark blocks of colour, green or blue in the light of the sky; in the sunlight the limbs glowed red. Tracy had heard that these pines were part of the great Caledonian Forest that once had stretched for leagues. What leagues were, in terms of the popular kilometre or mile, didn't matter. What mattered was that the great forest had not died out.

Martok ranged about as she climbed up from the car park on the ramblers' well-worn track. This part of Horncross was a nature reserve. All of it needed preserving, she thought, except perhaps for the northern fringe planted with spruces. Pines and birches grew elsewhere, with open stretches of bog or moor, heather or crowberry, or level rock to which the wild thyme clung.

Above the track, brown velvet butterflies danced in the fitful sunshine. Harebells bloomed beside the path. Tracy could hear a buzzard screaming somewhere out of sight. In a nearby tree sat an incredibly tiny bird with a bright red stripe on his head. Martok bounded past her with his nose to the ground, his hindquarters threatening to overrun his fore. She whistled and he came back to her.

When they reached the level the cool breeze met them. Tracy could see the buzzard where it wheeled above the pines. She was on a long outcrop of dark grey rock, sinuous like a snake's back skirting the trees, leading seductively out of sight beyond them.

Martok had his nose on the ground again and was snuffling to and fro. As for Tracy's nose, it caught a whiff of woodsmoke. The woods were bone-dry, this might not be such a great time for fire. She hurried on along the rock, bumping into the dog as he zigzagged about. Then she heard voices.

Martok was a scary-looking beast. A nice little dog, Frank often said, when you get to know him; but Tracy had noticed that many people preferred not to get to know him. Occasionally he bit Frank. What chance had anyone else?

Luckily Martok was smart as well as scary, and when you called him he generally came. He came now at Tracy's shriek of apprehension. Two children and a skinny black mutt were running towards them along the level. She collared Martok, fished his chain from her pocket and clipped it on as the mutt romped up with its backside skittering sideways in appeasement.

'Does your dog fight?' shouted the leading child.

Martok didn't fight. That is, he could murder anything that tried to fight with him, but fighting was not his hobby. Tracy didn't know this. She froze onto his collar, which made him growl.

'He's mostly mad at me,' she said. Martok backed up in her grasp and she gripped tighter to stop him slipping his collar. 'I think.'

The leading child, a red-haired boy of twelve or so, grabbed his black dog by the scruff of its neck. It had no collar. The second child was a girl with a long red pigtail, younger, or smaller anyway: Tracy couldn't tell. 'Sit,' said Tracy. Martok sat, but stood up again instantly. 'Sit!!' said Tracy. The dogs eyed one another in the stillness.

'They won't fight, mine's female,' said the boy.

'We've got a camp, would you like to see our camp?' said the girl.

'Our Gran hates Alsatians,' the boy said.

'She's not there, is she.'

'What sort of camp?' said Tracy.

Behind the pine grove the level of rock fell gently towards a meadow fringed by birches. To Tracy's surprise there was a road here, a foresters' track, deep-sunken and rutted and with birch and goat willow on its banks; but somebody had hauled two caravans along it, for here they were end-to-end in the meadow. They were handsome caravans, not large, but streamlined and sporting longitudinal strips of chrome.

The dogs frolicked and snarled as they whisked across the turf, falling down, rolling over, covering one another with flecks of foam. The little girl laughed and ran after them, pigtail lashing wildly. The black mutt was half Martok's size but she was much faster: a lurcher, wire-coated, with whippet in her bloodline. From time to time the creatures stopped to pant and grin into each other's faces.

The woodsmoke came from the chimney of one of the caravans, though there was also a burnt patch on the ground close by, with a ring of blackened stones around it. At right angles to the rear caravan stood a shiny late-model Shogun. Leaning on a low trailer just ahead of the front caravan were two bicycles, four cartwheels, a stack of Mini wheels and the arms of a small fore-end loader, among other objects that Tracy wasn't qualified to name.

The boy said, 'We came last week.'

'Oh....'

'We've got to go to school here,' he said. 'In Whixton.'

'Oh? Soon?'

'On Monday. Really soon.'

'Did you go to a different school before? Or do you....'

'We've always gone to Whixton,' said the boy. 'But usually we camp there. At the travellers' site. Cause we're travellers.'

'No,' said the little girl, flitting up. She stood with the flat of her hand on the ground, leaning over sideways with her leg in the air. 'We're gypsies.'

'Gran is. We're not.'

The little girl nearly pulled off a handstand. From the turf she said, 'Uncle Willy says we are.'

'Where's Uncle Willy?' said Tracy.

'Went to Whixton.'

'Everybody went to Whixton,' said the boy. 'Uncle Willy and Gran and our Mum and Vanessa and Uncle Oscar. They have to see the travelling people. We didn't want to go.'

'I don't want to go to school on Monday,' the little girl said. 'I want to stay up here.'

'I like it up here too,' Tracy said.

'Where d'you live?'

'In Marchbank.'

'Is it nice?' said the little girl.

'It's just a town. A bunch of houses. It's boring,' Tracy said.

* * *

'Let's go out,' Sandy said under his breath as Debbie passed his groceries across the barcode reader. 'Let's drive somewhere.'

'Sandy....'

'We haven't much time. We don't have next weekend....'

'I know we don't,' she said. 'Let's talk later. Look, people are waiting. This isn't a singles bar.'

Sandy's brows puckered up. 'I'm sorry,' she said, 'I really am, Sandy. That's twelve fifty-eight. Would you like any cash back?'

'No thanks,' he muttered, signing the slip. He stuffed his card and receipt and the transaction slip into different pockets, his face averted, and hefted his carrier bags.

She wasn't amused by his efforts to resuscitate their affair. She loved Sandy: but that was the point. Their relationship had hit the buffers. It was kinder to end it no matter how hard that was.

She loved her husband too but that wasn't why she needed to break with Sandy. Geoff didn't know about them and he'd never find out: like, when was he ever home? But Sandy could get hurt; he would get hurt, if this carried on.

He was being weird, acting like a teenager. If she wanted to sleep with a teenager she could go find herself a real one. It wasn't impossible by any means.

* * *

Linda sat at her desk that afternoon, typing a report for the procurator fiscal.

'That for the fiscal?' Armie said. 'Isn't this a bit premature?'

'Practising,' said Linda.

'You've done a lot though,' he said. 'You've been busy.'

She sighed. 'I can't get to the main guy. The fellow with the fists. I'm leaving a lot of blanks in here....'

Armie was reading over her shoulder. 'Who's Rashid? Was he beaten up?'

'No. The other guys were. Two of 'em, Milne and Reedie.'

'Pimps?'

'Mmm well, you could say so. Reedie's got four girls, I mean he used to, and Milne had two that we know about.'

'Used to? Ah! Scuse me.' His phone was ringing. 'DI Armistead.... Oh hello Mrs Third....' Linda's typing faltered momentarily. 'No it's no trouble. I could be there in say twenty minutes…. See you then, bye. That was your Mrs Third,' he said.

'She isn't my Mrs Third. You pray she isn't yours.'

'Remind me again, Linda. Those clubs, what are they called?'

'The Beggar's Belief. The Odd Spot. The Inferno,' she said. 'Or at least it was the Inferno last week. She changes 'em fairly often.'

'With names like those she'll want to,' said Armie. 'Well I'm off. I take it Fabe's not back yet.'

Fabe had been dispatched to Edinburgh, where the case against Andrew was building up. The lab results had helped a good deal. There was proof that Andrew had been in Beames's house; better still, the DNA from the Andrew murder matched Beames's.

'Haven't seen him. I expect the bus got lost. I told him he ought to drive,' said Linda. 'Couldn't the old cat have talked to you over the phone?'

'Aye she could. She wants to see me, she's that kind of woman. And I,' he said, winking, 'I want to see her, I'm that kind of man.'

When Armie reached the Thirds' house twenty minutes later, a low, slinky car stood crouched before the door. Armie parked where he was, and as he climbed out he saw Sandy Third creeping out from behind the car, bent double.

Sandy stood up with an effort and pressed his hands into the small of his back. 'Oh crumbs. Must be age coming on. Aye aye! It's Mr Armistead isn't it?'

'Hello Mr Third. That's a handsome car.'

Sandy grinned. 'Handsome? I know it looks a dinosaur, but it's a good 'un. You'd be surprised.'

'I must confess, I'm not into cars,' Armie said. 'I know I bought mine from you though. One of your minions, anyway. Is your missus about? She asked me to come.'

'Oh aye?' Sandy wiped his hands with a rag. 'Don't know what that's about. Arlene's a law unto herself you know.' He opened the front door. 'Oh honey! I'm off now, OK? Here's Inspector Armistead for you. I'll see you at eight.' He paused on the step. 'Oh I ought to've told you. She's got another visitor.'

51

He nodded at two Toyotas standing side by side on the gravel beyond the house. 'The shiny one's his. Some businessman, I forget his name. Pleasant sort of guy.'

As Sandy thundered into the distance, Arlene's voice floated from within. 'Come in the kitchen, Inspector, the door is open.'

So it was. Armie could see in. Arlene stood, dressed in ravishing denims, her hand resting on a chair-back. Her feet were bare, her toenails painted with pearl varnish; suddenly Armie remembered last week's dream of women. At the table sat a man, who rose now, beaming, holding out his hand and saying: 'Geordie!'

Armie felt his chest tighten. He gaped at the hand, then took it. 'Ronnie!' he said.

five

There it Was – Gone

'SO INTERESTING that you two know each other,' Arlene said, sitting down.

That's putting it well, Armie thought. 'Past times,' he said, 'lost youth….'

'Oh not lost altogether, surely,' said Arlene. 'Well! I should let you two catch up. But actually I did want to speak to you, Inspector.'

'That's why I'm here.'

'It's about my bouncer.'

Ronnie Goudie shot a covert glance at Armie, trying to exchange ironic smiles. True enough, some of Ronnie's youth was still with him. He was heavy-set, dark-eyed and grey-haired as Armie was; but anyone could see he must be ten years younger.

'The bouncer at your club?' Armie took out his notebook and spectacles. 'One of your clubs?'

'I've employed him at the Odd Spot but I sacked him. I sacked him for living off immoral earnings.'

'Did you happen to report him to the police for that, Mrs Third?'

'Oh no. No I didn't. I have to confess....' She twirled a lock of hair round a finger. Ouch, Armie thought, it's too short for that. 'I have to confess, I don't care. I mean live and let live. Someone has to.... I'm sorry Inspector, but you know, supply and demand? Long as it's not the people who work for me.'

'Supply and demand,' Armie said, 'it's an old, old story. What's the bouncer's name?'

'Dave Rashid. That's right, i-d. He's got quite a rep, used to be a boxer, that sort of idea. He even won titles. Amateur titles, but still!'

'What weight?' said Ronnie.

'Oh I don't know, middle? Light middle? I'm guessing,' she said, 'but he's not one of these lumbering heavyweight types. So Dave, anyway, last week he turned up at the Beggar's Belief and tried to wheedle his way back in. I mean as the bouncer. The manager hires the staff down there, he's in charge. Mikey Lamond. He's young but he's sharp, you know? He's got a free hand. Well – almost.'

'So Rashid,' Armie said, 'he'd have to apply to Mikey Lamond.'

'That's right. And Mikey, good man that he is... he told him to clear off! So no problem there! But the thing is... as I say, he runs whores. Immoral earnings – you know.'

'He runs whores.' Armie made a note. 'Hmm! In the plural?'

'By the half-dozen or so,' said Arlene.

'Well Mrs Third, there's not much gets past you. So what is it he did, exactly?'

'He's been knocking them about.'

'What, his own girls?'

She nodded. 'They won't go to the police. But I know.'

'Can you prove it?'

'No.' She shrugged. 'But it's true. I'd like you to get him. You'll easy get proof, if you look.'

'The girls won't indict him,' said Armie. 'I mean, maybe they will. You never know.'

'These tarts get jealous. Then they'll say anything,' said Ronnie.

'Well!' said Arlene. 'I can see you've been carefully brought up!'

Ronnie blushed: something Armie had never thought he'd see.

'I'm buying one of her clubs,' said Ronnie, once they were outside on the step. 'But this is rare – it's grand to see you, Geordie.' You too, thought Armie, like hell. 'So it sounds like you want to pick up this Rashid,' said Ronnie. 'Sounds a wee jobbie to me.'

'You mean, you want him out of the way.'

'I didn't say that.'

'Did you get Arlene – no of course you didn't.'

'Of course I didn't. How true,' Ronnie said. 'You're a good copper, Geordie. I know you. I'm not pretending I can put one across you. Want a drink? My house is quite near here.'

'No I'll pass, thanks, Ronnie. See me, I'm conscientious as well as good. Which club?'

'Am I buying? All of 'em – that's the plan. But not yet.... The Inferno, for starters. Got to lose that name eh? Terrible. Aye well,' Ronnie called as Armie pulled away, 'drop by and see me, don't be a stranger.'

The bloody man likes me, thought Armie as he turned out of the lane from Nellfield.

He likes me and he's actually living in Marchbank. If only I never had to come here again. He thumped the steering wheel feebly twice, then slowed and turned right towards the town.

* * *

'I know who his girls are,' Linda said. 'I thought I did.... Knocked about? Hm! I'd better get back on the street, so to speak.'

'Up to you,' Armie said. 'You're off duty in forty-five minutes.'

'And I was meeting Grassy for tea. Early for once. At his place – he's got the cookery bug.'

Armie knocked on Bob Marshall's door and when nobody answered he said, 'I've been disingenuous, Linda.'

She stood by the window: her face was in shadow, her fair hair a corona in the sunlight. 'You mean lying?'

'N – fair enough, aye.' He sat down on his desk. 'You remember when all this started? I said, let's imagine some new guy who's taking over the enterprises in Hornbridge.'

'For argument's sake?'

'Right. Well, he's real. And I knew he was here, I'm afraid.'

'Oo.'

'I should've said something, you've been working your socks off on this case. But I had my reasons. Not good ones but reasons. The guy's name is Goudie… Ronnie Goudie.'

'Ah.'

'Goudie was a villain in the old days and he's a villain today,' Armie said, 'but his style has changed. In the eighties he was banged up for armed robbery, he was lucky not to be charged with murder cause somebody was killed. You knew that.' She didn't speak. 'OK, now he's a businessman. He's buying The Inferno.'

'Oo, I didn't know that.'

'You would've found out in a minute, I'm sure. Now, the fact is I don't like Ronnie Goudie, but I don't think he knows that. He thinks I'm on his side. I haven't said I'm not… and it's clear he wants Rashid out of action. It's natural enough.'

'So if you lock Rashid up you're on Goudie's side,' said Linda.

'That's right. And Rashid, he probably never laid a finger on 'em. It'll be… well, Ronnie's not going to demean himself by beating girls up. He'll have muscle. You know what you said about Hendry?'

'Ahh… too big?'

'Right, well, Rashid's an amateur boxing ace. Retired.'

'Is he! It fits,' said Linda.

'So you might find Rashid didn't beat the girls up. Or you might find that he did. I don't know. But I think we could very well pull him in on spec.'

'Goudie'd be pleased.'

'Goudie would just think I'd done him a favour. I could do with that while I work out what to do. Of course Rashid wouldn't be pleased at all.'

'Wouldn't his girls be in danger then? If he was locked up.'

'I've thought about that. I don't see why. Goudie's Mr Muscle might've done 'em over cause he couldn't nobble Rashid – but we'll be nobbling Rashid for him.'

'I mean,' Linda said, 'danger from other guys. Pimps don't just cream off the girls' earnings y'know.'

'I'm sorry. I know what you mean,' Armie said, 'but it looks like Goudie's about to take their protection on himself.'

* * *

Arlene didn't notice at first that the car was gone. She'd got so used to its absence: Sandy's sports car, always away getting seen to. But of course he'd had it at home for nearly a week. So where was it?

Seven o'clock. She was later than usual. Ronnie Goudie had turned up at the Odd Spot, and suddenly work had become play. She'd lost track of the time.

But the car really was gone. She hurried upstairs. Well, Sandy was there all right. He smiled in his sleep. Too bad he wouldn't be smiling much longer.

'Nissan two hundred,' Ian Barclay said. 'Two hundred SX. Quite a beast. And you say you never left it locked.'

'I take the key out,' said Sandy.

'And you say you were back here at eight last night.'

'At ten past.'

'Ten past.' They sat in the conservatory. Arlene, who needed caffeine, brought a tray with coffee-things and collapsed into a deep bamboo chair.

'He was,' she said. 'I was here.'

'You went out?'

'I went out about nine. Always go Wednesdays.' She hauled herself upright and poured. 'Sugar?' You look like you need something sweet, she thought, what a gloomy-looking bugger you are. 'Help yourself to cream.' She yawned. 'Scuse me. And I got back at seven. And there it was, gone.'

'Is the key still in the house?' said Barclay.

'It's here.' Sandy took the key from his pocket. 'I had it in my pocket, there isn't a spare.'

'Didn't hear anything?'

'He sleeps like the dead,' Arlene said, tapping her forehead, 'touch wood.'

A little later, Barclay crossed the drive and climbed the steps of Nellfield Mains. He rang the bell.

He was thinking about women: specifically, about their primal urge to feed you tea and coffee at all hours of the day and night. He was sure it was part of a plot to make men uncomfortable.

Presumably, the lady of the house was at home. She'd have coffee on her mind as well.

* * *

Hands in her pockets, Tracy leaned against the workshop sink. 'You really have a thing about gypsies, don't you.'

'Why shouldn't I? Look at the way they live.'

'You don't even….' But why start a fight? You don't even know how they live: how would he? What did anyone really know about gypsies? Especially around here, where there weren't any.

In any case Martok had started to caper about and yodel. He could never stay out of an argument.

'Shut up,' Frank said. 'Martok I mean.' He picked up a service manual. 'I'm not going to talk about this. I've got work to do. These coffee breaks are taking up the whole bloody day.'

She'd never seen Frank look like that, ever. His face had crumpled as if he was going to cry.

57

She tried not to be all romantic and gooey about gypsies. It wasn't easy, but, she knew, the gypsies of tradition weren't the same as those of the real world.

But it isn't just romantics that hide from the world. The prejudiced do it too.

Rounding the corner by the showroom she piled into Guin.

'Oops. Sorry Tracy. Wasn't looking. You OK?'

'I'm... I wasn't looking either, sorry.'

'You OK?'

'Mmm.'

'Going somewhere?' Guin said.

'I don't know. Somewhere, yeah.'

'Well I have to take the truck out, I'll give you a lift.'

It mightn't be clever to tell Guin about the travelling folk. Fabe would get to know, then the whole of CID. But after all they weren't doing anything wrong up there... were they?

As the pickup rolled along the Hornway Tracy said, 'What is it with Frank and gypsies?'

'Frank and gypsies?' Guin yelped. 'You're kidding me.'

'No, why?'

'Oooh. He can't, he can't possibly still believe it.'

Guin dodged round a string of parked cars. Tracy waited in silence for whatever it was Frank couldn't still believe.

'It was when our Mum left, he's told you about that.'

'A little,' Tracy said.

'But I thought he must've.... Aagh! How do these people get a driving license! Hell's bloody teeth. Well... I'd never have thought he'd still believe that. Gypsies. Oh dear.'

Guin's pretty aggressive behind the wheel, thought Tracy: must be because she usually rides a scooter. 'So what was it?' she said after a while.

'Oh, our Dad, when our Mum went away. He told those two she'd run off with the gypsies. Just for something to say.'

'Oh my God,' Tracy said, 'no wonder. Oh poor Frankie, bloody hell. Oh poor Frankie. I didn't know...'

'Goodness,' said Guin. 'Never mind, Tracy. You couldn't know. I didn't! I mean I thought he'd forgotten about it. Not Mum, but the gypsy bit.'

'Was it true?'

'Of course not. There aren't any....'

'There could've been. There are travelling folk.'

'That's different. Travellers aren't the same thing. I mean, real gypsies are travellers, but travellers aren't necessarily –'

'Suppose that was who she went off with,' Tracy said, 'and your Dad just said gypsies.'

Guin took a left into the Safeways car park, parked, and sat, staring across at the trolley bay.

'What's kicked this off?' she said, at length.

'Some travellers I met in the woods.'

'I never thought of travellers,' Guin said. Still she gazed out at the trolleys. 'Dad said gypsies.'

'These were just children. They don't even know if they're proper gypsies or not.'

'Dad said gypsies, I thought he was kidding. Not kidding, I mean, but just making it up.'

'Have you ever... does he ever speak about this? Could you....'

'I'm not asking him now. It's better this way. Cause I still don't believe it.' Guin took her hands from the wheel and leaned back, folding her arms. 'It doesn't matter who she went off with or where... or where she is now. She went. Oh, Tracy, he was her baby.' She bit her lip, shook her head. 'To hell with it.'

They went inside and bought beer.

'You have to watch Dad,' Guin said, loading another twelve-pack on the trolley, 'he drinks a lot if you let him get depressed.'

* * *

Late that afternoon, Ian Barclay's quest for the Nissan led him to the travellers' designated site on the edge of Whixton industrial estate.

In all this beautiful countryside, thought Barclay, and given that tinkers are basically a country thing, couldn't some genius on the council have thought of a better place to put them? This could be Birmingham, for God's sake.

No one could be seen outside the vans, except for a dark-haired man in a brown leather jacket and high boots. 'Afternoon Inspector,' he said.

'Sergeant,' said Barclay. 'Sergeant Ian Barclay, Car Crime. You belong to this lot, do you?'

'No,' said the dark man. 'But I know them. Willy Smith.' He proffered a hand, and Barclay, to his own surprise, shook it. This fellow's a gypsy, he thought. Not a tink. Hard hand too. 'What's the car like?' said Smith. 'Nice, is it?'

'It's a white H reg Nissan 200 SX. A sports car,' said Barclay. 'Taken from Marchbank.'

'I've seen it,' said Smith. 'When did it go missing?'

'Sometime between eight last night and seven this morning. Probably after midnight sometime.'

'Well I saw a car like it, driven by a bloke,' said Smith. 'In Whixton. Did a handbrake turn into South Horn Street. Very noisy.'

'When was this?'

'Oh… two-ish? Say a quarter past.'

'And what was he like, this guy?'

'I think he was young. Short hair,' said Smith, 'like a bristle cut, maybe. Oh, and he was wearing a tee shirt.'

'Any tattoos?' said Barclay, with irony.

The gypsy smiled obliquely. 'No. No, I didn't see any tattoos. Nor studs in his lips nor hairs growing out of his nose.'

'You know cars, do you?'

'Oh I do, mush. I do. I know that one.' Smith's dark eyes studied Barclay, and all at once the angular smile faded. 'You ought to take a holiday, Sergeant.'

'What?'

'I beg pardon, a slip of the tongue. Please expunge it from the record.' Smith was smiling again; but his eyes were sad.

* * *

Up over the Fairyhill road, through the forestry, watch out for deer; slow for the logging machinery grumbling into the lay-by. Round the switchback flipping left, right, and merrily onto the Whixton straight, eighty-five, ninety: then let her back off, dropping down, and roll into town at thirty.

It was dusk, a time when you need your wits about you: things aren't as they look, Grassy thought. People, cars, cats, materialise beside you without warning. They don't see you. 'I'm sorry pal, I didn't see you!' Bikers have all heard that one. It's one thing for cats to act dozy, but humans, you'd think, would know better.

The white car materialised on Grassy's offside flank and he twitched towards the curb. 'Twat and a half,' he said inside his helmet, straightening out, letting the idiot in the Nissan – for Nissan it was – forge ahead, breaking the built-up speed limit. The car vanished round a bend ahead; Grassy puttered serenely on for a law-abiding circuit of Whixton.

Ten minutes later he was out on the Marchbank road. Whixton was dead tonight. What he thought he'd find there, he couldn't have said: he was at a loose end without Linda, that was all. She always made him promise to ride carefully. But he was too old and smart to take risks… except calculated ones of course.

The Nissan flashed past him on the straight.

Oh goody.

Grassy's Honda claimed among its ancestors some of the fastest road bikes there have ever been. It accelerated well, too. He opened it up. The car was in sight, diminishing fast; there was no one else on the road.

The car got closer.

The little chicane at the end of the straight was still a few hundred yards off. Grassy boosted the Honda onto the car's tail, hung on his quarter, and the Nissan actually began to draw away. The guy at the wheel was giving it some welly. He's nuts, or he doesn't know the road, Grassy thought. The question is, do I go through?

At the last moment he didn't go through. There was room but he couldn't see. The Nissan hurtled into the switchback ahead of him and out of sight. Even before he heard the bang he knew the guy had lost it.

* * *

'Calculated risks,' Linda said. 'You are the limit, you know?'

'Well,' said Grassy, 'maybe I am, but you were off cruising for a bruising in Polwarth.'

It was dark now. They stood in the middle of the chicane; it was cordoned off and full of flashing lights. The ambulance had gone. People were measuring skidmarks, swarming over the wreck; there was a disturbing smell of petrol. Barclay was waiting to take Grassy's statement.

'What bruising?' said Linda. 'I arrested the guy, big deal. I told him it was for his own good. He didn't get rough.'

'His own good? He swallowed that?'

'It happens to be true. Armie says.... Tell you later. OK Ian, you better have him now.'

The guy who'd taken the Nissan was lucky it hadn't burned. Sandy would say later that the Devil looked after his own.

The guy was called Cyril MacBride. When he woke up he gave an address in Lanark, and said he'd come down to Hornbridge to find work. In fact, he said, the manager at the Beggar's Belief had already offered him a fortnight's trial as bouncer.

He was out of luck there, Barclay thought. Not only had he broken his arm, he'd totalled his future employer's husband's car. He guessed MacBride hadn't connected the car with the Beggar's Belief, since Mikey Lamond did his own hiring and firing.

In any case MacBride was a pretty small catch: no hope that he'd turn out to be working for top-of-the-market car thieves. It wasn't as though that Nissan was much these days.

six

September

UP ON the heights there wasn't a lot to eat. Mice were scarce: it didn't take many nights to catch every one within range of her den among the rocks. But there was a little boggy tarn, shrunk to a puddle, where frogs were. Also the river was low, and she'd learned to fish.

That afternoon she'd taken a duck, springing on it out of the rushes by the tarn. The bones and little feathers, and of course the oil, had later made her vomit. Now she stood hock-deep in the river and drank. Her belly squeaked and burbled.

Rabbits were scarce, too, although they frequented the meadow where the little bitch and her men were living. The bitch had caught some and the scent of their livers had spread abroad: livers and urine and blood. But the foolish rabbits played in the meadow still. The men and their bitch would surely have them all.

She'd have to move, hunt in the grassy uplands: rabbits swarmed there, mice ran everywhere. She could find a new den close to the pasturelands, perhaps in the thick belt of spruces to the north, and from there she'd raid at night. The sun set early now. The nights were long.

As she walked ashore the rising moon, red and round, tipped the margins of her ears with fire.

* * *

Tracy awoke in the dark and decided it was morning. She went to the bathroom. The red numerals on her clock said 05:31.

She didn't switch on the bathroom light; the streetlamps leaked in, filling the room with a cozy sulphurous glow. She peeked out the window. Ian Barclay's bedroom light shone dimly behind the curtain. As Tracy watched, it went out.

After that, Barclay's place stayed dark. Tracy left the bathroom, put on a sweater and went to the kitchen to make coffee. She brought an Anglepoise lamp from the sitting room and set it up on the breakfast bar, then took out a sketch pad. The amateur drama group in Hornbridge had asked her to design some scenes. She was flattered: too bad they couldn't afford to pay.

The coffee-maker hissed and sighed and went quiet. Before she could rise to get a cup Tracy heard the slam of some door in the stillness, an outer door. She went back to the bathroom, leaped to the window: there, sure enough, was a shadow flitting down the path from Barclay's back door, away down the path and out of sight. A woman, she supposed.

* * *

'Trying to reach bloody Ian Barclay all morning,' Linda muttered.

'It's only nine-thirty,' Fabe said.

'Ever since I got here I mean. It's MacBride. I have to compare notes on him, Rashid's given me a description.'

'Any joy from the toms?' Fabe said.

'They're not interested.' She swivelled her chair round and looked up at him, balefully. 'Toms. There's something very offensive about that expression.'

In Bob Marshall's office, Armie said, 'You're having me watched, aren't you.'

'What makes you….'

'Every time I go out they leap to their feet and volunteer to come too.'

'It's loyalty.'

'No it isn't.'

'Armie,' said Bob, 'please don't go paranoid on me.'

'But you think I….'

'If you think your people are watching you, ask them. They'll tell you. It's all in your mind. Now if you can spare me a little time, we need to talk about Dunc Brown's case. Rod Andrew.'

Armie sat back and sighed faintly. Brown's case. They'd been knitting it together, like children in separate primary schools making squares for the same quilt. It made him feel slightly ill; but it was a welcome distraction from Ronnie Goudie.

Goudie kept inviting him to things. Come and see my club, take a look at my house. The door's always open – to you, pal, not to the world at large. We ought to catch up. It's been a long time.

Bob was saying, 'Your evidence. Armie?'

'Aye. I'm here, Bob. The transaction slip.'

'No,' Bob said, 'the forensic from the bedrooms.' Evidently, Andrew had stayed overnight. He'd left traces in two of the bedrooms.

'None of it says he's a killer,' said Armie.

'If anybody happened to be in Marchbank they could call round by Ian's,' Fabe said.

'You mean, let's go for a drive,' Linda said. 'Takes up too much time.'

'I didn't. I said if anybody happened…. Have you tried his people? Scottie, Jock Ord?'

'Course I have.' Linda swivelled back to her screen. 'They aren't worried, see, he does this. I mean, goes AWOL from time to time. Since he split with Jessie.'

'Oh aye.'

'But I don't know.' She nudged the mouse to get the screen to display, then whacked a few times at the down key. 'I mean he could answer his bloody phone.'

'Who's that?' said Armie from behind her. He'd ransomed himself from Bob's office with a promise to liaise more assiduously with Brown. 'Trying to liaise with someone?'

'To what?' said Linda. 'Oh yeah. I am, aye, Ian Barclay. Randy bugger.'

'I wouldn't know.'

'She means he's sleeping in,' Fabe said. 'In addition to sleeping around. And he's not answering his phone, either.'

'Ah,' said Armie, sitting down on his desk. 'That. Aye. Well we've all heard the stories. Let's not – hell's teeth. Hell's teeth.'

'What do you mean hell's teeth?' Fabe said.

Armie was on his feet again, staring at Fabe as if he couldn't see him. He blinked and shook his head. 'No,' he said, walking to the window, 'no. It was Andrew.'

'What do you mean it –'

'But all the same let's go, Fabe. I mean, I'm going out, and you want to come too, am I right?'

* * *

The harvest was over, the fields were shorn. On the road to Marchbank, Fabe gazed out the window at the birch-clumps, golden now, and the beech hedges dressed in cobwebs still wet where the sun didn't reach anymore. Even so, he thought, it's going to be another warm one. Nice.

'Armie,' he said. 'What the hell did you mean I'll want to come too? What's with you?'

'Bob's having me watched, isn't he.'

'No he isn't. Well not by me.'

'Ah, you would say that.'

'Oh you're hopeless,' said Fabe. 'If you can't accept anything anyone tells you…. Why would he have you watched?'

Armie didn't answer. He pulled over and parked in Mill Circle. 'I think the actual door's in back,' said Fabe. 'These places are really bijou. It's the ground floor.'

At the back they rang the bell and rattled the letterbox and hollered, 'Ian!' a few times, and peered in at the windows. There were only the two, and no one was in the kitchen. They could just see into the curtained room to the left.

'Bedroom,' said Fabe. 'Look.'

Armie stood on tiptoe with his hands on the ledge, and put his eye to the crack in the curtains. 'It's a bed all right. I wonder if this window will open…. No.' With his fingertips clutching the windowframe he hauled himself onto the ledge, kneeling and trying to make himself narrow like a cat. 'I can see

66

something. Fabe.... Damn it.' He fell off sideways, miraculously landing on his feet. 'Going in.'

'What did you see?' But Armie was already busy with the door. 'OK, wait up,' Fabe said.

The door had a glass panel. They broke it, turned the handle and went in.

In the papers you often read, 'Inspector So-and-so said it was the most distressing case he ever dealt with....' and you think, Really? Like, where's he been? Armie himself had read such things in the papers.

But he never found himself thinking, 'Where's he been?' Each case, he thought, might truly be more distressing than the last.

The sight of Ian Barclay with his throat hacked open was way beyond distressing, and Fabe was sick on the carpet. Armie wished he could throw up too. Instead he knelt beside the body and looked into the dead eyes for a long time without speaking, his own eyes running with tears.

He would have liked to tell Ian he was sorry. He was sorry he hadn't warned him. He was sorry he hadn't made everybody listen, that he hadn't foreseen this until after Ian was dead.

Fabe was calling the station now, getting the doctor and the SOCO, and blowing his nose like fury.

* * *

Bob took the meeting in the big room, because everybody was there: all the officers who'd been at the house, all the car crime guys and the uniformed people. Hornbridge would have to police itself this bright September day.

It seemed a long day now that the sun was setting. The tall windows of the detectives' base were edged with mellow gold. No one looked out at the sunset. The officers watched Bob, or talked in undertones, or sat with their thoughts.

'May I have your attention.'

Armie sat beside the whiteboard on a stool. Bob would want him to speak in a little while.

'As you're aware, our friend and colleague Ian Barclay is dead. Murdered,' said Bob. 'He was found this morning by DI Armistead and DS Finnie....'

Tragedy makes people formal, Armie thought. Suppose that was me there. Stabbed and left to bleed to death. Detective Inspector George Hope Armistead was a fine man and a fine police officer. Except he had this strange propensity for befriending intolerable villains like –

Bob was saying something. 'DI Armistead has the specifics so let me hand over to him. Armie?'

'Thanks Bob.' Armie got off his stool and Bob stepped aside, giving him the floor, except that he didn't sit down. Since he stood some five inches taller than Armie, he didn't appear to have relinquished anything.

'The time,' said Armie. 'Dr Greig puts the probable time of death at somewhere between two and seven in the morning. But we have a witness, a neighbour, Miss Wiseman, who was up at half past five. She looked out her window. She saw a light in the bedroom, which went out at about five-thirty-five. She also heard a door slam, and saw someone hurrying down the path at exactly – according to her kitchen clock – five-fifty-three. So the time of death is between two and say five-thirty-five.' He paused; people scribbled.

'Forensic,' he said. 'You've been working all day, we have lots to get through, but I'd like to mention this glove.' He held up a clear plastic bag with a dark-coloured object inside. 'It's a right-handed brown leather glove, driving glove, apparently a man's. Small to medium man's. Good quality, expensive. It's not bloodstained. But it hasn't a mate, as far as we know, so it could've been dropped by the killer. If he was stupid, or in a hurry.... It was on the kitchen floor, by the table. The lab will get something from it – there's a stain at the base of the thumb and index finger.... You know, where a guy might wipe his nose. So they'll get results, but take a good look at it now while you can. Cause we're looking for the mate to it. It'll be on my desk.'

He put the bag down and went on. 'The weapon. This we know, from Dr Greig's preliminary findings, to have been most probably a sharp slender-bladed knife. Like a boning knife, doesn't have to be a boning knife, but slim like that. We haven't found it. You're all still looking.'

He viewed their bent heads with misgiving. 'Now the way it was used. This isn't easy. For me either. The knife enters the left side of the neck and severs the jugular, passing right through and out at the right side. This is the fatal wound.... Sorry.' Several of the scribbling hands had fallen slack, and one or two heads wagged in protest. 'This is what Dr Greig's initial findings strongly suggest. And the conspicuous lacerations of the throat are post-mortem... mutilations. Unlikely in themselves to have been fatal. These... lacerations are of course reminiscent of the wound that killed Neil Beames a month ago.'

Bob shifted restlessly and Armie thought, just give me one second, damn you. 'As you're all aware, Beames was killed with a broken bottle, not a knife. And a man's been arrested and charged with the murder of Beames. He's in custody. So we're looking at what could be a copycat killing, given the differences – use of a knife. But we're also going to bear in mind the similarities... as both men were naked in bed when they were killed.'

There was a silence. Someone sniffed loudly. 'I think that's all I have to say,' Armie said. 'Except for – you know this of course – the presumed copycat is extremely likely to go on killing. Given that the usual psychology applies.'

* * *

Tracy hadn't given her statement out of any sense of public duty, nor was she scared of getting killed herself. It was what she'd seen through her camera lens that decided her.

Tracy's modest telephoto lens had been trained on the maisonette since she'd heard the sirens in mid-morning; then came the whole gaudy advent of the specialist teams. She hadn't taken any pictures: no film. But the live show was worth watching.

Most of the cops, some of whom she'd surely have seen before, were swathed in white suits and couldn't be recognised. She knew Fabe Finnie though, and Ferris turned up after a few minutes. They stood talking outside by the door. Where was their boss, then?

She'd spotted him in the kitchen. For a moment she looked down on his curly head as he nosed about the sink below the window. Then he vanished, to reappear in the doorway. The other two conferred, he stood apart. Tracy saw him reach into his jacket pocket and pull out a handkerchief, then take off his glasses and mop his face; he wiped the lenses, then mopped his face again. At length he turned from the young detectives and walked, head bowed, towards the rear of the silent ambulance.

I wouldn't have believed that if I hadn't seen it, she'd said to herself, stuffing her camera under some towels and running downstairs to him.

Frank had rung up at intervals through the day. At five he had left his workshop and driven over in the pickup.

'I think I should stay here,' he said now, as Tracy, in the bathroom, watched the polis packing up. 'I think I ought to just move in.'

'Hmmm?'

'I said I should move in here. There's some psycho going about. You shouldn't be on your own.'

'Oh Frankie.' She emerged and gave him a squeeze. 'I'm not on my own. It doesn't feel like I am.'

'Well I'm staying,' he said. 'OK?'

'Course it's OK. But no one's going to kill me.'

'No, that's right. Cause I'll be here.'

'Someone might get your Dad....'

'He's got Martok.'

They went to the kitchen, and Frank sat at the breakfast bar. Tracy put on the kettle. 'You know those pictures I took,' she said.

'Certainly do.'

'I'm going to burn them.'

'Thank God for that,' said Frank. 'You making toast?'

seven

Immorality I Know

RONNIE SAID, 'It's not about the toms, you know, Geordie. Or the clubs.'

'So you say.'

'It's not! Look, I was eight years in the old Bar-L. People respect me....'

'You got twelve,' Armie said.

'I know, it just goes to show that hope springs eternal. You're empty....'

Armie put a hand over his glass. 'No more for me thanks. I'm not a drinking copper.'

'Course you're not.' Ronnie sat back on his stool and regarded his guest with quiet pride. 'But I was speaking about respect, wasn't I. Aye. See me, I don't have to get personally involved these days. People are happy to be of service. Cause they respect me....'

'So it's about respect, that's what you're saying.'

'That's what I'm saying,' Ronnie said. 'It's not about the tarts. Good place this.'

They sat at the deserted bar of The Inferno. Ronnie owned it now, he had the keys. In the daytime the club had a curiously churchlike air: it awaited the worshippers of pleasure.

'I'm changing the name just like you said,' said Ronnie. 'I'm calling it Heaven.'

'No kidding?'

'You,' said Ronnie, 'you ought to think about respect. I hear you've got the youngsters calling you Armie.' He chuckled. 'You and whose Armie. They ought to show you more respect.'

'They think I have some terrible secret, don't they,' Armie said, 'from my big city days.'

'Then they ought to respect you for it. That's how it works. I was eight years in the Bar-L, Geordie.' Ronnie poured himself another Macallan, stopped himself offering Armie a shot – for that would hardly be respectful; instead he raised his glass in tribute, and remarked, 'Here's to buried treasure!'

'Here's to it,' said Armie. 'What buried treasure?'

'I have the strangest feeling,' Ronnie said. 'I have a feeling I'm going to tell you about it.'

I can't drink in the daytime, Armie thought, stepping out into sunlight from the gloomy bar. I can't drink in the daytime and now I feel like I need a bath, no, two baths.

He wondered who'd watched him go in, who'd seen him come out. He couldn't see any coppers about but that didn't mean they weren't there. Fabe, it was true, was busy talking to Barclay's recent contacts, the victims of car crime and its perpetrators. As for Linda, she'd had to stop harassing MacBride; she was interviewing Barclay's family, hunting out his girlfriends. Wattie was going over CCTV footage, the rest of uniform were still combing the maisonette.

Perhaps Bob's watching me himself, he thought.

This was ridiculous. Ian was dead. He'd been dead for a day and a half. High time to focus on the killer – the copycat killer, Armie repeated to himself. It fitted and yet it didn't fit, because if Andrew was the killer of Beames he'd eat his hat, not that he had one.

'Suze,' he said ten minutes later. The walk to the bank, in the cool dry air of autumn, had almost put the Macallan to flight. 'Had lunch yet?'

'Yes,' said Susie, reaching under her desk for the sandwich box. 'Salad or jelly?'

'Please.' He began with the salad. 'I had a drink with Goudie just now. Christ what a bullshitter that man is. Mind you, he'd never let you die of thirst. This the blackcurrant?'

'What did you think it was?' Susie rose and fetched him a coffee. 'You can't drink in the daytime.'

'No. Ah, that's what I needed, thanks. Well... I don't think it's drugs, thank God. Not yet.'

'Why ever not? Because you're watching him?'

'Maybe. And of course, Hornsdale folk are damned near with their drug money. Anyway if Linda can tie him to MacBride....' He swallowed coffee. The phone rang.

'Susan Ar – Hello Bob! Aye... here you go.' She handed the receiver to Armie. 'For you.'

'Hi Bob.' He listened, fiddling with the pens in Susie's desk-tidy. 'You know I was here?' He listened some more. The desk-tidy tipped over and the pens slithered out. 'I can't right now. I'll have to walk. I've left my –' Susie was picking up the pens, some of which had slid right under his chair. 'Right Bob, look, how did you know – pardon? I'll be there by two, no problem. Starting now. Right – goodbye.' Delicately he set the receiver down; Susie retrieved the last of the pens. 'Sorry about that,' Armie said. 'It's a press call. He wants me for two.'

'Another one? They had one yesterday.'

'Aye.' Armie brushed crumbs from his shirt. 'They did. It's a funny one this time though. Somebody's saying we've got a werewolf.'

* * *

When Guin got back to the showroom after lunch, she was thinking about twenty-eight-day cycles. There was the moon's cycle: she took a personal interest in this in the winter, when, thanks to the moon, she didn't always have to walk the dog in the dark. There was also the cycle of human female reproductive function.

It hadn't escaped her that Beames and Barclay had been murdered when the moon was full. But since she was almost sure Beames's killer was a woman, she was thinking mostly about the reproductive thing. She herself didn't experience much emotional swing round the menstrual cycle, but she'd known people who did. For example, her poor sister had got frightful cramps. That bore on your mood all right.

So when she heard on the three o'clock news that some nutter was shouting werewolf, she wasn't surprised. It was only a matter of time before some other crank blamed PMT. She listened to a recording of Armie saying he hoped that everyone would keep an open mind about it all. The sound of his voice made her smile; Martok, lying at her feet, stared at the radio and cocked his ears.

'He isn't in the radio, goofy,' she told him. 'He's on it.'

She'd known Barclay a little. Their acquaintance had been professional: he'd investigated her for vehicle crime, she'd shopped her brother to him. She remembered him as a reserved and saturnine chap. After Barclay and his wife broke up, Fabe had passed on some choice bits of scandal, like Barclay had got off with the teenage cleaner, had propositioned Mira, had gone curb-crawling on Polwarth Avenue. But it turned out that the teenage cleaner had gone to char for Ian, not to bed with him. As for Mira, she'd been dating a fireman called Sam.

The scandal wasn't funny anymore. Ian had been lonely and sad and now he was dead. Guin knew the details of his death. When her time came she hoped she'd go faster.

Martok rose to greet Tracy, prancing round her with lowered head, leaning against her and rubbing fur and slime on her clothes. Tracy gave him a squeeze. 'Frankie's got people in,' she said. 'Guys trying to sell him bikes or something.'

'He's really moved in with you,' Guin said.

'I don't know. He might have. Time will tell…. You hear about the werewolf thing? On the radio? What do you think?'

'I don't think it's a werewolf.' Guin wondered if Tracy herself might be the nutter who'd cried wolf. Better be tactful. 'I think it's a woman.'

'But they arrested a man. For Beames I mean.'

'So they did.'

'They don't know their own minds,' Tracy said. She stroked the dog's ears. 'Martok would make a good werewolf. He's trying to speak.' So he was, in a sort of grumbling warble. 'I should take him out somewhere, I've got nothing better to do.'

He was Frank's dog. Guin wasn't going to interfere. She only hoped Tracy wouldn't get him into trouble.

* * *

The press call over, Armie fled from the news hounds to his desk upstairs and plunged into the paperwork on Ian's murder. Bob followed him in.

'I thought that went well,' Bob said. 'Considering.'

Considering what? Armie thought. 'Aye… fine, fine…. You know, I think I ought to go out and help Fabe. He's got a long list of contacts….'

'Can you drive yet?'

'Bob, why are you shadowing me? I haven't done anything.'

'Who says I'm shadowing you?'

'Can I drive yet. And phoning me at the bank. Jesus Christ on stalks, Bob, you don't call me on a landline unless you know where I am. How else –'

'If you're going to be hostile and paranoid I –'

'I haven't done anything. The man is a villain and I am investigating him, OK? You think you know anything about it, Bob? Were you there?'

'You know very well I wasn't –'

'No. No you weren't. And you know less than nothing about me, and I resent all this cloak and dagger carry-on. How can I work with folk if they don't trust me?'

'For God's sake, Armie.' Bob didn't know whether to be angry or alarmed. 'All I said was can you drive yet. Wattie happened to see you coming out of the Inferno Club.'

'I didn't bloody see him.'

'I didn't imply that there was anything unprofessional about –'

'You'd better bloody not.'

It is a fact, Armie thought ruefully as he made his way downstairs, that if I drink in the daytime I get fair murderous later on.

He took a police car and drove towards the travellers' site at Whixton industrial estate. Barclay had come here last month, hunting for the stolen Nissan: like many policemen he'd associated tinks with stolen cars. His notes said he'd spoken to a Willy Smith.

The site looked deserted, but all the same Armie parked the car, got out and knocked on the door of a van at random.

'Oozat?' said a shrill voice. 'Go away!'

'Shan't,' he called back.

'Not a tome,' said the voice.

'Y'are though!' Who'm I playing silly buggers with? he wondered. The door opened, slapping the side of the van sharply. A little round woman stood in the doorway, chortling.

'You sound a right bloody idiot,' she said. 'Policeman? Are you?'

'That's right. Detective Inspector George –'

'Knew it, knew it! Inspector. What else!'

'Armistead,' said Armie. 'Hornbridge CID.'

'I'm Miranda. Miranda Herring. Sound a fishy customer don't I? What can I do you for?'

'Do you know Willy Smith?'

'Ahh!' said Miranda. 'Willy Smith. Snot about that copper who died is it? Is it! Eh! He said he'd spoken to him. And Willy saw.'

'Oh he did? What did he see?' said Armie.

'He saw didn't he,' she sat on the narrow top step, 'he was gonna die. Your mate who was murdered. Willy saw it all.'

'He saw that?' said Armie. 'When it hadn't happened yet? Isn't it a funny old world?'

'Isn't it?' said Miranda.

She sent him into the forest. She asked him not to mention her.

'You dint hear this from me,' she said, 'they're camped in the forestry, Orncross Forest. Willy's got a bee in his bonnet. You ask his Mum.'

It took him an hour to reach the encampment in the meadow. He would've been longer if it hadn't occurred to him, as he passed the forestry office, that the trackway would probably be barred. He pulled in and found a forester, who lent him the key.

'So how do the travellers get in and out?' Armie asked.

'Willy's got a key too,' said the forester. 'He's working for us. Casual kind of thing.'

'What, felling trees?'

'Why aye, just about everything, really.'

Then there was the track itself: deep, axle-destroying ruts, whiskery growths up the centre. At last the police car crawled to a halt beside the travellers' meadow. There were the vans, and the black lurcher he'd seen in town: it pirouetted round him and yelled like a banshee. He made for the van with the smoking chimney.

The door opened as he reached it. 'Shut up Squeeter! Shut it now! Down! Get down!' To be fair, the lurcher hadn't jumped on him, but it looked chastened now and lay at his feet.

The woman in the doorway sneezed, reached inside, and clapped a paper hanky to her nose. 'Scuse me,' she said through the tissue. 'Damn cold.'

She was about seventy, small and wiry with a shock of grey hair; her eyebrows were black, her eyes too. 'It's the kids,' she said, 'they bring home all the bugs in creation. So, you're the police, I see. Now what's happened? God forbid. I'm Josephine Stewart.'

'Pleased to meet you. DI Armistead. Nothing. Nothing's happened. I'm investigating the murder of one of our officers....'

'Oh,' said Mrs Stewart, 'you want Willy.'

But Willy wouldn't be back for hours. He was working in Fairyhill woods. The rest of Mrs Stewart's people had gone to Whixton to pick up the kids from school.

'My brother Oscar. Snfff.' They sat outdoors: less risk of infection, she fancied. 'His wife, Vanessa, except she never married him. They stay in my van. And in that one there, my daughter Maisie and her kids. And my son. Willy.'

'Willy Smith,' Armie said, 'not Stewart.'

'No, they had different fathers, Maisie and Willy.' She blew her nose. The lurcher put its paws on her lap and tried to lick her nose. 'Get to hell. And Willy, he was born in the south ... travels in Sussex, only came up last spring.'

'I wanted to ask him what he thought of Sergeant Barclay – if he seemed all right, that sort of thing.'

'He didn't,' Mrs Stewart said. 'He seemed miserable.'

Everyone says that, Armie thought; and maybe he was. 'I might come back and speak to your son... if that's OK.'

'He could come to you.'

'What, to the station?'

'Why not? It's not as though he had a guilty conscience.'

Now to get the car turned around. While Armie thrashed it and wallowed in the ruts, the travellers' Shogun roared up the track. The children tumbled out while it was moving, and raced off across the meadow with the dog.

The Shogun stopped, nose to flank with the police car, which nestled crosswise in the trackway. A man of about Armie's age climbed from the passenger seat; a red-haired young woman jumped out after him. Another woman sat behind the wheel.

The kids had red hair too, the man was dark. He stared down at Armie. 'Who the bloody hell are you?' he said. 'Got lost have you?'

'Right, and I nicked this car off a copper called Detective Inspector Armistead. He's going to be bloody cross when he finds out.' Armie got out and went to the driver's side of the Shogun. The window slid down; a woman of fifty or so glared out at him.

'I'm sorry,' Armie said. 'I may be a minute or two.' Where've I seen you before? he thought. He hadn't. Her yellow but greying mane was too distinctive: he couldn't have seen her before, and yet he had. But he couldn't think where.

'Stop goggling at me, your eyes'll drop out.' She reversed down the track and swung backwards up onto the turf, and getting down from her seat, slammed the door behind her and strode towards the vans without looking back.

* * *

After her last trip to Horncross Forest, Tracy had bought a large-scale map of the place. On it she could make out the travellers' meadow, and the track they must have used to get their vans up there. The track led in from the main road on the north side, through the strip of commercial spruces.

She'd also learned that the scenic route wasn't the quick way over there. If you followed the river, as she had before, the drive took twice as long as the dash along the trunk road that skirted the northern fringe. From this road you could take a

78

turning back towards the nature reserve, ending at the ramblers' car park at the foot of the plateau; or you could take the forest track, and get up onto the high ground from the north.

This afternoon she'd set off late, so she'd taken the main road to make up time. She bowled along in the pickup at fifty or more. Martok sat, braced with his forefeet, snuffling and slurping at the gap at the top of the passenger's side window. Tracy thought highway driving daunting, but in time she relaxed and began to mull over her problems.

It was all very fine saying you'd burn a pile of pictures. Her flat was heated by oil and she had no fireplace. Frankie's dad had one in the sitting-room, but she couldn't see herself using that. So she turned to the wilderness.

Here, though, it was dry as a bone: woods, grasses, moorland, ready to go up in smoke. True, the equinox was coming, with its promise of Atlantic storms; but she couldn't wait for those, even if they came.

There might be a safe place: perhaps by the river. She needed to explore.

By the time she reached the forest the spruces were thick with shadow. She wouldn't be able to go very far, after all. But it was good to be here. There was something exciting about commercial forests: the wood was a crop planted decades ago, grown and harvested on a heroic scale of time. Too bad she couldn't drive into it. A locked gate, made of a single pole, barred the trackway.

Wondering how the travelling folk had managed it, she stepped round the barrier and freed Martok from his chain. He bounded ahead a little way and stopped, looking back at her, hanging his tongue out and grinning.

'Go along, get some exercise,' she said. He shook himself and started up the track.

He could smell rubber and diesel oil. Men had been here, and squirrels, more squirrels than men. A fox had left droppings; a badger, too. As for his own kind: females, several females, none of them interesting, and a male. There were traces of deer, of mice; pigeons in places were cloying, and at a little distance a dead one was being consumed by maggots.

He paused and glanced back, his head low. Ought he to roll on that bird? Would it not be worth a quick.... Something was moving.

He raised his head, standing tall, his tail lifted; his nostrils quivered. The scent was near, and growing nearer. It was intense. It was female, his sort of female, but somehow, somehow not. His hackles lifted, long stiff black hairs, all along his shoulders and right down to the root of his tail, and he growled. But he didn't bare his fangs.

His tail began to swing slowly and he paced forward. Her pale eyes looked into his.

It wasn't afraid: she could smell that, the absence of any fear. It was male, huge, but nonetheless a dog. All the other dogs had run.

She could smell the woman on the trackway. She couldn't hang around and wait for that. Alas no; but she wanted this dog.

The woman was looking at her with burning eyes.

Perhaps the dog would follow her. She turned and fled some way up the winding path. When she paused and sniffed the air, she knew it wasn't with her. But she sat and listened for a long time.

Later, as the moon climbed above the pasturelands, she began to howl.

eight

The Lady is a Wolf

SATURDAY NIGHT: in the downstairs bar of the former Inferno, a woman who called herself Sylvie sat on the stool that had once supported Armie's behind. She was sipping tonic and lime.

Her eyes roved over the clientele, resting now on the proud new owner, now on some tarts at the end of the bar. One of them was only a teenager, perhaps even too young to drink here. But she might be on tonic and lime too, of course. There was little point in a working girl getting giddy this early in the evening.

Sylvie herself wasn't here to pick up men. She just wanted to feel good, and watch the parade of life unfolding. It was fun to speculate. What about the new guy, so cozy with the tarts: was he running them, as well as the club? The former owner would never have had the guts to do that.

She turned away, watched other folk: the band lugging their stuff through the crowd, their jackets spotted with rain; two couples in their forties sharing a table, the women whispering while the men conversed with wide gestures. A sound system played music, tepid stuff, she thought, but then this was the night spot for the slightly wrinkly brigade. What was it about middle age? People who were middle-aged today had experienced Jimi Hendrix: were they meant to forget all that as soon as they passed fifty?

But the real oldies' club had to be the Odd Spot. That place was so dead you could smell the lilies. At least here, you could pick up a tart, or listen to live music. You could pick up a musician if you fancied one.

'Can I buy you a drink?' said a voice at her shoulder. Ooh, what an original line. She glanced across the bar at the mirror that doubled all the pretty bottles of drink. The man standing at her side was a hunk, a lovely specimen... but still she felt lazy, disinclined. She smiled at him in the mirror, then looked up.

'No thanks, I'm good,' she said.

'How good are we talking?' He was too much. Too easy, and let's face it, men as a species were dire. But she was grateful to them in an obscure way: not for her old life, but for the new. She wondered whether caterpillars were aware of their destiny.

* * *

'So you don't mind about us not going to the woods,' Frank said, pouring phony draught beer tenderly from a can.

'A little,' said Tracy. It had rained all day; she still hadn't managed to get him to those woods. But since the place was crawling with gypsies it was probably just as well.

'Thought you'd like the rain,' he said. 'Especially when it's been so dry.'

'Oh I love it. Everything smells so good. But you don't have proper outdoor gear, do you? You'd have got all wet.'

He passed her a pint mug. 'So let's have a wet night in.'

Home at last, Tracy thought, with a tickly feeling in her stomach.

'There was a wolf there yesterday,' she said. 'Cheers.'

'You're joking.'

'No I'm not. It looked at me....'

'And I suppose Martok took one look and bolted.'

'No, he wagged his tail.'

'You're winding me up.'

'I am not. Ask Martok.'

'If he saw a real wolf he'd be petrified. There aren't any wolves,' said Frank. 'Want some crisps?'

'So what was it then?'

'Someone's husky or something. What happened to all those spicy ones?'

'You've eaten 'em all. I thought these scientists had probably started releasing wolves. In secret. You know, cause all the farmers are against it?'

'Everyone's against it. Except the fanatics. And they couldn't, I mean... they wouldn't.'

'They would.'

'OK, they would. But you know what it was? A werewolf,' he said, beaming and draining his glass. 'The rumours are true.'

* * *

'Saturday night,' Fabe said in pained tones, looking down at the gleaming wet street outside. 'Sunday morning.'

'I know, Fabe. I've got a home to go to as well,' Armie said. 'I want to wait for Linda. She was going to come in past... I should've gone with her, shouldn't I.'

'No. If I were a tom I'd run a mile at the sight of you. Linda's fine. I just thought.... This isn't helping anyone, is it. I'm doing sod-all.'

'You're not doing sod-all at all. You're helping me think. Let's look at it again – his last hours.'

'Christ Armie, there's nothing to look at, nobody saw him after he said goodbye to Ord.'

'Motive, then.'

'Oh please. We have no clue.' Fabe subsided into his chair with a groan.

'Tell me, Fabe.' Armie walked over to the whiteboard, which had sprouted a mishmash of dates and names. 'Why was I so afraid?'

'What do you mean why were you....'

'On Thursday morning. Here, on Thursday when Linda couldn't get him on the phone. Someone called him a randy sod. Randy. That scared me. Why?'

'If you don't know, who does?' Fabe said. 'I don't know, you thought... I mean he was spreading himself pretty thin and you probably thought... all those women.'

'But Fabe, that's what we thought about Beames.' Armie tapped the whiteboard. 'All those women.'

'That he'd killed,' said Fabe. 'Might have killed.'

'No. No, that might've killed him.'

83

'I don't get you.'

'Oh you do, Fabe, come on. That's what scared me that morning. Strange women in his bed.'

'Strange women.' Fabe stared at the whiteboard a minute. 'We've been checking out Ian's women. He slept with a lot, that's no revelation.'

'That's not what I meant.'

'So what in hell's name do you mean? I think I need some sleep.'

'Let's make coffee. Linda will be here soon.'

She'd found Zoe again. It had been a couple of weeks since she'd seen her to speak to. Coming out of the former Inferno with two friends, Zoe hadn't been quick enough to dodge Linda where she lurked under the club's scalloped awning.

'She knew Ian,' Linda reported now, hanging her dripping coat on its peg in the detectives' base. 'I thought she would. I used to see him in the Avenue sometimes…. Oo. Coffee.'

'Knew him how?' said Armie.

'He picked her up twice, she thinks twice. More than once anyway.'

'What does she say about him? I mean… I don't feel great about this, you know.'

'Can't hurt now,' Fabe said.

'No. It can't hurt now. What does she say?'

Linda sat, sipped coffee, sighed. 'Not a lot. He wasn't kinky. She knew he was a copper – didn't dislike him. Most guys she goes with, according to her, they're pond-life.'

'Like the guy who smacked her up,' Fabe said.

'She's not talking about that. Not even now. He's locked up… MacBride… and she still won't give his name. I mean I suppose she knows his name. It's Goudie that's her problem.'

Nice to have someone to share my problem, Armie thought. 'The Inferno,' he said. 'I mean Heaven. Did you see him?'

'No. I didn't go in. Anyway Zoe seems sorry Ian's dead. She has seen him with other girls and I have a note of the ones she can identify. Any one of 'em….' She yawned. 'More coffee.'

'Any one of 'em,' said Armie, pouring. 'We need to look further back.'

'We do? How do we?' said Fabe. 'I need sleep.'

'Beames,' said Armie.

'Bullshit. Beames is just history.'

* * *

After the rain the colours of pine and rock had deepened, as though a varnish had been laid on the pastels of the long dry spell. To a city man, vexed and winded by the climb, it was wholly unexpected: the plateau opened before him like a flag.

Some folk, Ronnie thought, wouldn't approve of Sunday morning treasure-hunting. But they couldn't know, could they, how like a church this was: the reverent hush, the overarching sky. He stood a moment, leaning his metal detector against his hip.

On his map the place was different. He'd studied modern maps, trying to match them to the one his great-great-grandfather had made. Now the terrain itself confronted him and, to his surprise, he recognised a lot of it from his map-reading. He was getting to be quite the outdoorsman. Well, he thought, I already was a survival expert.

Great-great-grandfather Blythe had drawn his map for his own use, never thinking he wouldn't be the one to come back here. All the same, he'd foreseen that he might be held up, with his flair for being detained for this reason or that. He'd had a compensating flair for wriggling out of things, but at last that gift had failed him; and before he could come for his gold he was dead in prison of a fever.

Ronnie turned from the plateau's edge, and made his way slowly westward across the rock.

He trudged along the shelf, thinking: Stanley. Funny how Stanley had never believed in the buried treasure story. Stanley, he mused, going daft over that bank job, that day when Geordie Armistead had popped up out of nowhere. Slippery Stanley who'd disappeared, leaving Ronnie to go down for twelve years.

Stanley's Dad, thought Ronnie, Uncle Stan: he had the map all along and just sat on it. Why? Devious old bugger. More of the gypsy in him. The Blythes, the real gyppoes, the further back you go the more devious they become.

The rocky shelf curved northwestward, round the fringe of pines. Ronnie paused, took out his map and traced the line of the plateau. Sure enough, there was a bend before you reached the path that Great-great-grandpa Blythe had marked with dashes.

All at once he realised he'd been smelling woodsmoke for awhile. He put down his metal detector and padded across the rocks, stepped in among the trees, sniffing.

They didn't see him. Somehow or other their scrawny black mutt hadn't yet caught his scent. From his hiding-place he made out two vans, two children and two trucks. Hence, two or more adults.

The dog, which was playing piggy-in-the-middle with the children, left them and ran to the foremost van. A man stepped out of it, wearing high boots. Ronnie's face grew long.

* * *

On Monday morning Willy Smith dropped by the police station and asked for Inspector Armistead. Wattie sent him upstairs.

'About the chap who died,' said Willy.

Armie couldn't recall having met a gypsy before. He didn't know if he was meeting one now; there weren't any gypsies around here.

On the other hand Ronnie Goudie thought there were. Maybe he wasn't such a bullshitter, after all. 'Thanks for coming,' said Armie. 'Take a seat.'

'He was looking for a stolen Nissan 200 SX and I told him I'd seen it. I had seen it. He was an unhappy man,' Willy said. 'A desperate man.'

'Why did you think that?'

'I didn't. I knew it. It was in his face.'

'You mean desperate in the sense of having no hope,' said Armie.

'That's it exactly.'

'No hope of what?'

'Of love.'

'God, that's hellish,' said Armie. 'Did you know he was going to die?'

'How would I?'

'Did you?'

Willy smiled lopsidedly. 'Someone told you I have the sight. Right?'

'Sort of. Have you?'

'Everyone foresees something sometime.'

'Is it something gypsies have?'

'No. It's a Highland thing. I should've thought you'd know that,' Willy said. 'I have some MacGregors a way back. They'll be to blame.'

'I expect there's a lot of folk who'd like to have second sight,' Armie said. 'They probably think it'd make 'em rich.'

'It doesn't, mush,' said Willy.

* * *

Sleeping, Guin looked younger than her thirty-one years, although Fabe forebore from asking himself how much younger. He loved to wake up with her. At this stage in a murder investigation he didn't often get the chance to stay all night.

Between them they had two unprepossessing homes. Fabe lived in a converted garage in a run-down section of Hornbridge Industrial Estate. He'd bought it from a cousin of his who speculated in property – disastrously, as it now appeared. He wondered how Guin would like to live there, instead of in her second-storey Marchbank flat with its view of privet hedges and far-off hills, and its odours of dogs and petrol.

Ah, the mystery of woman, Fabe thought.

But Guin wasn't a mystery at all; she was perfect. The woman of mystery was this other one, who Guin believed, and evidently Armie believed, was cutting men's throats in bed. Did she exist?

He'd asked Guin last night and she'd told him: yes, as far as she was concerned it was the same killer, and a woman. They hadn't discussed it: now he asked himself why. Guin was too tactful to push it, that was why. But what called for tact? His own hang-up, that's what. He asked himself what that could be.

Did he want to believe that Dunc Brown had Beames's killer locked up, because he himself had helped to nail the guy? Maybe. But surely the problem went deeper than that.

Perhaps, after all, Fabe thought, I idealise women.

So, when he strode into the detectives' base that Tuesday morning, he was overjoyed to find that they had a male suspect for Barclay. The lab results had come, early by the standards of most inquiries: but of course this one was special.

'From the glove,' said Armie, proffering the report. 'A match straight away, would you believe.'

'You don't sound ecstatic,' said Fabe. He looked over at Linda, who was typing, but she made a face and kept bashing away. Fabe scanned the print-out and burst out laughing.

'Why is that funny?' Armie demanded. 'It's no bloody use at all, is it.'

'Why not?' Fabe said. 'You've said yourself that he's the worst villain for a hundred miles.'

'It's inconceivable. Goudie has no motive, he'll probably have an alibi –'

'Oh come on. He'll buy himself an alibi. Don't be such a defeatist. Do you really think he didn't do this?' Fabe snorted. 'You're mad.'

Respect, Armie thought. 'Let's say for argument's sake that he did. Not Beames, he probably wasn't here yet... but Ian. Sat they had something going or he had a grudge, that'll do for motive. So, what evidence have we? A lost glove. What does it prove? Nothing.'

'OK, it's a clue,' Fabe said.

'Well OK, it is. We'll follow it up. But it's not evidence. I mean what do I pull him in for? Permitting his gloves to roam at large?'

'The left one's still on the rampage,' Linda said, typing.

nine

Chickens Come Home

IT FELL to Armie to make the arrest.

'Ronald Henry Goudie. I am arresting you on susp –'

'Geordie, you're not serious.'

'Believe me, Ronnie, I am serious,' said Armie. 'We have evidence that puts you at the scene of a murder. The murder of a policeman.'

'That's impossible. I was never there, are you crazy? What evidence?'

'All in good time. Thanks, PC Chandra.' Mira escorted Ronnie down the steps of his house, a pretty two-storey cottage: it was down the lane from Nellfield, where the Thirds and Chalmerses lived.

'What evidence? There can't be any evidence, that's crazy,' Ronnie said as they rolled through Marchbank, and on into the countryside.

'So convince us,' Armie said. 'Convince us and you can go.'

'I have a club to run.'

'You have a manager. You told me so yourself.'

'I don't do murders,' Ronnie said. 'Murders are for toe-rags.'

His face was purple by the time they got him to the interview room. Among other woes, he missed his lawyer. He hadn't acquired a local one yet, not one he could trust. In other words, Armie thought, not one who's in your pocket.

Charlie Henderson had acted for him in the purchase of the club, so Charlie it had to be. He was a cheery man, with honest blue eyes: incorruptible, most likely. 'Thanks for coming,' said Armie. 'Take a seat.'

'Morning Charlie,' Ronnie growled, 'who'd have thought it.'

'Be cleared up in no time,' Charlie said. 'Won't it Mr Armistead?'

Armie had no answer to that one. He switched on a little cassette recorder that stood at his elbow, and said, 'Interview begins 10:35 hours. Present are Ronald Goudie, Charles Henderson, Detective Sergeant Finnie, PC Chandra and me... DI Armistead. Ronnie....' He took the glove, in its clear plastic bag, from Mira, who stood behind him. 'Can you identify this? Ah – I'm showing Mr Goudie a right-hand leather glove,' he added, for the benefit of the tape.

The tape recorded a short silence. Ronnie stared at the glove. At length he said, 'Where the hell was it? They cost me a packet, these. Got the other one?'

'Fraid not,' said Fabe.

'Cost an arm and a leg. I lost 'em sometime last winter. Not winter but March or April. The weather was diabolical, I needed 'em to drive.'

'You mislaid them, did you?' said Armie.

'I don't know. I thought some toe-rag had run off with 'em. Fellow I had driving for me, I've sacked him now.'

'Thought you said you needed gloves for driving,' Fabe said.

'Aye well, I don't always get guys to drive me, do I? I'd be a right bloody pansy if I did.'

'Can you explain, then,' said Armie, 'how this glove of yours – it's been matched to you by DNA fingerprinting – how did it come to be in the kitchen of Sergeant Barclay's house? Where we picked it up on the day he was murdered?'

'DNA bollocks. I've told you it was mine. I don't know do I? Maybe Barclay picked 'em up somewhere.'

'But when you lost the gloves, back last April....'

'Whenever,' said Ronnie.

'Whenever,' said Armie. 'Were you here in Hornsdale? Or in the city?'

'How the bloody hell would I know, Geordie? If I'd known I was losing 'em I wouldn't have been losing 'em, would I?'

'Did you come to Hornsdale last spring, or not? Can you remember?'

'I was back and forth all the time, wasn't I. Course I came here. I was buying property, you know that.'

'So sometime last spring,' Fabe said, 'you missed your gloves.'

'Right,' said Ronnie. 'Now we've cleared that up –'

'They may have got lost here, they may have got lost back home in Glasgow. Or they may have gone missing somewhere in between,' said Fabe.

'So what?'

'So why is one of them at the scene of a murder? You still haven't explained that.'

'Well what am I?' said Ronnie. 'Clairvoyant?'

'I'll tell you what you are,' said Fabe. 'You're a killer.'

'Hear that, Charlie? Slander,' said Ronnie. 'I've never been convicted of murder.'

'True,' Armie said. 'Did you kill Ian Barclay?'

'No, would I tell you if I had?'

'Probably,' said Armie. 'Wouldn't you?'

'Not where this hatchet-faced long streak of piss could hear me.'

'That isn't going to get you anywhere,' said Fabe.

* * *

Linda faced an unpalatable truth. It was time for a talk with Arlene.

It was weeks since she'd locked up Dave Rashid and charged him with procuring. He could've been out on bail, except Goudie probably would've sent someone after him again. Dave had confessed to pimping, but he wouldn't admit to smacking up his girls, as Arlene claimed he did.

Linda left her colleagues grilling Goudie, and drove out to Arlene's place. She hoped the old cat would be out of bed by now: it was only half eleven, after all. But Arlene answered the bell, barefoot as always, wearing leggings and a red silk top.

'Oh! It's you,' she said. 'Wondered who the hell it was.'

'May I come in, Mrs Third?' said Linda.

They went through to the kitchen. Arlene didn't offer to make coffee. She stood with her arms folded, watching her visitor and thinking, police officers shouldn't be gorgeous, it's the end of law and order.

'It's about some allegations you made last month to DI Armistead concerning Mr Rashid....'

'Little thug. Haven't you locked him up yet?'

'I have. He is locked up. He's on remand.' That's told you, you old cow. 'On a charge of procuring. The thing is, he won't admit assault, and you alleged....'

'I had it on good authority. You ask the girls.'

'Well, but which girls, Mrs Third? That's what I wanted to ask.'

Arlene frowned. 'Which girls. Good God, Constable, it's been weeks. Don't expect me to remember everything for weeks and weeks, I lead a full life y'know.'

'So you do. I'd have liked to pick up on this sooner, but as you'll be aware,' Linda said, 'we're also investigating a murder.'

'Oh don't I know it. Your colleague, that long drink o' water, asked me all about poor Mr Barclay. I must say I was surprised it didn't turn out to be suicide.... I never saw such a gloomy-looking Gus. But there, it wasn't.'

'No. Well.... So are you saying that one of these girls told you she'd been assaulted, but you don't remember which one?'

'No I'm not,' said Arlene. 'I'm not saying that at all. I haven't the time or the inclination to hang about talking to prostitutes. It was a rumour.'

'You took it seriously though, DI Armistead says.'

'It came from someone reliable, yes. Hang on, I can think who it was if you'll just.... It wasn't Mikey.... Dave Rashid, Dave Rashid. Hang on a minute. It's coming.'

Linda waited. Her eyes roved round the kitchen: oak table, solid fuel stove, knife-block and silver teapot on a counter beside it. Knife-sharpener screwed to the wall above, the kind you draw the knife through, makes it hellish sharp.

'Mikey's brother,' said Arlene. 'That's who it was, Gerry Lamond, the keyboard player.'

'Oh, who's he play with?' said Linda, taking a note. 'Local band?'

'Rantin' Pipe and Tremblin' String. There! Got it right. I've had to practice that one.'

'And that's Gerry.' Linda put away her pen. 'Well I'll talk to him. Thanks very much, Mrs Third.' Nice set of knives you have there, Linda thought, forcing herself not to stare at them. Don't be so silly. Everyone's got knives.

Step by step. She went round to Beggar's Belief and spoke to Mikey. His brother the keyboard player was a forester by day. She drove out to the forestry office, only to be sent back to Fairyhill where the felling was going on.

She parked in a layby where fresh logs were piled; the green and yellow van from the forestry office stood near them. As soon as she switched off her engine, the zipping and ripping of saws filled her ears. Luckily it was nearly lunchtime. Presently the racket stopped, and men began to emerge from among the trees.

'Gerry Lamond?' she said to a sunburned edition of Mikey.

'Ahh – aye.' He looked startled, but then lots of men looked startled when they first saw Linda. Gerry got over it fast: he was in show business, after all. He opened the rear of his van and sat in it to have lunch.

'Girl called Sonia,' he said through a mouthful of sandwich. 'She's on the game.'

'I think I know Sonia,' said Linda. 'Fair hair, permed, nose stud?'

'Aye that's right. Working girl. But she comes to our gigs, I suppose she's a sort of groupie. Said something about this guy of hers, Dave. Like, if he finds out I'm hanging around you lot he'll give me another good hiding. Have a crisp.'

'Oo. Thanks. Did she have any bruises, or anything?'

'No. But I said, you know, did that bastard hit you? She said yeah, the bloody coward, he used to be a boxer and everything. Knocks us about a bit. You know he's got a few of 'em? Aye well! Iffy character.'

Funny, Linda thought, driving back to Hornbridge. I thought Sonia had some other guy. Barney, she calls him: whoever he is.

* * *

'The thing is,' Fabe said. They'd adjourned the interview. It hadn't been going anywhere. In any case Ronnie claimed he had an alibi. He said he'd been with a girl: they could ask her. Now he was snugged down in a cell, and Charlie had gone back to his office in the Cornmarket. 'The thing is, the way Ian was killed. So professional.'

'I see what you're saying,' Armie said.

'I've seen Goudie's files. He's been a pro in his time.'

'Never convicted.'

'Aye, so you both kept saying,' said Fabe. 'What is it with you two?'

'It isn't anything, Fabe. I nicked him for armed robbery and that's it. We go back a long way, cop and robber stuff. I grant you he's been a pro. He's been most things.'

'Well, in his file....' Which you've studied because Bob asked you to, Armie thought, I didn't. 'It's interesting that he spent three years in the nick with Bill Patrick,' said Fabe.

'Scissors Patrick.'

'Aye. Why'd they call him....'

'Little fingers,' said Armie. 'See Bill, he used to believe that folk don't need little fingers. He lent money, had a protection racket... sometimes he'd get impatient. They say.'

'Well,' said Fabe. 'It caught up with him in the end. Somebody knifed him.'

'I heard.'

'He died in the nick. No one was ever caught. Well I mean, who'd bother? And the wound was just like Ian's. Through the jugular from the side.'

'Ronnie was out by then.'

'You know all about Ronnie, don't you.'

'I don't like knowing about him,' Armie said, 'he's just hard to ignore.'

'All I'm saying is that that's a very professional hit,' Fabe said. 'So how about it? Whoever killed Beames, Andrew or whoever, had a completely different style. They trashed his throat. But Ian was killed clinically. Then the killer hacked him about to make it look the same.'

'I'm still with you, Fabe.'

'So why do you keep on saying the same person killed Beames?'

'Och well,' said Armie, 'I can't explain it. What you're saying makes perfect sense. Now... say Ronnie's going to kill Ian. For a start he doesn't, he'd pay someone else. Fine... and they go along and do it. Why have they got Ronnie's gloves there? To incriminate him?'

'Maybe.'

'Why not just denounce him, then?'

'I don't know, do I?' said Fabe. 'Look Armie, what about this. You keep on saying it's a woman. So – Goudie hires a woman. She gets Ian into bed and.... That make you happy?'

Armie looked at him a moment, knitted his brows: you literally could, Fabe thought, they're very woolly. 'Get him into bed,' Armie said. His face cleared. 'You're sharp as a razor, you know that?'

'You could live with that?' said Fabe.

'It isn't the simplest explanation, mind you. It isn't simple. But I love it.'

Driving over to Polwarth Avenue Armie thought, it's special pleading. Too neat. No, I'm just prejudiced, it's brilliant really.

Ronnie had had just the fuzziest clue where his alibi lived, this girl he'd left the club with, Sonia McHardy. He was pretty sure she lived in Greenbank Road. It was a street of semi-detached brick houses, each with a little paved area in front: no green banks in sight. The house had a name, Ronnie said. What was it? No idea. But it was on the left-hand side, about halfway up.

Armie checked out the houses on foot. Number thirty-eight had a name: Bogniebrae, in blackletter across the fanlight. He wondered if Ronnie really could have forgotten a name like Bogniebrae. Number forty was Bracobrae. He supposed he'd better try Bognie first.

There were five doorbells. Two had tenants' names above them, three hadn't. She lives upstairs, Ronnie had said: first or second floor. Not the loft. Well, probably not the loft. Supposing the bells to be in order of ascent.... It doesn't have five floors, so much for that theory. Armie pressed the second bell from the bottom: McHardy, it said. He couldn't hear it ring.

A window creaked open overhead. He looked up and called, 'Hello! Miss McHardy?' For all I know, he thought, it's Mr McHardy and a big angry one at that. But he heard a woman's voice from above.

'Oh for Christ's sake why bloody now?' it said. 'Jesus. Just a minute.' The window banged shut.

Sonia McHardy was small and painfully fair. Her fine bones were prominent for such a young girl; blue shadows framed her eyes. 'What's the deal?' she said. 'I can't be doing with – oh. The pigs.'

'DI Armistead, Hornbridge CID…. Pigs?' said Armie. 'I think I'll die of nostalgia.'

'I read too much, I don't know what century it is. What do you want? Jesus, I'm trying to write an essay here.'

'I'm sorry, Miss McHardy. I need confirmation of a statement by a man we have under arrest. His name is Ronnie Goudie.'

'Oh God. Come upstairs.'

She had the second floor front: two rooms. One was mostly bed. She ushered Armie into the other one, evidently a study, with bookshelves from floor to ceiling. Books covered the mantelpiece and the windowledge and large areas of floor. A laptop whirred among the books and papers on the desk. Sonia lifted a printer off a chair, so Armie could sit down.

'Why thank you,' he said. 'I don't want to take up your time. Goudie –'

'What's he done?'

'He's helping us with a murder inquiry. He says –'

'Helping? Did he kill someone?' She rolled her eyes. 'God, who needs enemies?'

Who indeed, Armie thought. 'The thing is, he says he was with you. It was early Thursday morning.'

'Last Thursday?'

'That's right.'

'I don't….' She rubbed her chin, frowning. 'Well, OK. I was out Wednesday night….' What's she trying to remember, Armie wondered: where she was, or what Ronnie told her to say? 'I was out, and at some point I went in a night club. It would've actually been Thursday morning by then.'

'Ronnie Goudie's club?'

'Well he acts like he owns it. It used to be the Inferno....'

'Heaven,' said Armie.

'Oh yeah. Heaven. It is his, cause he said he renamed it, that's right. But we left before closing. He drove me home.'

'So what time was this?'

'Oh Christ. I don't know, I'd had a few drinks. But you know, it was still dark... and actually it felt late, so... fourish? Five-ish? He stayed a while. Not long, but... you know.'

'Was it dark when he left?'

'Yeah, I think.'

'And you'd be willing to swear to that, would you? That Ronnie was with you, here in Hornbridge....'

'Is he a friend of yours, Inspector?'

'No. Absolutely not.'

'Good,' said Sonia. 'Cause he's bad news.'

* * *

Back at the station, Linda found Armie getting ready to go out again.

'We can search Ronnie's,' he said. 'Fabe's there now. Want to come?'

They took his car. 'I've been following up the Rashid story,' Linda said, 'Arlene's allegations. It seems to have come from a girl called Sonia.'

'Oh dear,' said Armie. 'Bugger, I've just come from her. Isn't that weird, she's Goudie's alibi.'

'Well let's go see her. I have to talk to her too, come on. I don't know where she lives....'

Armie drove resolutely towards Marchbank. 'Not till she's finished her essay.'

'Eh?'

'She's doing an Access course at the Tech, this is the thing. And I've already interrupted her once today. Her time is tight.'

'You mean she's whoring her way through college?'

They crossed a little humpbacked bridge. 'Whoops! Well it's not uncommon,' Armie said. 'In university towns at least. But I think Sonia was already on the night shift. She wants to read English Literature.'

'Well,' said Linda, 'what else is it good for? God, I need to ask her about Dave.'

'I almost forgot,' Armie said as they threaded their way through Marchbank. 'Fabe's had a brainwave. Try this. Goudie hired a woman to kill Ian. Isn't that a beauty?'

'Oo,' said Linda. 'What if it's Sonia?'

They pulled up at the cottage. Fabe and Wattie were out on the front step, talking.

'Aye aye,' said Armie, joining them. 'All done, are we?'

The two men gazed at him in silence.

'Well,' Linda said, 'I'm not done. Let's have a look in there.'

They stood aside; she went in. They'd turned the place over. But, she thought, it was a nice wee home for all that.

She glanced over her shoulder. What was keeping Armie, anyway? But never mind. She'd have a wander round, starting with the kitchen. There might be knives.

'Something you want to tell me?' Armie said.

'No, no, Inspector,' Wattie said, 'we were just, er.'

'Just saying what a strange guy Goudie is,' Fabe said. 'Where his head's at.'

'Wherever that is,' said Armie.

'Thought you'd know,' said Fabe. Wattie looked embarrassed.

'The ideas some folk have,' said Armie, 'about my acquaintance with Ronnie Goudie and his ways are highly misleading. Find anything useful, did you?'

There were knives. He kept them in a drawer. What he did about sharpening them she couldn't guess, since there wasn't a stone or steel, nor a sharpener like Arlene's. The knives were all new, and some were blunt. She figured he'd bought them when he moved in, and would buy more when these became unuseable.

She went back to the passage and tried the next room along: a study. Goudie had a laptop computer on his desk. It was running its screensaver: probably the guys had had a look at Goudie's files and left it. She sat down and moved the mouse, the screensaver vanished, and in its place a magical vision appeared. It was Armie, in black and white; instead of grey curls he sported dark ones.

It was a newspaper photo. Underneath it was the line: 'George Armistead: didn't see.'

He was looking up at the camera. His face was troubled – and so young. He looked up at her out of the depths of time.

'Didn't see,' said Armie's voice behind her.

He's going to be young, she thought, turning. He wasn't.

'That's true,' he said. 'I didn't see. They picked the right bite. By accident or design.'

'Armie, why are you Goudie's desktop wallpaper?'

'No accounting for some folk's tastes.'

'What does it mean, didn't see?'

'Don't you know?' said Armie. 'Doesn't everyone know this? I thought Bob would've briefed you all.' He stepped to the door, looked up and down the passage: no one there. 'That's from when I nicked him. Goudie. The caption's about my testimony… or lack of it. I didn't see who fired the shot.'

The screensaver came on again. 'Thank God that's gone,' he said. 'See, at the end of the day Goudie was all we'd got. There was a girl dead. Twenty-four she was, bank worker.' He roamed about the small room, poking among the disordered papers and floppy disks. 'Just come back from her break… so had I. Heading back to the cop shop, past the bank. And there was this kerfuffle going on. When I saw it was a raid in progress I… well, obviously… I mean what luck, you know? What a stroke of luck.'

Someone had emptied the waste-paper bin onto the floor and now he turned it upside down and sat on it. 'They were coming out when I showed up. They had masks, balaclavas, but you could tell 'em apart. Four of 'em…. Not sure who, we have a pretty good idea though. Ronnie's cousin Stanley, they were always together. But we only got Ronnie, so… can't be sure. But you must know all this, it's history.'

'No I don't,' said Linda, 'tell me.'

'Well… they were coming out backwards. One had the gun – a shotgun, and he was pointing it into the bank. The girl…. She ran up from the other side, I mean, on the other side from me, and she yelled something. Only twenty-four. A mad thing to do. He swung and fired… and she fell.'

He looked over at the door. Still no one.

'I don't know which of them it was, I don't, to this day, because his mates were between him and me. I was running along the pavement. But then, whoever it was tossed the gun to the man behind him. I made a grab for him, this guy who'd got the gun, and he hit me on the side of my head with the butt – better than being shot, I suppose. So I didn't get him. But because they were moving out backwards, and one of them was lugging the money in a bag, somehow they started to bump into each other. Then they scattered. I just grabbed the nearest one.'

'You say you could tell them apart,' said Linda.

'You could, a bit, from their clothing. And the people inside the bank told us that when the gang came in, the one who was holding the gun had on blue jeans. Two of them had on jeans, and the other two... slacks or something. So you could tell them apart a bit. And when they came in, the one with the gun passed it to another guy and he held it on the people and told them to get on the floor. Some of them told us afterwards that this man also wore jeans, but a couple of them said he didn't, he wore cords, or something. So that didn't help. And anyway the gang kept on handing the gun around. And outside... outside it was just the same. And of course they all wore gloves.'

'So nobody knows which one shot her,' said Linda.

'Oh... someone knows. The person who did it knows. Unless it was Stanley – he's dead. And the other gang members, they'll know.'

'You collared Ronnie,' said Linda. 'Do you think, I mean you must've had some idea.'

'Some idea doesn't cut it,' said Armie. 'Not with murder.'

The doorway darkened, and there was Fabe looking down at him.

Adventures of a Tree Hugger

WHEN GUIN got back to the showroom after lunch on Wednesday, Fabe was sitting in his car outside.

'Hang on,' she said, unlocking the showroom door to let the dog in. Martok didn't want to go in: he wanted to see Fabe. He dragged Guin back to the car. 'Coming inside?' she said.

'Maybe for a minute.'

'How's it going?' She switched the lights on, opened the till to check for change. 'Hmm, should've gone to the bank. All bloody twenties.'

'It's going nowhere. We can't shake Goudie, and he's got an alibi.'

'So it's not Goudie.'

'There must be a connexion. Must be. Must be a hitman... hit-person. Armie's acting weird again.'

'In what way weird?'

'Bends over backwards to confirm the guy's alibi. Won't look at options.... You know if I didn't know him better.... I thought I knew him.'

'He's just trying to play straight,' said Guin.

'Goudie wouldn't play straight. He's an evil bastard. It isn't playing straight to unleash him on the public and at this rate we'll have to.'

'So when's your time up? If you don't charge him?'

'Tomorrow.' Fabe sat heavily in a spare chair and put an arm round the dog. 'If we could just find a link to Ian.'

Tracy peeked through the glass door and wondered if she ought to go in. She'd be interrupting them and they looked serious. But they were probably only talking about the murder. In any case, Martok had seen her and was slithering towards her across the polished floor.

'Can I borrow him?' she said, opening the door a crack. Martok rammed his nose into the gap and she caught his collar. 'Just going up the forest.'

'It's OK with me,' said Guin. 'Here, take his lead.'

'She do that a lot?' said Fabe, as the two slunk out of sight.

'Lately. Horncross Forest, she's got a thing about it.'

'Long way to take him walkies. Doesn't she ever work?'

'Probably works at night,' Guin said. 'She's sort of nocturnal.'

* * *

Oscar the traveller could take an old Mini axle and wheels, or at a pinch, the mere wheels, and with some other bits and pieces he'd make you a handy little trailer in no time. Since he'd come back to Hornsdale, early this year, he'd found lots of people wanting trailers: more than he had wheels for. So whenever he spotted an old Mini or its parts, he was interested.

That afternoon when Vanessa set out for Whixton, he got her to drive along the edge of the spruce plantation and drop him off. He thought he'd glimpsed some little wheels at the back of a layby there. She and Maisie were picking up the kids; Oscar said he'd walk back, taking a shortcut he knew. If there were bits to carry home he'd bring Willy's pickup later.

There were wheels, as he'd thought, tucked up behind the litter-bins. He rolled them under a tree and covered them with cut branches left by the foresters, and walked into the wood to where his shortcut began.

Oscar was mildly disgusted with Willy for perching them up on the plateau like crows. If they'd used the designated site at Whixton, he could've got his materials far more easily; he could also have sold more trailers, simply by building them and displaying them for sale. But Willy was set on spending the winter in the forest, and Josephine wouldn't hear of staying on a different site. Maybe it was for the best, anyway. The families at Whixton were nothing but a bunch of pikeys.

His path led through the narrowest part of the plantation near its western end. Coming out of the trees, he turned east, and followed the rise of the plateau's edge. By this time, cloud had spread across the fine blue autumn sky: the breeze was bringing up rain. Oscar hadn't brought a coat, but he put on a tweed cap, turned up the collar of his waistcoat, and strode contentedly onward.

Presently his way climbed above the old quarry. The southerly breeze caught him here, dampening his face. Automatically he glanced down at the overgrown workings: people throw rubbish into quarries, and sometimes Minis, you never know. But no one came here. Long ago, at the start of the First World War, the old laird's quarrymen had marched away forever.

Oscar moved away from the edge. He was leaving the spruces, seeing more pines, more open glades, where lichens grew. He was halfway home. Just as well: his right sleeve was wet and sticking to his skin. The rock underfoot was giving way to turf, short but sopping, and the wind was rising. It whistled in his right ear. But his left ear caught something else, a scraping or scrabbling across the rock behind him.

There was also the breathing.

Oscar hated Alsatian dogs. He'd seldom admit it, but he feared them too. Instinct now told him to be afraid, and as the dog burst out of the wood beside him Oscar stooped for a stone. Too late: it was nearly on him, a huge black brute of a thing.

But it hadn't seen him. It was running for the hell of it. Oscar froze, aware of the quarry's lip at his back, and then the creature saw him. It let out a roar and skidded into a turn. Oscar had a fleeting notion of dodging and sending it over the edge: out of the corner of his eye he'd seen a tree, a lone pine just showing its top where it grew up from below. A bad idea, suicidal, the tree would simply collapse and fall. But he couldn't run.

The dog bared its fangs and came on. Oscar found himself backing towards the lone tree. Then he saw the second animal: it raced from the wood, flung itself on the dog, disengaged and sprang aside, and the dog followed it. The animal romped away and the dog ran after, gasping and yelping, into the dripping wood. Saved, thought Oscar.

That's when he realised he was hugging that tree, dangling over the drop.

* * *

Bob Marshall nearly started his meeting without Fabe. Sometimes he despaired of his detectives: always stealing kisses or whatever on the fly. But that's youth for you, he thought as his sergeant finally bounded into the office and sat down between Armie and Linda.

'You're wet,' said Bob.

'I've been standing in the rain,' said Fabe. Bob didn't need to know that he'd just been all the way to Horncross Forest on a rescue mission. Martok had bolted, Tracy had rung up in despair and Fabe and Guin had rushed off to console her. But all was well now: the beast was back.

Bob cleared his throat and leaned forward with his elbows on his desk. 'A week ago tomorrow morning, Ian Barclay was murdered. A week tomorrow. What have you come up with? Please tell me you have something solid.'

'Goudie,' said Fabe.

'Goudie's glove at the murder scene,' said Armie.

'His alibi checks out,' said Linda.

'Alibi,' said Bob. 'He's sent in a hitman. Work with that. There's got to be a link.'

'That's what I keep saying,' said Fabe.

'Then it's what you'll have to be finding,' said Bob. 'Bring me up to score on Ian's last movements. What's Wattie got from the video?'

'Ian doesn't appear on any video,' Armie said.

'Anyone see him? He hasn't been invisible all that time.'

'He may have been in a night club Wednesday night,' Linda said. 'Beggar's Belief. I've only just got that, by the way, off Sonia –'

'The alibi girl,' said Bob, 'she's dodgy as hell. Say anything for money. Who was he with, then?'

'He was talking to a woman. An older woman. She was dressed in black and silver and Sonia thinks her hair was red.

How she could tell in what passes for light in there I don't know.'

'How much older?' said Armie.

'Just older. Sonia's nineteen. I mean I'm an older woman to someone her age.'

'Chase it up, Linda, good work,' Bob said. 'You charging Goudie?'

'Aw Bob, hell's teeth,' said Armie. 'That'll just end in tears.'

Whose tears does he mean, Bob wondered. 'You've got a few hours,' he said, 'keep trying. Listen, Armie, Ronnie Goudie has killed men for no better reason than because he could. You know that.'

'I don't get it,' said Fabe. 'If Ronnie's killed all these guys, why's he got away with it?'

'Cause he could,' said Armie. 'OK, here's an example, he kicked a guy to death. This was in the eighties, before we put him away. There were three or four guys watching and none of 'em would ever say a word. But everybody knew it! And another fellow, he got drunk with him and Ronnie filled him up with pills, a guy who never took drugs, only drink, so you know it has to have been done to him. And he had his pals lug the poor bastard downstairs and left him to die out in the rain. And – d'you want to hear more? We could never get him, ever. I – Sorry. Don't get me started.'

'This stuff's not in his file,' said Fabe.

'No, cause he was never pulled in for it. I'd love to do him for murder so I would. But his damned glove isn't evidence. Like it or not.'

'And in your book,' said Bob, 'that makes him innocent.'

'It does not. It makes him unassailable. Exactly as before.'

* * *

Oscar crouched by the quarry's rim, staring down at the pine. He'd got himself back to earth by reaching out, wedging his fingers in a crack in the rock and inching his body round the trunk until he could shift his weight little by little off the tree. With both hands grasping rock, and his feet walking heels up, toes down on the trunk, he'd made it finally, on his stomach. Then he'd turned to see what had made that chinking sound.

He'd shaken the tree so hard its roots had nearly let go. They writhed into a crack, not too far down: twenty feet perhaps, or less. Oscar saw how, above the roots, the quarry face was loose scree. It looked as though the tree had long ago slid from the level of the plateau, and established itself on a tiny outcrop lower down. The scree could have chinked like that, he thought. But it had sounded more like metal, like a light hammer on steel.

Daylight was fading. The quarry was a pot of gloom. Still the wet rock gleamed in places, reflecting the wet sky. At the roots of the tree, too, something brightened, as Oscar peered this way and that. The gleam wasn't white like the sky, but yellow.

He'd grown tired of listening to Willy's treasure story. He didn't even believe it: but Willy did.

It was the reason they were living in the meadow. Willy's famous second sight had shown him last winter that the gold was in this forest. Before that, it hadn't had a precise location: it was just Great-grandfather Joseph's treasure that he'd buried somewhere. It was down in the Borders, in Galloway, in Cumbria or wherever you liked. Willy was Joseph Blythe's great-great-grandson, so actually Oscar had the better claim.

Joseph Blythe had been a horsey person and a gambling man. He'd bet with anybody, especially rich men: he hobnobbed with sporting types from all levels. One day at Ayr he'd won money from somebody, a minor Royal maybe; some said it was the Prince of Wales. Whoever it was had been well heeled. Old Joe had scored two thousand guineas, or so the legend ran. A long shot that must've been.

The Prince or minor Royal had paid up in gold: two thousand golden guineas. Then Joe had run into some bother, and foreseeing that he'd be in worse trouble with the gold on him, he'd buried it, drawn a plan of the place, and gone to meet his fate.

When he didn't come back, his exploit and his map passed into legend. People assumed that the map had been handed down through the Blythe line. The Blythes weren't saying.

Oscar's mother had been a Blythe, but now the name seemed to have died out. It had descended through one of old

Joe's sons, Henry, who'd come home from the war and settled down. Henry's brothers didn't come home, and they left no children. So Joe's name had passed through the settled line, and no travellers bore it now.

Oscar mused on all this as he stared at the glint of gold. Now he regretted scoffing at the notion of second sight. Still, the sight wasn't any good if it didn't show you where the treasure was. Now what he needed was not second sight, but a long rope, and of course Vanessa. He didn't need Willy, that was for sure.

He picked himself up, and took the darkening path, thinking it was time those kids of Maisie's learned a lesson about this end of the woods. Snakes, cliffs, all the rest of it, you couldn't tell those kids a thing. But they'd damn well listen when they heard there was a wolf up here.

* * *

Night fell on Polwarth Avenue and Linda started prowling. She didn't have much hope, but she'd promised to talk to Sonia.

Sonia wasn't at her place in Greenbank Road, and the night clubs wouldn't open for hours, so Linda dropped by the Goat. Early evening was a key time at the Goat. It was a big pub with a mixed clientele, where respectable gents might go unremarked as they checked out the talent. But you could easily spot them, because try as they would to look urbane, their eyes bulged.

There were two bars and a lounge in the hotel. Linda chose the saloon bar, and there was Zoe, sitting on a stool with a man beside her. She noticed Linda in the mirror and instead of pretending to be invisible, as she liked to do, she said something to the guy, got down from her stool and headed for the ladies'.

'Come on,' she muttered as she passed.

Linda followed her in. It was a good-sized powder-room, suitable for fancy functions, such as the Goat hadn't had in years. They checked behind various partitions to make sure they were alone and Zoe said, 'The thing is, there was a girl I forgot about. I honestly forgot all about her till today.'

'You mean with Barclay?'

'Yeah, I saw her with him in the Avenue. It must've been in the summer cause it was still light at ten. That's one time I can remember. I don't think it's the only time.'

'What's her name?'

'Sonia. Skinny, flaky looking, fair hair.'

'Oo. Thanks loads,' said Linda, passing her a twenty.

All roads lead to Sonia.

Linda got back in her crumbling motor and puttered slowly towards home. She'd get a coffee and something sugary and come out when the night clubs opened up. She could've gone to the station but she'd been there enough lately. Maybe she'd give Grassy a shout.

She'd asked Sonia yesterday about Dave Rashid and the girl had just said That's right, he clobbered me. No reason, he just clobbered me. Makes him feel manly.

Linda wasn't comfortable with it. It wasn't that she knew Dave well, or thought he'd be nicer than that. But Sonia didn't talk like that ordinarily, not that she knew Sonia well, either.

But normally when Sonia spoke, her face came alive, her smudgy eyes sparkled. When she said Dave clobbered her, her eyes and her voice went flat. She was like a puppet.

Then again, when she'd talked about seeing Barclay with a woman at the club, why hadn't she said that she'd known him, as it were, professionally? What did her eyes do then, when she talked about Barclay?

Would I tell? Linda wondered. After the guy was murdered, would I say I'd been with him? Probably not, no.

But this kid was a far from reliable witness. That alibi stank. Linda stopped outside her maisonette, pulled the handbrake on wearily and took out her mobile to call Grassy.

* * *

'Hello Geordie man. A human face at last.'

'Aye aye Ronnie. How's the service?'

Ronnie cast an eye round Hornbridge nick's best cell, and sniffed. 'It stinks. But I'll be out tomorrow. Right?'

'Possibly.'

'You're never going to charge me for losing my damn gloves.'

'Possibly not.'

'Listen Geordie, at the risk of repeating myself, I didn't kill Barclay. I didn't have him killed. You do know that. And please don't say possibly.'

'But how did that glove get there?'

'No idea. I'm being straight with you, Geordie, what's your problem? Have you never laid your gloves down in a shop or something and left 'em?'

'No.'

'Well, everyone else has. Trust me. Listen....'

'I'd be a damn fool to trust you, Ronnie. I would.'

Ronnie sighed. 'You're not glad I came, are you.'

'No, I'm not. How'd you guess?'

'Look, don't sweat it. You know what I'm really here for.'

'But you're settling in, man. Your other business, this treasure-map stuff.... A guy doesn't buy a house just for that.'

'No of course not. I never meant to buy the place, I just.... It's pretty. I like it here, Geordie. Don't you?'

Ever so much more before you came, Armie thought. 'It's a good place to live. And it had better stay that way. You hear me?'

'Nothing's changed, has it? Same tarts, same punters. What's eating you? Think I'm dealing?'

'You mean you're not,' Armie said. 'You're asking me to believe.... OK. But procuring's still illegal.'

'So charge me,' said Ronnie. 'Go on, Geordie, you haven't a bit of evidence. Where's the evidence? Who's going to testify? No... I'm just a night-club owner, Geordie. A businessman.'

'Good,' said Armie. 'Happy to hear it. So Ronnie... how's that other thing coming along?'

* * *

The woman who called herself Sylvie stood in front of her mirror and combed her hair straight up. She liked the way it stuck straight up, red and irregular like grass in a winter landscape. She also liked the way it made her into someone new.

She wondered, though, if she oughtn't to change it yet again. Keep people guessing. Who am I? Down the club, if she wasn't careful, they'd be taking her for granted. But she liked this look; maybe she ought to try a different club.

Guinea For Your Thoughts

IT WAS four in the morning when Armie got to his bed. He'd promised to find a way to charge Ronnie, he'd tried all night and he'd failed. There was no more he could do.

Susie was sitting up in bed, reading an old paperback. She had a heap of them on the duvet: all the old sci-fi from the attic, it looked like.

'What's to do?' said Armie. 'Can't you sleep?'

'No, I'm in love with Philip K Dick. I was worried. Thank God you're here.'

'You never worried before.'

'Don't be too sure,' said Susie. 'No, I wasn't expecting you to come home in a box... it's Goudie... I mean it's hard on you. Want some cocoa or something?'

'No, I'm knackered. Thanks.... I can't believe you waited up. You never wait up.'

She put her book down, and hugged him. 'You're letting him go, aren't you.'

He couldn't get to sleep. After half an hour or so she said, 'Geordie....'

'Go to sleep, Suze.'

'It's emotional blackmail, that's what it is.'

'Not at all. He isn't blackmailing me at all. It wouldn't change anything.... You know it wouldn't change anything. And he hasn't said anything. I mean, nothing like that.'

'You're thinking it though.'

'No... I don't think so,' Armie said. 'I think I'm just... aware that he knows. He won't tell me. I don't think he'll even bring it up. Not if I don't.'

'You trust him,' Susie said. He didn't answer; it was too dark to see his face. 'You OK?'

'I'll be OK when he gets the hell away from here. How I wish he hadn't got mixed up in this. Oh God, Suze.' He held her for a long time, without speaking.

* * *

Debbie Chalmers awoke to feel sunlight on her face. She rolled over, sat up and looked reproachfully at the alarm clock; but it wasn't its fault, she'd forgotten to set it. She'd just have time for a shower.

Geoff's back tomorrow, she thought suddenly. Thank God for that. Tomorrow night, but still tomorrow.

In between times she could give the place a clean, and slap a coat of paint on the spare bedroom. Then when Liz came in October, it'd be all nice and new.

If Sandy came nosing around, she could always hand him a roller.

Sandy opened his eyes. What had awakened him, where was Arlene? It was after seven. She couldn't still be at the club.

Then he heard her. She was in the bathroom, dropping things and whistling. He listened for a moment: could that once have been 'Mull of Kintyre'? Debbie whistled sometimes, too.

He threw off the covers and stood up. This was no time for thoughts like those.

'You're up?' said Arlene. She had a towel round her stomach; as she came through the bedroom door she pulled it off and began to rub her hair. 'Early birdie.'

'You just get in?' he said.

'Well – no. I haven't been streaking, believe it or not. I got in half an hour ago or something…. Geoff's up early, I saw his light. You're all on the go this morning.'

'Geoff's still offshore.'

'No, really?' said Arlene. 'Thought he'd be back by now. What a life.' She draped the towel on the bedside radiator and hopped into bed. 'Mmm, still warm…. I suppose I should sleep….'

'I have to go, babe. I overslept.'

She rolled herself in the blankets. 'If you want a shower there's a towel on the other one.' Her voice filtered through the wool. 'The other radiator. And if you don't want a shower….'

'It's there all the same.' Sandy picked up some shorts, and shambled out.

* * *

'I found her,' Linda said. 'I asked her. She lied.'

'Hell's teeth,' said Armie.

The forty-eight hours would be up after coffee. Ronnie would be free to go.

'Otherwise it's a beautiful day,' Linda said. It was, too: the tall windows showed a pure blue sky, their steel frames were edged with gold. 'Great day to be half alive. I must've had two hours' sleep.'

'You shouldn't have run round all night like that.'

'She bloody lied, Armie. We ought to hold him.'

'I know, hen. But be scientific about it. She lied about Barclay, OK, you've shown that…. Doesn't mean she lied about Ronnie.'

'Oh sod you, Armie. She lied about everything. She doesn't know what truth is.'

She'd found Sonia at a pub in Whixton. By sheer luck, the third time she'd gone back in desperation to the Goat, Linda had noticed a sheet of pink A4 pinned to the bulletin board in the lobby. The Wheatsheaf, Whixton, it said. Wednesday 17 Sept – Rantin' Pipe and Tremblin' String. She'd launched her old car for Whixton like a rocket.

The gig had finished by the time she got there. The band were carrying amps out to their van. Sonia was helping. She couldn't do enough for the roadie: she had hold of one handle of a monstrous bass bin, and the strapping roadie had the other one, when Linda drove up behind them.

Sonia hadn't been too keen to talk just then.

'For the love of Christ,' she'd said. 'Can't you people tell when you're not wanted?'

But Linda had had only one question. 'Do you know a guy called Ian Barclay?'

'Called who?'

'Ian Barclay.'

'I don't think –'

'That's the guy who was murdered last week,' the roadie put in.

'I didn't know.' In the sodium light of the street, Sonia's eyes would've looked flat anyway. 'I never met the guy. Or if I met him I didn't know his name, you know? Goodbye. So long. Farewell. Hasta la Vista, like never again.'

'OK,' Armie said. 'You say she lies like a ventriloquist's dummy. She didn't look like it when we spoke about Ronnie.'

'You believed her.'

Armie just stopped himself saying he didn't believe, he found out. 'She convinced me,' he said. 'But I have to consider the possibility that it was a total crock of shite.' He gazed unseeing out the window, trying to picture Sonia against the blue sky: a fragile gambler, opportunist, survivor. Or not.

'Time's up, Armie,' said Fabe from the doorway. 'Go talk to Goudie. Tell him we're watching him. Tell him to watch himself.'

* * *

At noon Oscar and Vanessa slipped away from camp with a length of rope in a rucksack. Vanessa carried the sack.

'Looks more natural,' she said. 'Josie knows what an idle bastard you are.'

'You just like flashing your muscles around, Popeye,' said Oscar. 'Listen, this is going to be a bit heavy, this stuff.'

113

'You hope.'

Oscar got cramps in his shins from walking too fast. He couldn't breathe, he was so worried about his gold: but they met no one on the path, and the quarry's edge was deserted.

'Too good to be true,' he panted.

'Jesus, will you stop moaning and give me a hand.'

They tied the rope round a little rowan that grew at the forest's edge. Oscar put on his gauntlets and tested the knot, looping a bight round his waist and straining. 'Quit buggering about,' Vanessa said. 'I'm lighter. I'll go.'

'It's heavy.'

'That's the point. You pull it up, dickhead, I don't.'

Once more they looked around. Nobody was there, neither wolf nor man. 'Damn funny about that wolf,' Vanessa said, hanging the empty rucksack on her forearm.

'Funny my arse. OK, now for God's sake be careful and don't start a landslip in that scree there.'

'Oh shut up, Oscar.' She pulled her gloves on. 'How hard can it be?'

But it was hard. The scree was treacherous, so was the pine, but from time to time she had to trust her weight to both of them. At last she was down at root level.

When she looked up, Oscar was hidden by the cliff-top. She began to feel sympathy for the clinging pine.

'See it?' came his voice.

'It's here.'

'Is it in anything?'

'It's rotten.'

'Is there a lot of it d'you think?'

'Oh for shit's sake, Oscar, stop asking silly questions.'

It was tricky, winning those guineas from the soil: much trickier than it had been to win them from the Prince of Wales.

'If that's who it was,' she gasped as she crawled back onto the cliff-top. She'd had to pick the coins out with her bare fingers and now they bled. The rope had played hell with her lower back and ribs. It hurt more when Oscar unfastened it.

'The damn roots had grown right through the bloody things,' she said. 'God, I'll get triple blood poisoning.' She grinned suddenly. 'Be nice to me, and I'll give you a guinea.'

114

Guin and Martok took their lunchtime walk in River Park. Must be pretty tame for him after yesterday, Guin thought.

What a nut her future sister-in-law was turning out to be. In spite of herself Guin felt a glow of pride. She was proud of Martok too: he'd come back, when he could have stayed out with his wolf all night.

'Best dog in the world,' she said to the top of his head as they paced back along the Hornway. But he didn't look up. He'd begun to pull and his ears were straining forward. A white van stood outside the showroom: deliveries at lunchtime, bloody nuisance, keep the bloody dog from eating the drivers, no bloody time to yourself.

But Martok liked this driver. At least, he wagged his tail and only growled a little.

'Got one at home,' said the man. He handed Guin a ballpoint. 'Here please love. Ta very much. Turned out fine again, haven't we been lucky! Hey big pup,' he stroked Martok's ears, 'you're what they need over at Whixton. Got a wolf loose over at Whixton. If you believe it.'

'Oh no kidding,' Guin said. 'Really?' She ruffled Martok's long black hackles.'What next eh!'

Wonder why I didn't say we knew that, she thought as the van drove off. I must be getting it from Tracy, secretive to the point of paranoia. She let the dog into the showroom, and picked up the box the driver had left on the pavement outside.

It was a shredder, of all things. She hadn't ordered that.

'Dad,' she said, carrying the thing into his little glassed-in office at the back. 'You order this?'

'No, that'll be Frank. Apparently the Council's trying to get people to shred before they recycle.' Big Frank took the gadget and unwound its cord. 'Trying to save the planet. And burning up electricity to do it, I don't know.' He stuck the plug in a wall socket, and looked about for something to shred.

'The driver says, the delivery guy,' said Guin, passing him some old catalogues, 'there's a wolf roaming around.'

'These staples'll have to come out,' said her father. 'Got your knife? Mmm. Werewolf, more like.'

'Ha ha.'

'Well don't blame me.' He hoicked out a staple and dropped it in the waste-paper basket. 'It was on Dalesound again, they call it the werewolf murders. Your lot must be fed up with that crap.'

'My lot,' said Guin, 'that's another laugh.'

To tell the truth, Fabe and Armie weren't asking her for her opinions these days. That didn't mean she hadn't any. That villain they were holding, he was a red herring just like the wolf. Each of the creatures had its private agenda; neither was the killer.

I'm not being very scientific about all this, she thought. I need to reason. Test some hypotheses.

She sat at the showroom counter, a stack of invoices at her elbow. They had to be dealt with, but all the same she pulled the telephone pad towards her and began drawing a little diagram. Here was Marchbank, here was Beames's house. She had a vague idea where Barclay's was: near Tracy's, wasn't it?

The street door bumped shut. She looked up, and there was Grassy Knowles in his ancient leather jacket.

'Hi Grassy, you on holiday?'

'No no,' said Grassy, 'not in term time.' He was the school janitor in Hornbridge. 'Just taking the afternoon off. There's a pile of evening classes – I'll be faffing about all night.' From an inner pocket he took a sheet of lined paper folded in eight. 'I was thinking, while the bike's off the road I'll rebuild it. Strip it down and give it an overhaul. You can get me some of these weird Honda special tools, can't you?' He unfolded the paper, revealing a long smudgy list. 'They cost the earth but at least when you've got 'em, you've got 'em.'

'I can order all right.' Guin lifted a thick catalogue onto the counter. 'So when do you get your license back?'

'Five months, one week.'

'Long time,' said Guin.

'Yeah… but it was inevitable. As far as the polis were concerned I'd been riding like a maniac. I mean at least they didn't blame me for the wreck, they could have. They were definitely easy on me. Their way of saying thanks for the villain I gave them.'

'So what's Linda say?'

'Get a skateboard if I want kicks. Did you know she was a skateboard wizard? So... I actually managed to see her last night – two whole hours, we had. Between prostitutes.'

'Eh?' said Guin. 'Oh the prostitutes, right.'

'And then she went out in the wee wee hours. Still looking for this one girl who'd given that guy his alibi. That heavy guy, you know?'

'Goudie.'

'Right. And she was depressed because she said they'd have to let him go today, they can't charge him. I said what if Barclay was killed earlier, and the man Tracy saw wasn't the killer? But it didn't help.'

'Oh? The man... our Tracy? No. How did Tracy see the killer?'

'She saw him leave. Early in the morning.'

'God, Fabe didn't tell me that.'

'Put my foot in it have I?' said Grassy. 'Whoops!'

'No, he did tell me someone saw the killer leave,' Guin said, 'but not that it was Tracy. But I can't believe she'd do that. She never tells anyone anything. She's a human oyster.'

'Well I could've always got it wrong. Wouldn't be the first time.'

'But how could she have seen him? Wait a sec. She lives near him, doesn't she.'

'She lives right by him, that's the thing,' Grassy said.

'My God.' Guin stared down at the telephone pad. Next to it was Grassy's shopping list. 'Oh I'm sorry. I'm holding you up here.... What, like next door?'

'Not next door exactly, more like opposite. It's funny,' said Grassy. 'I thought you'd have been over to her place, detecting.'

'I've never been there. She hasn't asked me. Frank's actually moved in, you know? But I.... How weird. Tracy was the witness, that is weird. Sorry,' said Guin, 'Honda tools. I'm neglecting you, aren't I.'

* * *

117

On Friday morning Mrs Miller, who ran the Red Cross shop in Marchbank, got to work at five to ten. A black plastic bin bag awaited her on the doorstep.

People always left bags of stuff there for Mrs Miller to find. The shop opened too late for them to go in with their donations; they were rushing to work, or taking kids to school. She often wondered about these unseen donors, especially when the things in the bin bags turned out to be valuable.

But this was only a bag of women's clothes. They were nice, trendy, for going out clubbing perhaps: a bit skimpy, but clean and newly pressed. Someone was thoughtful.

She thought she'd just put some of the clothes on sale right now, as they were clean. She picked up a little green leather jacket, gave it a shake, held it up, and then went through the pockets.

There were no nasties in the jacket, no fuzzy old tissues or sweets. But in one side pocket there was a leather glove. She was sure it was a man's glove: a good one, but old, so she didn't feel sorry when she couldn't find its mate.

eleven

What's Mine's Mine

SHE COULD hear the man's voice. 'Little vermin,' he was saying.

She kept her eyes shut, shut tight. 'How can you speak like that in front of her?' said the other.

'Well it's hardly a problem. It can't understand.'

Her heart started to pound. She had to keep her eyes closed or she'd be sick.

'Pukes if you look at it,' the man said.

Her eyes flew open and she felt her stomach heave: then panic flooded in. Whose body was this? In the bed... whose bed? Whose room?

The ceiling, he'd papered the ceiling last spring. It matched her blue duvet, her blue pillowslips. He was only asleep. He was breathing. Stealthily, so he wouldn't awaken, she moved close to him.

* * *

The two kids, Armie thought, that's the trouble.

It was Saturday morning. Ronnie had been on the loose for two days. No doubt he'd been catching up with his business affairs. Pretty soon, though, he'd be back in the forest looking for that treasure of his.

Ronnie hadn't said it, but he'd dropped ample hints. He needed Armie to get those tinks chased off. Ronnie knew all about Willy's second sight, believed in it too: so, why else would the gypsy be there? The thought of him up on the plateau was driving Ronnie crazy.

But the tinks were there by invitation. Willy was working in the forestry. He had keys to the gates. Why would anybody dream of disturbing him?

Ronnie's got no favours coming to him, Armie thought as he drove across to Marchbank. Whereas Willy, now, him I could probably learn to like.

All the same, he wouldn't have bothered about it except for the children. Ronnie was such an utter bastard.

The stack of logs in the lay-by was growing. Armie drove on a little way and squeezed his car up onto the grass verge, and walked back.

Saws still zipped, for it wasn't yet lunchtime. The smell of slain trees lay on the air. So much for these guys' weekend, Armie thought: the overtime had better be worth it.

As the log-pile grew, so the spruce wood shrank. Instead of the green gloom he remembered, Armie looked across an open slope, pale under the sky. Here and there stood patches of timber with high crowns and stark straight trunks. From the lay-by, Armie could see three men working at the edge of a stand; he watched them bring a tree down, wondered at the force with which it fell.

'Hoy,' he shouted, waving. 'Mr Smith?'

'Ronnie Goudie,' Willy said. He'd taken off his orange hard hat, and now he waved it at a large black-and-yellow insect that droned past on shimmering wings. 'See that bloody thing? Wood wasp. The size of 'em. Harmless, mind.'

'Goudie isn't,' said Armie.

'I know who the Goudies are. They're cousins of cousins of cousins…. My mother could work it out.'

'He's an evil bastard, Mr Smith, just so you know. He thinks you're after something… a certain thing he's after. In the forest.'

'Old Blythe's gold,' Willy said. 'It's OK to say it. What a nice kind cousin. So what's he going to do about it? Get you to chase us off? Never.'

'No,' said Armie, 'but it's what he might do himself that worries me.'

'So why aren't you up there looking for treasure? You afraid of Goudie? Sorry mush,' said Willy, 'I'm out of order. You know, it's good of you to trouble yourself. But don't.'

Armie shrugged. 'Just so you know.' He looked across the clearing: how long, he wondered, before you'd be able to see clear to North Fairyhill on the other side? Soon. How strange.

Willy put his hat back on. 'This is a dark place, mush.' He tightened the strap. 'Just so you know.'

* * *

Make the summer last as long as you can, was the children's motto. There was a corollary: make Saturdays long.

It seemed longer if they stayed in camp while the grown-ups went to town. There was more to do in camp. Lee wanted to make a trebuchet, Moira was thinking of a tree-house. But she shelved it when she learned what a trebuchet was.

They had their lunch early. At noon their Gran, Uncle Oscar, Vanessa and their Mum drove away down the forest track. Uncle Willy wasn't back yet from his work. Hours of self-rule stretched ahead.

120

'I need tools,' Lee said.

'What tools? A hammer?' Moira had already found the hammer: she handed it over. 'What tools?'

'I have to have a saw.'

Uncle Oscar had two sorts of tools, the ones he kept locked up in a steel box, and the other kind, which were distributed around the site: under his caravan in a fish-box, under the trailer to keep out of the rain. Even so, the saw was rusty. But Lee didn't care.

'I need a long, long plank,' he said to his sister. 'You go find me the weight.'

Eventually Lee decided it was time to make the pivot. He could picture in his head the thing he wanted: a thick black steel bolt with a chunky head at one end, and threaded at the other. At that end you'd have a nut.

'I need a nut,' he told Moira, 'you'll do.'

'You're a banana,' she said.

'I know the thing I'm looking for. Uncle Oscar has them. They're black like giant bolts. Where does he put everything?'

'Maybe in Granny Josie's van. We can't look in there,' said Moira.

'Why not?' said her brother. 'You help me look.' He opened the door; they stepped in, softly as cats, even though no one was home.

Moira searched the kitchen. She found a screwdriver and a pair of pliers. In a cupboard was an old chisel and a can of nails. 'No,' she said. 'Not here.'

Lee's voice came back to her from the forward end of the van. 'Know what I bet?'

Oscar and Vanessa had a room of their own up forward. Lee had never been in there, it was off limits. But Uncle Oscar might have a cupboard or a chest for his extra tools and things.

Under his own bunk Lee had a locker. Uncle Oscar had one too, he saw: there was the same sort of little door on the side of the double bunk. It was locked. Lee rattled the catch in vain.

'You're crazy,' Moira said from the doorway. 'You're an imbecile. You will get killed so dead that your guts will be sticking –'

'Sshh. Don't burble, I'm trying to listen.'

'Squeeter will bark if anyone comes.'

'I know, stupid, that's why I'm trying to listen.'

'If you lift up the mattress it might open from the top,' Moira said.

'Don't be a dick.'

'Well how can I be a dick? If you lift up the mattress —'

'Oh all right, dickbrain.'

Willy finished at two and drove home to Horncross. His brain was zipping like the saws. The copper's warning had unsettled him, for one thing. Then, he'd seen something.

The trees they were felling were some fifty years old. The plantation had once been pasture. Before that, the ground had been tilled in strips; but it was rocky, and in places springs issued from among the stones. Long ago, perhaps even before men had tried to cultivate this soil, someone had improved on one of the springs by digging himself a well. It was six yards deep, narrow, and lined with rubble.

Willy had uncovered this well in the usual way: he'd stepped in it. For a while he'd sat there groaning, staring down at the well-head by his thigh, where an iron ring was leaded into the stone. Lucky he hadn't come down on that at least. At length he hauled his leg out and looked in. The well was dry. At the bottom was something round and pale.

It was a skull all right. He'd made out some long bones too. No wonder Fairyhill felt evil.

It didn't matter. The gold, that was the thing. Against the twilight of the well-shaft, Willy had seen more than bones. He must get back to Horncross, to the quarry.

With any luck the camp would be deserted till teatime. He'd find some rope and get going at once. Bouncing up the track to the meadow he almost prayed, please, Lord, grant me a little peace and quiet and no Oscar.

His mother's caravan door hung open. Bloody hell, thought Willy, what did that copper tell me? Where's that Squeeter?

But the little dog sat peacefully in the shade of the heap of wheels. She rose to greet him. He stepped silently to the door of the van.

The kids were in there. He heard Moira say, 'You can't put it back. We have to tell....'

'Sshh!' said Lee. 'Listen!'

The dog jumped into the van and trotted noisily up front. 'Go away,' squeaked Moira. Willy smiled his angular smile.

'Oh *Moi*raaa....'

'Eeek!'

'Hah!' said Willy. 'Thought it was Oscar, didn't you.' He leaned round the bedroom door, and gasped. 'Oh my sainted Auntie Harriet. God almighty, look at that.'

* * *

Vanessa had talked Oscar into letting her take one coin, just one, to Whixton that afternoon. She wanted to see what their treasure was worth. She'd get someone to make her an offer, and then all she had to do was multiply by two thousand.

In the wynd off the square was an antique shop: Oldroyd's. A bell tinkled as she went in. One thousand, nine hundred and ninety-nine of 'em under the mattress, she thought: Oscar shouldn't sulk so.

'Guinea,' said Oldroyd, squinting. 'By gum, so it is. Excuse me just a moment.'

He dived into a back room. Vanessa waited. Oscar hung around outside, looking in the shop window as though pondering Oldroyd's wares: the wind-up gramophone might have been useful, back in the days when you could get records for it. Vanessa waited.

Oldroyd reappeared with a much-thumbed catalogue. 'Guinea!' he said. 'Interesting.'

In the back room, Mrs Oldroyd dialled her old-fashioned phone. The answering voice said, 'Whixton Police.'

'Davie? Meg Oldroyd.' She spoke huskily: cripes, thought the copper at the other end, I hope she doesn't fancy me. 'Antique coins?' she said. 'You said –'

'Oh aye right, Meg, right enough. Still there is he? Can you keep him talking? I'll be five minutes.'

* * *

123

That afternoon Tracy and Frank finally got away together to the forest. They took the pickup, with Martok sharing the cab.

They weren't going over to Horncross straight away though. Guin was about to shut up for lunch when Frank ducked into the back office, and came out with the shredder. 'Got to take this to Tracy's for the weekend,' he said.

Guin watched him back and turn the pickup into Horn Crescent. How long would they be away, she wondered; mightn't they stay out after dark? She was ready to take drastic action.

It would've helped if she'd known Ian Barclay's address, or Tracy's. She didn't know either of them. The phone book was no good: poor Barclay hadn't been in his maisonette long enough to get listed, while Tracy used only her cellphone. Guin felt an idiot asking Fabe for her own brother's girlfriend's address: so she didn't. She didn't ask Tracy or Frank either, since she was, after all, investigating.

But the night before, Friday night, she'd got on her scooter and tailed them as they left her Dad's. It had been dark by that time. She was almost sure they hadn't seen her.

Now, after they'd left the showroom, she let them get a couple of hours' head start. Then she stuck her head round the office door.

'Dad? I'd really appreciate an early dart tonight.'

'Early dart?' said Big Frank. 'Night? It's the middle of the day, woman.'

'It's an hour and a half to closing.'

'Youth will be served.' He picked up the magazine he'd been reading, and took it to the showroom counter. 'Let's have your keys then. Don't suppose you'll be back by five.'

The sometimes faithful Lambretta purred its way through the thronged Saturday streets. Mill Circle seemed dead by comparison. That's fine with me, thought Guin.

Now she wondered what she was doing here. She couldn't get into the flat; she couldn't even get into the building, so she had only the sketchiest idea what the view from the windows was like. Which windows? Where was Barclay's place?

She was fairly sure the upper flats faced the rear. She'd work out which windows were Tracy's. She dismounted, took her helmet off, and wheeled the scooter along a flagged path that led round the back to a green lawn between the buildings. On the path, alongside a young whitebeam, she parked the scooter on its stand. She could see Barclay's house, just across the grass: it had blue and white police tape around it still.

You could imagine how those upstairs windows looked down on the green, and on some of the other properties too. Even if you stood here at ground level you could survey the lower windows after a fashion. You'd hardly see in. But that window to the right of the door was a kitchen window: a bottle of washing-up liquid stood on the sill. So the left-hand window was probably the bedroom. The curtains were closed.

As she watched, someone lifted a corner of the bedroom curtain. She saw eyes. Then the curtain fell. She had an urge to flee: stupid, she thought. Then the door opened.

'Guin,' Armie called from the doorway. 'Fabe's inside. Don't go away.'

Together they peered in over the kitchen windowsill. 'You made me jump,' she said. 'Why didn't I see your car on the street? I hadn't a clue you were here.'

'It's there,' said Armie. 'You missed it. Clean your visor. Fabe is inside, he's seeking inspiration.'

'So was I.'

'Tracy isn't home.'

'I know.'

'We'd love to see what she saw,' said Armie. 'From her window.'

'Me too.'

'You've never looked?'

Guin turned from the window to look at him. 'Firstly, I've never been in her flat. Secondly, I didn't know her address until last night. Thirdly, I didn't know she was the witness until two days ago. Fourthly... I mean, what's the big secret? Fabe might've said.'

'Well I thought he had,' said Armie. 'Don't fourthly me.'

They settled on Barclay's kitchen stools. 'You found us,' Fabe said. 'Neat work, Sherlock.'

'What did you come back for?' Guin said. 'I mean aren't you finished here?'

'We're in trouble,' said Armie. 'No one in custody. Thought we might find something… a link between the crimes. Or to Ronnie.'

'Between the crimes,' said Guin. 'Isn't there a woman….'

'Zoe,' said Armie. 'The prostitute, Zoe. She was in Beames's little black book. She knew Barclay.'

'I was in it too,' said Guin, 'and I knew Barclay, and I'm not a link.'

'Arlene Third,' Fabe said. 'Same on both counts.'

'She's out of it,' Armie said. 'The Odd Spot, remember? She spent all that night there, the Wednesday.'

'Tracy Wiseman,' said Fabe. 'She knew Beames and she probably knew Barclay. About time we asked her. Did she know Barclay, d'you know?'

'Don't know. No,' said Guin. 'I mean maybe.'

Armie's phone trilled. 'Armistead…. Davie! What can I…. I'm in Marchbank. Say twenty minutes? I'll go like the clappers. Bye.' He put the phone away and stood up. 'Davie Howat. He's got a woman in custody there – it's to do with that antiques thing. You know.' He headed for the door. 'Victorian coin collection, you remember…. Scuse us Guin, won't you? Mmm… gold coins.'

They trooped out of the maisonette, and Fabe locked the door. 'See you tonight, princess,' he said. 'I hope.'

* * *

The blonde from Horncross Forest glared at Armie from across the table. They sat in the small room where the Whixton police took statements. Occasionally the Whixton guys got to question suspects here: more often, they sent them to Hornbridge.

Davie Howat sat with Armie; Fabe leaned against the wall. Vanessa folded her arms. 'It's mine,' she said.

'Can you prove that, Mrs Garden?' said Armie.

'I don't have to. If anybody has to prove anything it's you. You know that perfectly damn well too. Don't try to bully me.'

'Only asking. We are checking you know. And if it turns out that's not one of the missing coins then –'

'I've told you it isn't. Are you deaf?'

'I heard you, thanks. But you see the trouble is, you're not willing to explain how you came by it.'

'It's an heirloom, that's more than you need to know.'

'And you're not saying who it's inherited from.'

'Well I don't know,' said Vanessa, 'it's my husband who inherited them. It. Inherited it.'

'That isn't what you said –'

Someone knocked at the door, then opened it a crack. 'Sergeant Howat. Inspector,' said a soft voice.

'Scuse us,' said Armie, rising.

'It isn't his,' said the constable who'd called them out. 'It isn't any of the missing coins.'

'Oh bloody Nora,' said Davie. 'Now they tell us. Now what? Let her go I suppose.'

'And the coin,' said Armie. 'Since we've no proof....'

'Did I hear her say them? Inherited them?'

'You did, Davie.'

'Them.' Davie shook his head. 'Golden guineas? It's bizarre. But... I suppose the things could genuinely be theirs. I mean stretching a point. Couldn't they?'

'Why not?' said Armie. 'Keep an open mind. I try to. Want to face the music now?'

'Fabe,' said Armie as they motored past the northern boundary of Horncross. 'She looks like someone. Mrs Garden I mean. Who is it? It's driving me mad.'

'She looks to me like a hardfaced tink who's going to end up in Cornton Vale.'

'Not like someone we know? Think hard.'

But Fabe didn't feel like thinking hard; at least, not about Vanessa Garden.

twelve

Annals of a Quiet Neighbourhood

AS HE shaved, glancing in the mirror, Ronnie realised he'd have made a good cop. Not that he'd ever come up to Geordie's level; but then, few men did. But Ronnie was razor sharp himself. Experienced, too, and widely connected. The force could do worse than sign up Ronald Henry Goudie.

In the matter of these whores, he knew, he was lengths ahead of lovely Linda. Of course she hadn't had much experience, but she might've figured Sonia out by now. He had.

As a one-woman vice squad – and that'd be tough work for any girl – Linda needed to match whores to pimps. Soon she'd have no problem, all the girls would be Ronnie's, but they weren't yet. Sonia isn't, anyway, he thought peevishly, peering into his nose.

Sonia had once worked for Dave Rashid, but that was history. It hadn't even been serious. She'd been Dave's girlfriend and put herself about a bit, Dave had lived off her for quite some time and then he'd dumped her. She'd been seventeen then, and it had hurt. So when Cyril MacBride had asked her to drop some hints about Dave she'd been very obliging. Cyril had paid her, which made it all nice and tight.

The trouble was she'd never had a pimp after Dave. She pretended to have one. It wasn't hard, since practically no one gave a damn: only Ronnie and Linda, in fact. Sonia had given her imaginary pimp the name Barney. Ronnie reached for a towel. What sort of a stupid name was that?

But Ronnie wondered if he oughtn't to give Sonia a nudge. He'd made her a nice proposition and she'd turned him down: what a flake. But he hadn't yet, as it were, asked her formally. It couldn't hurt to try some persuasion. Too bad he had no one reliable here, since sacking Cyril.

A man shouldn't have to run his own errands. On the other hand he shouldn't let himself go soft; and after all, this wasn't the city. You have to do the best you can on the wild frontier.

It was wild now all right. Listen to that rain, whipped against the bathroom window. He could see leaves, green and yellow, plastered to the glass outside. September was dying hard.

Ronnie buttoned his shirt. He'd buy a Stanley knife. So appropriate, that name; poor Stanley had loved those gadgets. Ronnie smiled in spite of himself, thinking how his cousin had died, his veins cut open. They'd called it suicide. But people get cut, Ronnie reflected; Scissors did; and he was like a father to me. You couldn't have a better.

Stanley knife, then. And let Sonia think it over.

* * *

Debbie poured Geoff another cup of coffee, and placed it beside him on the breakfast bar. She kissed his hair, but didn't sit down.

'Aren't you having one too?' Geoff said.

'No – no time. And I'm floating anyway.'

'Everything's floating. Just listen to that rain. It'd better clear up before Liz and the kids get here.'

'Oh, I live in hope,' Debbie said. 'I have to. Imagine them mewed up in the house all week. Now let's see where my waterproofs are, after all this lovely....' She lifted the seat of a pinewood bench by the door. 'Aha!'

'God's sake Deb, let me drive you over,' he said, 'it's wild.'

'I don't care. You stay here and live it up.'

'You get Arlene to commit?'

'Hm? Yes. Yes, they're coming. Tomorrow. I'll see you soon, sweetheart.' She kissed him again.

'Ahh. Essence of waterproof,' he said, sniffing. 'You sure I can't give you a hurl, honey.'

'No! I'll be fine. You come by and see me. I'll sell you a bottle of gin.'

It's OK in the rain, she thought. Wind too. Of course it's harder, and you get in a sweat. But exercise is addictive.

Her waterproofs rattled in the gale. Funny, she thought, how much you miss your ears, riding a bike. Then you look over your shoulder and there's the inside of your hood looking back at you.

The spray from her tyres hissed softly as she coasted to a stop behind the supermarket. She hopped off and darted through the service door.

An island of light, weird artificial light, in an eerie sea of rain. Eerily quiet, too, the Safeways at this hour. Debbie sat for some minutes before anyone came through her checkout.

'Oh hi!' she beamed. 'Not very nice this morning!' She passed things over the glass panel: sandwiches, yoghurt, the *Mirror*, the Hornbridge *World*. Smart to get the local paper, she thought, when you're staying somewhere new. She keyed in the price of his croissants, and pressed the total.

'Oh I don't know,' said the customer, meeting her eye. 'Seems nice to me.' She lifted an eyebrow and smiled.

Crossing the car park, Ronnie bunched up his carrier bag to stop it twisting in the wind. Debbie, he thought. Hmm. A jewel in the Safeway's crown.

He dived into his car and set out for Hornbridge. He had business to sort, loose ends left over from his holiday in Geordie Armistead's best cell; he'd like to replace Cyril, he'd like to do a lot of things. This weather wasn't helping. Even the poor bloody sheep in the fields looked miserable, and in Hornbridge each street was a tiny torrent. Ronnie parked as close as he could to the former Inferno Club, and bounded through the puddles to shelter.

Each week since he'd moved to Marchbank, he'd read the Hornbridge *World*. Local names, local obsessions: a businessman needed to learn such things. But you couldn't help laughing at the *World*'s idea of news. A war could be going on –

in fact one was going on – but that couldn't keep Wally Gibson's heifers out of the headlines.

The coffee maker he'd inherited from Arlene gave a hiss and a sigh. In stocking-feet, he shuffled to the bar and poured himself a cup; he sat and inspected the headlines of the *Mirror*. More troops, he read. Friendly fire? Some friends, those. He shoved it away and opened the *World* instead.

Woman in Coin Theft Probe, said a small header on page three. Theft? At least there was something worth reading about.

* * *

Day after day, Lee would wake up and remember why he felt like shit. Then he'd think, Right. Let 'em go to hell. It wasn't my fault, I don't owe any of them anything.

'What's up, sourpuss?' Uncle Willy would say over breakfast. Lee would maintain a superior silence, hoping his uncle would take the hint.

'Saturday today,' said Willy a week after the catastrophe. Only a week, thought Lee, feels like centuries have passed. Willy handed him a plate of porridge and said, 'What you doing today?'

Lee stared down at the porridge with distaste. 'Staying here.' Duh, he didn't add. 'Moira's sick. I have to stay with her.'

'Sorry mush,' said his uncle, 'I wasn't thinking.'

Maisie came in from the kids' room, where Moira was having breakfast in bed. 'God's sake, Lee,' she said. 'Sweeten up.'

No more trebuchet building. Oscar's tools were off limits, and the campsite was soggy from Thursday's gale. No trip into Whixton. But that was no hardship, since everyone was so mad at each other you wouldn't dare open your mouth. In fact, thought Lee, I'd rather be in hell than trapped in the Shogun with them.

He was sorry for Moira. After all the adults' shouting and stamping, she'd been so unhappy she'd caught the flu. Well, fever anyway. On Thursday afternoon as they'd stood outside school, she'd started to shiver. 'I hurt all over,' she'd told him in

131

a small voice. Now she was eating: that was something, but she still had to stay in bed.

'Stay around,' said their mother, pulling a woolly hat over her ginger curls. 'Make Moira some cup-a-soup for lunch, OK? You can take Squeeter round the site to poo.'

Thanks a great big steaming heap, Lee thought.

But after soup, when he and Squeeter were loafing outside, the dog saw a rabbit. Off she went at whippet-speed into the pines. Lee whistled. She was gone.

He jumped back in the van and grabbed his jacket. 'Got to find the dog,' he called to his sister. 'Back soon.' Squeeter's trail led towards the open rock, the edge of the plateau. He'd better hurry.

He caught up with her on the path to the car park, where tourists used to come in summertime. She'd been all the way down there and was coming back up to him, her tongue flopping like a wet sock and her ribs heaving: a dog who could grin all over, so that even Lee had to smile. He rubbed her head. 'Let's go, shitbrain.'

'Hey Lee!' someone yelled from below.

'Malley? That you?'

'Lee, is that your dog? Hey, come down.'

Malley from third year: Lee knew him slightly, admired him like most people. 'Come on Squeeter.' Lee started down the path. 'What you doing Mal?'

'You know the wolf? We're going to hunt him. Me and Boney.' Now Lee could see down into the car park: Malley's pal, Boney, waved at him, flourishing a stick with a knob on the end. 'So Lee, you know the forest. You better come too.'

* * *

Ronnie didn't know if he should laugh or cry, but he thought: laugh, it's cheaper.

Thursday morning, when he'd learned that the bloody tinks had got his treasure – although the paper hadn't said it in so many words – he'd just stopped himself from putting his fist through the panelling, settled for shouting in anguish instead.

Then he'd seen the light. The buggers had saved him the trouble of looking. After all, he hadn't been having any luck.

The article said that some travelling woman had been hauled in on Saturday. She'd tried to reset a valuable antique coin: a golden guinea. She said she'd only wanted to see what Mr Oldroyd would offer her. It was her guinea. It wasn't stolen. But the dealer had called the police.

One Sunday last summer, the paper said, an antiques fair had come to Whixton Town Hall. One stallholder dealt in coins. He'd brought along some valuable collection in its own Victorian glass-fronted case, and placed it on the floor in front of his display table. Then some scrote had walked off with it. All the antique dealers for miles around had been after the culprit ever since.

Ronnie didn't know who this Vanessa Garden was, but she must be with Willy Smith. He knew where Smith was. The rest should be simple.

Gale or no gale, he'd have loved to go straight to the camp on Thursday. But he'd had things to do. In any case Saturday would be better: that's when the tinks would go off to town, and he'd have a free hand. He'd better hurry.

On Saturday, after lunch, Ronnie pulled in to the car park at Horncross. He sat for a moment, thinking. He had no weapon – except for the Stanley knife; but never mind, no one would be there. If he was wrong about that, he could wait. He got out of his car.

Beyond the low stone wall of the car park he could see some kids. A skinny black dog was with them: the dog from the camp. There was the red-haired boy, too, with his jeans at half-mast – that was him, all right. So the kids weren't in Whixton. But they weren't in camp either. Ronnie made for the plateau.

* * *

Moira woke up in the curtained stillness. Her fever had broken; she'd slept it through.

But she could hear noises. Where was Lee? She lay without moving. The van rocked slightly. Someone was inside.

They were flinging things about in the kitchen: saucepans, spoons. Cupboard doors clunked open. Then footsteps started down the van, through the sitting-room. There were muffled cushiony sounds.

She was trapped. You couldn't get under these beds. In any case whoever it was would look under beds. They were hunting for something, just like her and Lee last week. Three guesses what they were looking for.

Uncle Willy had told Uncle Oscar that the gold had disappeared. He'd simply told a lie. While Willy was working, and the other grown-ups were in town, and while Lee and Moira were meant to have been in camp with Squeeter, someone had snuck in and stolen the gold, Willy said. So Uncle Oscar had told Lee he'd murder him and why couldn't he have stayed in camp? Lee had said something rude. Mum had said something else. Vanessa had called the kids a name, and then their Gran had shut Vanessa up. But the grown-ups were still fed up with Moira and Lee.

Moira loved Uncle Willy, but this was not fair.

The footsteps again: they were coming to her room. She froze, staring at the half-open door.

Ronnie could feel his face turning red as he sought among the sofa-cushions. Bloody, flaming hell, where was it. The pile of junk outside perhaps: should've started with that, what a bloody fool he was. So damn hot in here. Why'd they keep it so hot?

He flung the last door open and shouted, 'My Christ!' There was a kid here! He dived on her, got her by the pigtail and said, 'Where's the gold?' He felt in his pocket for that Stanley knife. So lucky he'd brought that.

She squeaked. 'What?' roared Ronnie. He slid the blade forward. 'What?'

'Don't know.'

'Is it here? D'you know what this is? It's a knife, feel that? Where's the bloody gold? Where is it?'

'It's gone,' said Moira. 'It isn't here!'

'Where the flaming hell is it then?'

'Don't know. Don't know!'

'Ah come on, don't know!' said Ronnie.

Before he'd stopped, before he'd switched off his engine Willy saw that his caravan door was open. He started to run, sprang inside without touching the step. Moira was crying. Cold with terror, he bounded through to the bedrooms. There on Moira's bunk was the man Goudie, grasping her hair, with a mat-knife at her throat.

'Now we'll have it,' the bastard said. 'Where's the gold, Willy? Come on, get your jeep, it's easy.'

He couldn't think what else to do. He had to let Goudie bring Moira, too: she had on pyjamas, her feet were bare and she'd had a fever since Thursday. He felt like sobbing himself.

Goudie held the knife too close, the road was bumpy. 'For the love of God put that bloody thing down,' said Willy. 'I can't do this if you don't.'

'You can do it, Willy.'

Moira was brave but her tears kept flowing, her nose ran but she didn't dare to sniff. She didn't dare to move. Goudie had her on his knee and he gripped her wrist with his left hand. She shook and shook, looked steadily forward without a sound.

'Hurry up,' Goudie said, 'this kid is minging.'

At the forest gate Willy stopped the truck. 'Got to unlock this.' He reached for the door-handle, and heard Moira gasp. 'Watch it, Goudie.'

'You watch it. Just open it, Willy.'

Willy took off the padlock; he swung the gate open, got back in the cab, and drove through. He kept trying to look at Moira. 'Watch out!' Goudie shouted, too late, as they slammed into something: another truck turning in towards the gate. Willy banged his chin on the wheel, and Goudie nicked Moira. She squealed. 'Jesus Christ,' Goudie shouted.

Shocked by the impact, at first Tracy didn't see who it was: the girl from the meadow. But Frank was bellowing, climbing from the cab, storming round the back of the truck because the vehicles were head-to-head. The other truck had hit him at an angle, smashing its own headlamp. He was sure he'd come off worse.

Martok sat in the middle of the seat. Tracy would've liked to get out. But Frank and the other driver were blocking her door, and Martok sat like a statue. So Tracy stared across at the little girl, and the little girl stared back.

The child was sitting on some old guy's lap, her face swollen. Blood trickled from her chin. Tracy got out, shoving past Frank, and Martok flopped out too. The other driver, a dark man in high boots, shrank away when he saw the dog. Tracy ran round behind, and advanced on their truck.

The little girl mouthed something. Help, it was, Help Me. Tracy put on a big smile.

She knocked on the window. The old guy glared, so she opened the door: he didn't try to hold it shut. But that would be because he was holding the little girl's wrist, and he had something in his other hand.

'Hi!' said Tracy. 'You again! Want to come see my doggie?'

The guy let go. He gazed past the little girl, past Tracy, studying the doggie. The child squeaked and jumped from the truck, and ran to Martok, who growled and wagged his tail.

She put both her arms around his neck and started to sob. He wriggled backwards so he could lick her nose.

'You'll pay for this,' Frank yelled. It felt good to yell. Look at this idiot in his damned boots.

'OK,' said the idiot, 'you got it, no problem.'

'Eh?'

'Get us away from that nutter,' said the dark man. 'Please mush? He's cut my niece. He's a killer. I'll fix your truck.'

Ronnie slid from his seat and stood up. The dog stepped away from the kid and came forward, two paces, three. In the twilight of the spruces the dog was almost black. Just the ivory grin, and copper moons for eyes: the dark mask swallowed up the rest. Ronnie felt in his pocket for that knife. Futile, puny weapon. He got back in the cab and closed the door.

* * *

Arlene spent most of Saturday wondering why she didn't feel anything. Funny: last night she'd been in agony. She'd lain quite still and listened until Sandy dropped off, then cried,

136

secret and silent beside him. But she'd fallen asleep at last. Waking at noon, finding herself alone, she'd thought, that's amazing. I can't feel it now.

Strange, she thought as she took a shower. Weird, as she painted her toenails peach. Bizarre. She wriggled into a useful little turquoise number. It's going to be OK, how strange. After seventeen years of marriage.

At last, at half past five, the pain came back. It wasn't exactly pain, though, more like panic. Her heart slammed and she found herself swallowing, like the first time she'd taken a plane.

But there was pain too, of course; by six-fifteen, when Sandy got home, it had settled deep in her belly. She sat at the kitchen table, drinks all ready, listening as the front door opened and closed.

He didn't know, she'd bet on that. He hadn't seen a thing. Last night as they'd sat with Geoff and Debbie, laughing and talking, Sandy hadn't noticed a thing. But she'd seen him.

Laughing and talking and looking, that was it: Sandy and Debbie, looking across her into each other's eyes. They'd looked across her as though she wasn't there, or maybe they thought she was blind. How long, she wondered, would it take to invent a whole language of looks?

He came in now and leaned over her, gave her a clumsy squeeze and kissed her hair. 'Hey tiger, you look fierce.'

He doesn't know. There must be something in that, Arlene thought. Advantage, Me.

* * *

Bob Marshall sat at his desk, Monday morning, Monday the twenty-ninth of September, eighteen days after the murder of Barclay. He'd started to measure time against lack of results. The investigation was going nowhere.

Poor Ian. Forgive us all, wherever you are.

Bob realised he had his head in his hands and he straightened up. He lifted his phone. 'Armie?'

The detectives assembled. 'I'm worried about Sonia,' Linda said as she sat down. 'I can't find her anywhere.'

'Sonia?' said Bob.

'Prostitute.'

'Ah. Well... I'm sorry. Sure you're doing your best. Now... speaking of that....'

'You want results,' said Armie. 'Ian Barclay.'

'Well?'

'No new leads. There's no link to Goudie. We've got to try a new approach.'

'A woman,' Fabe said.

'Did that witness see a woman?' Bob said. 'Thought she saw a man.'

'Who can tell, Bob?' said Armie. 'She didn't say it was a man. She said it was a person. But I think she assumed it was a woman, actually. Not sure why I think that. Something she said. It's not in her statement.'

'Why would she think so?' Bob said.

'Well let's be honest,' said Fabe, 'he had ten squillion girlfriends.'

'Did she know that?' said Bob. 'What's her name again?'

'Tracy Wiseman,' Fabe said. 'The girl who found Beames. You know. Guin's brother's girl.'

'So she did,' said Bob. 'She did find Beames. Hmm! Had she slept with Ian?'

'No evidence. Didn't say she had,' said Armie. 'Naturally.'

'Hmm! But you're sure she thought the killer was a woman. The person she'd seen,' said Bob.

'No,' Armie said, 'not entirely. But I think she did.'

'You could be wrong, Armie.'

'Course I could.'

'But you're probably right,' Bob said. 'Which means she probably knew he had ten squillion girlfriends. Which means she's a nosey neighbour, at the very least. Which means...?'

'Ian nicked Frank last year,' said Fabe. 'Guin's brother. Remember?'

'Thank you Fabe,' said Bob. 'Well I think you investigate Wiseman. I think this is promising, don't you? She's got form, hasn't she, I seem to remember.'

'Only trying to save the planet,' Linda said.

'OK,' said Bob, 'but this girl's got the courage of her convictions. No, I do not mean that as a pun. She takes direct action. What about it? How well do you know her, Fabe?'

'Direct action,' Fabe said. 'That's true enough. And she doesn't like the polis – can't blame her. So I don't know her well. She's – well, I'd call it reserved, or… secretive, even. But no, I wouldn't, cause it's Guin who says that. Guin admires her, by the way. God knows why.'

thirteen

A *Herald* Reader Sings

'I LIKE what you've done so far,' Arlene said. 'Though I wouldn't have had quite so many little booths.'

'It's for intimacy,' Ronnie said. 'I think folk like an intimate feeling. A sense of adventure. Like we've been having.' He beamed and lifted the flap to get behind the bar. 'This is meant to be Heaven! Go on – take a seat for God's sake. Drink?'

'Mmm. I do have to get back… open the club.'

'Aww. Delegate, woman. Get a manager in.'

'I have,' said Arlene, 'but the Odd Spot's kind of a pet.'

'Let me be your pet. Look, I'm wagging my tail!' He filled the ice bucket. 'G and T all right?'

There were times when she liked Ronnie. She liked having a boyfriend, for one thing. But she'd also begun to notice him as a person. He had hidden depths; and as a man of the world, he might be helpful.

'You know,' she said, 'I wonder. What's a good way to get even with somebody? Really make them feel it.'

'Feel what?'

'Like, oh... feel the way I feel. Get them back.'

'What'd they do?'

'Put me through hell,' said Arlene. 'Trashed my self-respect....'

'If you mean your man cheated on you, say no more.' Ronnie clasped his hands over his heart. 'Babe, I knew I'd caught you on the rebound.' He came back round the bar, sat beside her and tugged gently at the short red hair above her ear. 'You're doing it, lovely. You're going with me.' He kissed her cheek. 'Best medicine too.'

'I don't mean him, I mean her,' she said. 'What's the worst feeling you can have?'

'Losing your man. Do a malky on him.'

God, she thought, he's serious. 'He hasn't done anything.'

'Well,' said Ronnie, 'if you hurt the bitch he'll feel it too. But.... Shall I tell you what the worst thing is? The worst feeling of all? That no one will save you.'

'From what?'

'From your nightmare,' said Ronnie. 'Everyone's got one. I have a nightmare sometimes, me. But I always know someone's going to save me... and that makes it all right, you see.'

* * *

Debbie thought she was an early riser. She was nothing compared to her sister's kids.

'Made you some porridge, Auntie Debs!' shouted little Sean. 'With milk!'

'Sweetie,' she said. 'Aren't you clever.' She reached over little Pete for the sponge at the back of the taps. 'What's to do, Pete?'

'I'm filling the kettle.'

So he was, but it was too big for him. He'd set it in the sink to fill. 'You know, darling, that bottom bit doesn't want to get wet,' said Debbie.

Liz shambled in, wearing jogging bottoms and a long flannel shirt. 'God, boys. You're like a plague.' She hefted the kettle from the sink, and dried the outside with the hand-towel.

'They're helping,' Debbie said, unsticking the porridge. 'Still picnicking?'

Liz looked out at the sky. 'Oh I think so. Aren't we, lads?'

'To the seashore!' Sean said. 'I'm going to the sea!'

'Bit fresh for a picnic,' Debbie said.

'No,' said Liz. 'These don't feel the cold. It's all you can do to stop 'em going in swimming. Got any oranges? I'll buy you more.'

'Oh don't worry about that. There's a supermarket full of that.' Debbie went to the pantry and rootled around until she found a basket. 'Take anything you need. How about some cheese?'

'I like cheese,' said Pete.

* * *

'Aye aye, Inspector.' Wattie held out a bundle of letters. 'Monday morning junk mail.'

'Oh right,' said Armie, taking the bundle, 'thanks Wattie. Who knows. Someone might've written to me to confess.' He headed up the stairs.

Seated on his desk, Armie put on his spectacles and tore the envelopes open one by one. He threw the contents in a heap beside him, dropping the envelopes on the floor.

The seventh letter was in a small square envelope, and so unlike the rest that he unfolded it at once. Then he got off his desk and fetched thin rubber gloves. Wearing these, he retrieved the envelope, and read the note again.

'Love letter?' said Linda from the doorway.

'Ah… no. No,' said Armie, 'poison pen.'

'Eh?'

'Anonymous tip-off.' He handed her the letter. She noticed his gloves, gripped the small sheet by a corner and read, Ian Barclay Was Murdered By Deborah Chalmers.

'Deborah Chalmers,' she said, 'isn't that one of those folk that Ian interviewed?'

'That's right. About Sandy Third's stolen car. The Chalmerses live right opposite.'

'Bits snipped out of a newspaper,' Linda said. 'Not too keen to identify themselves.'

'Well I think we've narrowed it down already. It's a *Herald* reader seemingly…. I wonder if it's true.'

'Have you met Deborah Chalmers?'

'Not yet,' Armie said.

He started by getting a search warrant, so Fabe and Linda could get on over to Nellfield. Meantime he collected Debbie from her checkout at Safeways.

'Just routine,' he said as they threaded their way through the mid-morning shoppers.

'Oh right,' said Debbie. 'Every day.'

Interview Room One: not exactly five-star. Armie found himself wishing someone could have put a vase of carnations there on the table along with the tape recorder.

'Your solicitor's on his way, Mrs Chalmers.'

'I don't need him,' said Debbie. 'I didn't do anything.'

They heard footsteps in the passage outside. 'Mira,' said Armie, opening the door. 'Could you ask Wattie to come? With some coffee? Thanks. And when you're ready, just join us, OK?' He sat down opposite Debbie and sighed. 'Well. And there was me wishing I had somebody in custody.'

'I still can't work out what all this is about,' said Debbie. 'I haven't done anything.'

She studied Armie in silence while they waited. She couldn't remember ever seeing such curly eyebrows. He looked tired, and worried.

So he should. He'd made a mistake. But he must have warrants for all this. So, were they actually searching the house? Liz and the kids had their stuff in the bedrooms. It was lucky, on balance, that they'd gone out. Imagine if they'd been there.

The door opened. A copper in uniform brought a tray; the girl constable ushered in Charlie Henderson. He too looked worried. He hurried to Debbie and took her hands.

'What's going on here?' said Charlie. 'Mr Armistead, this is bizarre.'

'Well I shouldn't worry,' said the Inspector. 'We've done bizarre before.'

* * *

They were searching the house. Arlene could hear them if she tried: and she did. She caught little alien sounds.

She was sorry they hadn't broken the door down. They'd done something clever with the lock instead. Finnie, the walking hat-rack, had sauntered boldly in, followed by that blonde. Their silhouettes crossed and recrossed the windows. There – that was the kitchen. Someone looking at the knives: after all, the poor guy's throat was slit.

So Ronnie's plan was a good one. Had it been Ronnie's? He was the one who'd brought up murder – an accusation of murder. His story was that it happened to a friend of his. Silly man: obviously he was speaking about himself.

Now Debbie was to be accused of murder. No one would save her: not like Ronnie, who always knew that someone would rescue him.

* * *

'I can't think who would send something like that,' Debbie said. 'It's unbelievable.'

'Someone's done it though,' said the Inspector.

She shook her head. 'It's so vicious.'

'Could you have an enemy? Someone with a grudge?'

'Oh don't be ridiculous,' said Debbie.

The detective's brows curled up. 'OK look. In your past. What did you use to do? Before you were married for instance.'

'I was a teacher. Games – PE.'

'Ah!' He smiled ruefully. 'I wonder how many kids get traumatised by PE teachers. You know? Not that it's your fault. But at school… kids demonise you.'

'Demonise teachers?' Debbie said. 'You mean cops.'

'Oh absolutely, I know that. But think. Were you ever aware of resentment, or….'

'Resentment. OK, not hatred! For goodness sake. Someone would've had to hate my guts. I actually think I was popular, as teachers go.'

'Don't you miss your teaching?'

'No!' Debbie said. 'It's just the past. Everything's changed since I married Geoff.'

'For the better,' said Armistead, 'I presume. What does he do? Where is he now, at work?'

'He's offshore. He's just gone, last night.'

'An oilman?'

'For his sins.'

'Thought they all lived in Aberdeen.'

Debbie smiled. 'Oh no, his sins weren't as bad as that.'

Can't afford to relax, she thought. He's putting me at ease, he's good at it. And Charlie, the trouble with Charlie is, he trusts the guy. He shouldn't.

The truth doesn't matter, they want a result. They need to put someone away. Me.

'Who the hell could've sent it?' she said aloud.

'That's what I'm asking,' said Armistead. 'We'll trace it, the lab will come up with something – but meantime....'

'You can't take it seriously. I didn't even know Ian Barclay.'

'You met him.'

'That's right, and your... colleague, the tall guy, he asked me about it before. I couldn't tell him much, I only met Mr Barclay that once. We talked about the Nissan, I hadn't seen anything – heard anything – so off he went.... I might've given him coffee. I don't even remember what Barclay looked like, except he had dark hair and I thought he looked sad.'

'You didn't see him again after that.'

'Why would I?'

'He didn't get in touch with you, say....'

My God, thought Debbie, it's like a bad script. I'm not going to say it, you better not either.

'Why the hell would he get in touch?' She glared at him, felt her face getting hot. 'Damn it Inspector, I am not going to say it.'

'You're not going to say what, Mrs Chalmers?'

Christ, she thought, why can't they open a window. But there weren't any windows in Interview Room One.

'Ian Barclay was a friend of mine,' Armistead said. 'But I didn't understand him. He'd had problems with his marriage – many coppers do. And he'd begun to console himself by, well, basically sleeping with just about everybody. Female,' he added absently.

'And what has that to do with....'

'I found him, you know. There in his bed. I remember.... I'm not trying shock tactics here, Mrs Chalmers. But I wish.... I'd like you to understand this. I remember thinking how sorry I was.'

Debbie waited, and thought how sorry he'd be when she got around to suing him black and blue.

'So if I seem to pry, Mrs Chalmers, it's probably just my way of trying to make it up to him.'

'A bit late,' Debbie said.

'Too late. OK. Someone's accused you of murdering him: I haven't. I'm not accusing you of sleeping with him either. How could I? It wouldn't have been illegal.'

'I wasn't sleeping with him. All right? I've said it. Will that do you?'

'It'll do me fine. And how about Sandy?'

She's a nasty colour, poor girl, Armie thought. Pretty woman. So fair, nice complexion, too. Then she spoils it all by first turning purple and then going sort of green.

'I mean Mr Third of course. I like Mr Third,' said Armie, 'don't you?'

'Oh, now it's Sandy Third I'm screwing,' she said. 'And who else while you're about it? Why not just get out the phone book and start....'

Charlie said, 'Debbie, just tell him you haven't.'

Better tell me the truth, Armie thought. But let's not hassle Charlie.

'I have not been sleeping with Sandy,' she said.

'I wasn't being impertinent,' Armie said. 'See Arlene, she might actually think that you have. If you have or not, she might actually think so.'

'You're scraping the barrel,' said Debbie. 'You're making up fairy tales.'

* * *

'Not a sausage,' said Linda, patting the pillows on little Sean's bed and smoothing out the duvet. 'Not a damn thing.'

'Well what were we expecting,' said Fabe, 'a wolf skin?'

'Maybe.'

They trudged downstairs. 'There's still hope,' she said, holding up a polythene bag full of knives.

'But none of 'em looks right,' said Fabe. 'It's just been a hoax. It's too easy, a tip-off like that.'

'Why?' said Linda. 'Suppose someone knows? And they want to remain anonymous, not stand in a witness-box.' She closed the front door gently; the lock snapped shut. 'Listen, if I wanted to tip off the cops I wouldn't just send an anonymous message. I'd plant evidence.'

'Well don't ever try it then. False evidence is the most obvious –'

'I'd plant good evidence,' Linda said. 'And I'd get away with it. You'd never know.'

'You're a master criminal. I surrender.' Fabe took out his phone and buzzed the station.

* * *

'So that's it?' said Debbie. They'd talked through lunchtime; she was famished. 'Thank God. I'll just go see if I still have a job, shall I?' She stepped to the door.

'Yes, thanks for your time, Mrs Chalmers.' Armistead hadn't risen. At the door she paused and wriggled her shoulder blades. She tucked in her hips and stood tall. He looked up at her gravely.

'Be careful, now,' he said.

She has no alibi, thought Armie as he looked down from the window at the top of Debbie's head. Wattie was taking her back to Marchbank. The doors of the car swung open like fish's fins, closed again, and the car nosed towards the street.

No alibi, no motive either. But I'm looking for a wifie who kills for fun. Or no, not fun, but for its own sake, so she needs no other motive.

So maybe she's not that wifie. She just has secrets the way folk do. Let's say she's been shagging old Sandy. That'd make a girl blush.

She's livid with me too. But she can't shout false arrest. There is that note, and I had to act on it. The lab will probably trace it to Arlene Third.

I wonder who else might've sent it. It could be serious, if it's not Arlene.

fourteen

October

GET UP soon, she thought. Get out of this. But it's so good. Not yet... not yet.

She needed to go: put clothes on and work out how to clean up. Clean herself up, get herself home. Not yet. She lay in the sweet stuff, lingered at the moment when it had flowed over her, hot, rich, drenching half her body. Still warm: a sweet-smelling river, his blood. Life's blood.

Their clothes were in front, on the passenger seat. Back here were some waterproofs and things, a blanket, the sleeping bag on which they'd lain. He'd carried a roll of blue paper wipe, the kind that filling stations hang by the pumps. That'd be handy.

So that was it then. She'd sobered up. The art of the possible was back: bits and pieces, ifs and buts.

She was miles from town. But the keys were here somewhere. In the ignition! Happy day.

Two weeks to the day, Ronnie thought. I'm losing my touch.

He sat in his car in the foresters' lay-by at Fairyhill. He'd pulled in beside the log pile, which hid the car from the guys working in the wood. The sun was low: it got in his eyes when he peered out across the plantation. But he'd seen enough, he realised with joy, just by following Willy here.

What worried him was the time he'd taken to track the gypsy to this place. Should've been simple, it's where he was working. Well, he thought, maybe Willy's been dodging me with his second sight.

But he was too hard on himself. Being a businessman took up his time: and Arlene did, too. He didn't care now if she never sold him the Beggar's. He'd rather she kept the place.

* * *

Gingerly, on account of last time, Tracy made the turn into the forest track. But after all there was nothing, no rampaging four-by-four. She parked the truck where, with luck, it wouldn't get bashed again by passing foresters or travelling folk.

The polis had been persecuting her. Armistead had started it, last month sometime. He was kind on the surface but she didn't trust him. You didn't get coppers that nice.

Fabe had questioned her too but he'd been embarrassed. That might mean he was halfway human, but let's face it, he didn't have to be a cop. There were other jobs for tall guys, he must know that.

Did she spy on Barclay? No. Did she know Barclay? No. Had she slept with Barclay? It was weird, but she never did sleep with guys she didn't know. The detectives had seemed unconvinced.

It was just as well she'd shredded those photographs.

She had Martok for company. Frank had stayed home. The gypsy – that was what he was – had put him off coming back here. Frank really had a thing about gypsies. But the little girl's Uncle Willy had turned out to be sweet. He had contacts, too. He'd arranged to have the truck fixed faster than Frank could've done, and Frank was in the motor trade. Then Willy had paid for it all because, he said, it had been his fault.

But Frankie was missing a super afternoon. The air was like spruce wine: if there was such a thing as spruce wine, Tracy thought, it'd be blue like this day. Not much day left now, that was the trouble. As always under these trees, the light was fading.

She let Martok out at the passenger side. They were near the road, so she reached for his collar: but he pulled away and plunged into a thicket by the gate. Tracy ducked under the bar. 'What've you got this time, you devil?' she said.

Last night's moon had been a wolf moon, rising blood-red. She'd tried to get Frank to come out for a look but he'd stayed inside. She'd wandered into the town and just for the hell of it, caught a bus to get out into the country away from the street lamps. The moon had been orange when she'd got off the bus, silver when she'd headed home: whenever that was. She'd lost track of time.

'Martok. God almighty.' She could hear him crashing about in there but she couldn't work out where he was. She whistled. The crashing stopped: no dog though.

She struggled through the prickly stuff, bent double. He was in here somewhere. He'd used a path made by animals, too low for a person. But, Tracy saw as she burst through into a space among the trees, you could do it an easier way. The main track was just to her left.

Martok was here too, guarding something on the forest floor: a dark grey woollen blanket. At one end of the blanket was the top of someone's head, with thick brown hair. A bit of red sleeping bag concealed the rest of the head. The sleeper lay still.

Martok sat by the head, watching Tracy, his ears low. He whined. She squatted beside him and reached out a hand towards the brown hair.

* * *

'Gerry Lamond,' Linda said. 'Poor guy. I met him once.'

Blue lights sparkled in the twilight under the trees. The sky above was blue too, pricked here and there by stars. White-suited SOC officers floated in and out of the gloom.

'Gerry Lamond,' Linda said again. 'Keyboard player.'

'You OK?' said Fabe.

'I'm fine.'

'Where's Dr Greig?' he said. 'I want to know.... Ah, sorry Doctor, didn't see you. Was it here?'

'No,' said Greig, 'definitely killed elsewhere. The blood loss – well, there's nothing.... There's a stain on the bag, mind you. If I were a detective....'

'Killed on or near the bag,' said Fabe, 'but not here.'

'Gerry Lamond,' Linda said. 'His brother's called Mikey.'

'Linda, hen,' said the doctor, 'why don't you sit down.'

'There isn't anything to sit on,' said Linda. 'We're in a forest. What's Armie up to? Where's Wiseman?'

'Still at the road end. He went to speak to her,' said Fabe.

'He look at the body?'

'Better go ask him,' said Greig.

'I know you don't trust me, Miss Wiseman,' said Armie. 'But I don't know why... or why not.'

He sat with Tracy and Martok in the pickup. Martok was in the middle as usual. Armie had to speak round him. The dog kept trying to lick his nose. 'Best dog in the world,' Armie said.

'Frank says that.' She sounded resentful.

'The Cattos all say that to their dogs. Why are you so browned off? See Martok, he still likes me.'

'Martok hasn't had you interrogating him.'

'Interrogating?' said Armie. 'Miss Wiseman, this isn't helping. There's a young guy dead there, he's got a brother and a semi-pro band and folk who care about him. I need your help. Did you know him?'

'No.'

'OK. Never saw him before?'

'I haven't seen him yet, except the top of his head.'

'Fair enough,' said Armie. 'We'll get back to that. Now – about this place. This trackway. Do you often come here to walk the dog?'

'That's got nothing to do with anything.'

'That's a yes then.'

'It's not a yes,' said Tracy. 'Yes. I've been here with Martok and we've been for a walk. Except today, when I called you to come and see a dead body and haven't been able to escape from you since.'

'We're almost done. I only want to know if you've seen anything on your walks here. Anything, anyone, any vehicle. It'd help – anything would help.'

She paused too long. 'Never seen anyone else here. Sorry.'

'You sure?'

'Why would I say so if I wasn't sure?'

'I beg your pardon,' Armie said. 'I meant, are you sure you won't change your mind about telling me who you saw. Or what.'

'I didn't see --'

'Fine. But if you should think of something you want to tell me –'

Tracy wiped steam from the windscreen with her sleeve. 'You don't leave off, do you?'

'No,' he said. 'Would you like to know why?'

'I don't think so.'

'I'll tell you anyway. You may find this useful. I don't leave off, because the truth is not served by my taking the path of least resistance. Nor is it served by evasion.' Martok, who'd been lying bunched up with his chin on Armie's trousers, raised his head and began a sing-song of small growls. 'I need all the facts I can get, all of them, and if they lead me to something you don't want me to know, so be it. If you think your something is more important than the capture of a murderer – shut up, dog! Then you think like a murderer. Because a murderer is anybody, he's not special. Or she's not special. She just thinks her something is more important than another person's life.'

He was watching her; but the light was dim. 'You finished?' she said.

'Aye.' He opened the door and climbed out. 'Goodbye. Thank you. Bye Martok, old pal. Till we meet again.'

Linda watched Armie disengage from the dog, close the door and step clear. Tracy switched the headlamps on; the pickup swung majestically towards the highway.

'So what did she say?' said Linda. 'Anything?'

'Bugger-all, really.'

They watched the taillights recede. 'Bloody little clam,' Linda said.

'She has secrets,' he said. 'She doesn't trust me, it doesn't help. So, you know what this is.'

'The same killer. At least….'

'At least these two last. Lamond and Ian.' His phone chirped. 'Armistead. Oh hello Mrs Herring. Nice to – Well well! I will, right away. Has anyone touched it? No – no, that's quite right. Right away. Thanks so much. Bye. That's it,' he said, pocketing the phone, 'the travellers found the van. Gerry Lamond's, the forestry van. Mrs Herring found it. It's on the industrial estate.'

'They know about Gerry?'

'No – who can say! But no,' said Armie, 'it's just that it's full of blood.'

* * *

'Honey, angel,' Frank said, pouring a beer, 'don't worry. Believe me, these tinks look after themselves.'

'Didn't look like it,' Tracy said. 'I mean my God. He'd have slit her throat.'

'But he didn't. Cheers.' He raised his glass and took a pull. 'No. If your gypsy pal said keep quiet, keep quiet. It's his decision.'

'Should've told bloody Armistead, I know I should.'

'No,' Frank said, 'you go with your instincts. You have great instincts. Cheer up, OK? But you know,' he passed her a bowl of nuts, 'Armie's pretty reasonable.'

'That's what I used to think.'

'He is. He's stiff-necked as hell of course. But that's cause he's old. I don't think he'd bother your pikeys really. And he'll find 'em anyway, so I mean, it's not like you'd be blowing their cover.'

'Well,' said Tracy, 'yeah, but Willy. I said I'd keep quiet.'

'Fair enough then. You're doing fine.' Frank set down his glass and got to his feet. 'Got to go stir that curry, babe. Things are hotting up.'

* * *

At six the next morning, Mira carried a tray of coffee into the detectives' base and set it down on Armie's desk. She yawned. 'Coffee's up,' she said, taking a cup. She sat down beside the window and sipped, blinking up at the whiteboard.

The detectives assembled. Fabe and Linda drank coffee drowsily, waiting for Armie to call the meeting together. Wattie lugged in a stack-a-box of evidence; Armie brought a sheaf of statements. Bob Marshall showed up about ten past six. It was obvious he'd been to bed.

'So Armie,' he said. 'It's your woman again.'

'This is what we have,' Armie said. He put his coffee down on the tray, went to the whiteboard and cleared a little space. 'Gerry Lamond, twenty-four. Forestry worker; a semi-pro musician. Well known around here – Rantin' Pipe et cetera, they're actually doing all right. T in the Park, that sort of thing.'

He'd written two dates on the board. Now he added another. 'Twelfth August, full moon. Tracy Wiseman finds Beames's body – thirteenth. Tenth September, full moon. We find Ian's body next morning, the eleventh.' He tapped on the board. 'Tenth October, full moon. Tracy Wiseman... again... finds the body of Gerry Lamond. On Saturday the eleventh, yesterday. Now,' he turned from the whiteboard, 'I'm not saying this is more than coincidence: it simply is. OK. What we know....'

He flipped through his notebook, blinked, put on spectacles and read, 'Time of death. Twelve hours at least, says the doctor, before Tracy found him, so four o'clock... four o'clock Saturday morning. And anything up to six hours before that, although it's probably not anything like six hours.'

'Not?' said Bob. Someone stifled a yawn.

'No. You see, they'd a gig Friday night. They were playing in Whixton – Souter Johnnie's, the place is called, it's a pub. So we've asked the rest of the band when they saw Gerry last, you know, when the gig was over. And the roadie, Vince Barnard's his name, he thinks he might've been the last one to see him. Barnard was ready to go by about ten past two. He had their van at the rear of the pub, him and his cousin who was helping him.'

'Speak to him too?' Bob said.

'Haven't caught up with him yet. He's a young guy... he's more or less dossing down at Barnard's, comes and goes. So before they drove away, these guys saw Gerry go back in the pub. He went in at the back door, the fire exit. But by then the others had gone off in their own cars.'

'So if you believe Barnard,' said Linda, 'time of death narrows down a lot.'

'Right. Now, we still need somebody who saw him leave the pub. He was driving his forestry van. If only we knew who he'd left with....'

'If he left with anyone at all,' said Linda.

'Ah!' said Armie. 'He was with someone most of the night. The band members saw her, the two barmaids did too. A woman with red hair, medium length, in a butterfly clip. That's what they called it, pulled up at the back, you know? She was wearing a black and silver jumpsuit.'

'Good God,' said Linda.

'Slim, medium height, large hands, dark nail varnish... thirty to forty. The barmaids are both in their forties so they're quite objective. Anyway – she picked him up. They both saw it.'

'She picked him up?' said Linda. 'At the bar, you mean?'

'Absolutely. Well, the barmaids thought so. That was quite early, before the band went on. They kicked off about a quarter to ten.'

'So after that,' Linda said, 'she and Gerry stayed together?'

'During the breaks, aye.'

'So they'd have left together.'

'It depends. He went back inside alone. The barmaids missed that; they were clearing up. Well,' Armie said, 'that's all I got myself. The vehicle evidence – we've got some already, they're working on it now... and the statements from the travellers. Let's just go over what Linda and Mira got out of 'em.'

It could be nothing, but Armie wondered why Willy's people had moved. There they were with Mrs Herring and the rest, on the designated site at Whixton. Could the gypsy have taken his warning seriously?

Miranda Herring thought Willy had a bee in his bonnet. Maybe the bee had flown away.

Miranda had discovered Gerry's van when she went to fetch water. The travellers' site had water laid on, but she didn't like the taste. The standpipe outside the body shop was nicer.

A chain-link fence ran alongside the body shop on the side where the standpipe was. In this fence was a gate, which the panel beaters almost never locked. They didn't work Saturdays, so they didn't know that the van had squeezed through into their compound, where Miranda had found it in late afternoon. She'd walked past it with her jerrycans to the tap, then noticed the puddles of water round about. The puddles were drying, and their edges were rusty red.

Puddles or no puddles, she could see that the van hadn't been cleaned. It was bloody inside. The detectives agreed: so the puddles were made by someone washing blood off of themselves.

'Himself or herself,' Linda said before Armie could say it.

'So in conclusion,' Armie said. The morning was passing. The high room was filled with the skirl of empty stomachs. 'We don't actually know where the murder took place, except it was in the victim's van. We have no weapon, but the doctor is certain it was a knife very like the one that killed Ian. Narrow blade, fine entry, very very sharp. The wound was similar in all respects to Ian's, and as in his case, the throat was slashed afterwards, probably after the victim had died.' Someone gave a small squeak of protest. 'Really,' said Armie, 'I'm sure he'd died. He had died. So... he may have been killed at the forest gate or elsewhere, but he certainly was dragged in the blanket from a point near the gate to the spot where Martok found him.'

'He was killed on the blanket?' said Bob.

'Probably. There's quite a stain on that and the sleeping bag as well. And of course the poor fellow had most of his clothes off. Everything in fact, except for his briefs… and his socks.'

'And the clothes – gone?'

'His trousers are gone. His trainers, a waistcoat and a pink denim shirt were found in the front seat. Unstained. He wore those at the gig, his friends tell me.'

'What about women's clothes?' said Fabe.

'Not a shred,' said Armie. 'But it's early days. So – we need everyone we can get…. Search the estate, skips, rubbish tips, bins… the forest gate… after breakfast. So if you've no more questions – '

'If you've finished, Armie, come in my office,' said Bob.

* * *

'One,' Bob said, 'Beames. He's not part of this. Two, moons. What's all that about?'

'I think it's interesting,' Armie said. 'And it's Beames as well, I mean it makes him a part of it. Don't you think?'

'No I don't. I think, I know that Rod Andrew killed Beames. If there is a connexion it's like you said, a copycat killer who's started to repeat herself. Himself.'

'With the full moon,' said Armie. 'It was full when Beames died. Would a copycat pick that up? I mean….'

'If they noticed the moon was full that night, they would,' Bob said. 'What's the problem?'

'What if it isn't a copycat?'

'What if it's two?' Bob countered. 'The third imitates the second imitates the first. It happens.'

'What if it's not, Bob?'

'Oh for bloody hell's sake man. Next you'll tell me it's the flaming werewolf. You may as well, everyone else will say so. I tell you what. You find the killer and then we'll know. And I'd like to see some progress on Goudie, wouldn't you?'

* * *

It had taken time and a lot of luck but at last Guin had them: the keys to Tracy's flat.

The lucky part had been Frank asking her to take the pickup for tyres. He couldn't be bothered. When Guin got in the truck, she found his keys dangling from the ignition: all his keys, including the two that he'd just had cut so he'd have his own set for the flat.

The tyre fitters told her half an hour. They needed the keys; she couldn't take the bunch, but she could take off the flat keys and pop round to the ironmonger's with them. But it'd be simpler to go on to the flat when the fitters had finished. The thing was, had she the time? Frank and Tracy were pretty much grounded while she had the truck. But she'd have to be fast.

It was Monday. The day before, she'd joined the search team of cops and volunteers, walking the verges between Whixton and the foresters' track at Horncross.

'Anything,' Fabe had told them. He didn't mention jumpsuits or slim-bladed knives. 'Just stick it in the bags provided. If it'll fit.'

But although the verges were now much cleaner, none of the searchers felt they'd made a breakthrough.

'Who goes through the stuff?' Guin had asked Mira, who'd led the verge party.

'Probably muggins,' said Mira, 'as per.'

The searchers in the industrial estate hadn't done any better. Today the police would inspect those premises that had been locked up on Sunday. They'd all been closed, except for the Council's recycling place, where the officers had eyed up the clothing bank with interest. But the man on duty couldn't open it. It had to be someone from Oxfam.

Mill Circle was as dead as before, or deader. Guin parked the pickup and hopped out with the keys. She got into the building, went up some stairs; here, if the key fitted, should be the door. It fitted.

She didn't feel great about sneaking into Tracy's place. She told herself she was doing it in order to eliminate Tracy from her inquiries, but that was bollocks and she knew it. She wished she'd never seen Tracy's roll of film.

She looked from each of the flat's three windows. The bathroom overlooked Ian Barclay's place right enough. But this wasn't about that: it was about photographs. Guin moved carefully, quickly, caught herself holding her breath and tried to breathe slowly. She had to focus, there was no time. No darkroom, she noted: but that's no surprise. She just rents it.

No darkroom, so processed where? Boots, chemists, camera shops. In Marchbank? In Hornbridge. Boots in Hornbridge? Or one could send films away, I would, thought Guin. You get a free roll back.

No drawer, no cupboard, no carton, no file: that film was nowhere in this flat. Not in a shopping bag stuffed in the pantry. Not behind the settee in a cheap portfolio. Not in the wardrobe – Tracy had some really unusual clothes; Guin hadn't seen her wearing these – but don't get distracted. A suitcase on the upper shelf... empty, what a waste of space. Put it back. Large poly carrier bag, upper shelf. Take it down. Two of these, different but both large, stuffed full – curtains in them. In one of them, poking through the plastic, corners. A wallet-sized thing stuck down the side.

Little fat wallet, dear sweet little fat film wallet. Boots Film Service. Now put carrier bags back... now get out of here.

fifteen

... As It Isn't Heaven

SYLVIE'S BED, that's where she was: so warm, so soft it felt like floating. Her head beneath the covers, secret, dark.

He wasn't there, was he? No snoring. No smell. She listened to Sylvie's breathing. Maybe he wouldn't ever come.

A thump and sudden movement: 'Hey Syl. Shove over. Is IT in here too? Chuck out the vermin, there's a good girl.' Chills crept up her arms and legs. She wanted to jump out and flee but she couldn't move.

No one touched her. No, and the covers weren't over her face: it was pitch dark, that was all. Pitch dark and the end of her nose was cold. No Sylvie.

It's not real. Only a dream. But the chill on her limbs died slowly. For some minutes she heard her own small voice, crying: Sylvie, look at him. Look at him, Sylvie, *look at his mouth.*

Be damned to that. She got out of bed and quietly opened the curtains. Still early; tough, she was getting up. Coffee and rolls would be good, and a shower.

The damn dreams would stop, she could deal with it. She'd deal with it.

Better do under her arms and so on, there was the club tonight.

* * *

Ronnie watched the dancers jerking and twitching round the floor and felt like a benefactor. He'd given them a place to go daft in. Well, Arlene had, really, but now it was his: his little contribution to the greater good.

In no way did he want to go to the city this week. He was busy, busy, busy: the gold, Arlene, the club. He'd have to go, though. You can't do everything over the phone, or by email. You have to look into people's eyes and they have to look into yours. That way they give you respect. Then things run smoothly.

He needed to sort out Cyril MacBride. After wrecking Third's car and the rest of it, Cyril was on remand at the Bar-L. In the nick he talked about nothing but Ronnie, which might make for pretty dull listening. But one of the listeners was Ronnie's nephew Todd, and he'd got word out to Ronnie.

'Helloooo....'

'My gorgeous princess. How deadly you look.'

'Deadly?' said Arlene. 'That's a new one.'

'Beautiful and deadly, like a sleek shiny blade. I was just thinking about knives,' Ronnie said, 'and then there was you. Babe, I hate to say it, but I have to be in Glasgow for a couple of days midweek.'

'Coming back?'
'Absolutely.'
'Dance?'
'Why not?'

* * *

'Barlinnie for you,' Wattie said as Linda stepped through the front doors of the station. 'On the phone I should say.'

'Oo.' She took the receiver. 'Ferris. Hi! Is there -- oo. No. I never.... God, no. I'll try.... Is he really not.... Somebody could maybe record, or take down.... I'll try. I should be there before lunch. Oh and thanks, thanks a lot.... Seeya.' She put the receiver down. 'Bloody hell.'

'Why, what's up?' Wattie said.

'Bloody Cyril MacBride's been stabbed in the stomach. He's not gonna make it. He wants me.'

She phoned Armie from the prison that afternoon. 'He's gone,' she said. 'Just closed his eyes.'

'Did you talk?' said Armie. He stood by the window: little knots of school kids passed by on the street below. 'Was he making sense?'

'He was making some sense. That kind of wound, they pump you full of morphine or something.'

'Aye right. So, what do you think?'

'I think you better see this statement,' said Linda. 'Look, I'll be back.'

'You couldn't by any chance fax it here?'

'Oh well,' she said, 'OK, if you can't wait.'

* * *

Guin sat behind the showroom counter, watching a couple of fellows look at bikes. They weren't serious. In fact they'd stopped looking, and now they stood talking superlatives: quickest, fastest from nought to sixty, greatest horsepower, quite a debate. Guin herself knew all these statistics but she didn't join in. She wished they'd argue out on the pavement.

She hadn't seen Fabe at lunchtime. She was actually relieved that he hadn't shown – and all because of those photographs. She'd looked through them. They were disturbing. She couldn't think what to do.

She didn't like keeping secrets at the best of times – whatever the best of times might be. Perhaps they were over. She couldn't talk to Fabe.

A police car drew up at the door and the two bikers sidled out and away, even before Fabe had unfolded himself from his seat.

'Can't stop,' he said, 'just wanted to say hi. We've got Goudie again. Should be good, this.'

'What've you got him for?' said Guin. 'The murders?'

'No! Running whores. And conspiracy to commit. Well, to cause GBH. Not sure how Armie'll play it cause that guy MacBride is dead. And Goudie won't know. So it's complicated.'

'I'll say it is. You lost me already.'

'I just wanted to see you today. With any luck we'll be questioning him for ages. I only hope…. Well, he'll be OK. It's probably his own fault,' Fabe said.

'Who will be OK and what is probably whose own fault?'

'Armie. This thing about Goudie. He's finally got him, I only hope he'll have the sense to be pleased.'

* * *

By the time Linda got back to Hornbridge, they had Ronnie in the interview room.

'Detective Constable Ferris has just entered the room,' Armie remarked to the tape recorder. 'Here Linda, take a seat. We need you. We were just asking Mr Goudie about one of your working girls.'

Ronnie sat next to his solicitor, his regular one from town: Jock Neill, a sixty-year-old with watery eyes. He looked harmless until he snapped, 'Are you getting to the point at all, Inspector? My client has a business to run.'

'Exactly,' said Armie. 'I've been asking about his business.'

'You've been making unsubstantiated and harmful allegations,' Jock said.

Linda settled herself against the wall, facing Armie and Fabe. She caught Fabe's eye fleetingly. Careful, his look said: wait and see.

'The word of some scrote locked up in Barlinnie isn't any sort of evidence at all,' Jock went on. 'Go ahead, prove to me that he's ever even seen my client.'

'All in good time,' said Armie. 'The young woman in question, Zoe Davis. On August thirteenth, DC Ferris and I spoke to Miss Davis concerning an assault on her by some person unknown. That is, she didn't identify him.' He glanced at Linda.

'Wouldn't identify him,' she said.

'That's right. Now our informant, MacBride, says he assaulted this girl.'

'Fine,' said Jock, 'so charge him. What's it got to do –'

'MacBride claims that you, Ronnie, induced him to attack her. You paid him.'

'Geordie man,' said Ronnie, 'that's nonsense. Nonsense. I don't know the guy.'

'I can prove that you do.'

'No you can't. Cause I don't,' said Ronnie. No he can't, thought Linda, you're right: I've been trying to prove it myself for ages. He's bluffing or something.

'And why would I want him to do that?' said Ronnie. 'Beat a girl up?'

'To persuade her to work for you,' said Linda. 'And now she does.'

'She doesn't,' said Ronnie. 'You can't prove any of this.'

'Let's sort that out later,' said Armie. 'You remember Dave Rashid?'

'No... yes I do,' Ronnie said. 'The guy that Arlene Third doesn't like. The bouncer.'

'That's the one. You remember, we locked him up. Arlene said he was pimping, and he'd been knocking his girls about.'

'And?'

'MacBride says he paid a young woman to start that story about Rashid. And he did that because you'd paid him to get rid of Rashid. So that was his method. Ingenious, wasn't it?'

'Not very,' said Ronnie. 'Just gutless. Rashid was too hard for him, that's all.'

162

'How'd you know he was hard?' said Fabe.

'Rashid? He's a boxer. He used to be some sort of champion, Arlene told us that. If MacBride likes a quiet life, he'll not mess with him.'

'True,' said Fabe. 'And true to type, MacBride also left Zoe's pimp alone. Hendry. He's a huge guy, is why.'

'He's told you all this?' Ronnie said huskily. 'He must love the sound of his own voice.' He took a sip of water and glanced sideways at Jock.

'So Sergeant,' said Jock. 'Is that all you've got? Obviously your informant was acting in his own interests. He'd ambitions to corner the sex trade in Hornbridge and this is the way he went about it. It has nothing whatever to do with Mr Goudie.'

Ronnie shuffled his feet. The little cassette recorder turned, squeaking on its tiny bearings. Jock tapped the tip of his pen on the table. Otherwise the room was silent.

Bloody Todd Harper, his sister's kid: he ought never to have let Lena marry his twat of a father. Todd was away in the Bar-L too and Ronnie had thought he was handy, he could do something in return for an uncle's indulgence. So now young Todd had screwed up, or else he was taking his time. All Ronnie knew was that MacBride was still talking when he should be, perforce, silent.

He waited for Jock to come up with a fix but the silence went on. Geordie had something. He wasn't about to rescue anyone today either, you could see that.

Their eyes met for a moment. Oh Christ, Geordie man, you've aged, thought Ronnie.

'DC Ferris,' said Armie. 'You have the statement there. Would you read a bit out loud for us?'

'Which?'

Armie looked through his spectacles at his own transcript. 'Page five. Top of page five, from, Thinks he's it….'

'Thinks he's it,' Linda read. 'Bloody Goudie. Thinks he's how do they cry him? Lord Muck. I mean look at the toms. He's a nutter. Empire builder. And all the clubs. Little, manky wee clubs, I don't know why… all manky and mingin and stinking of piss.'

'The man's well away,' said Jock, 'must be on something.'

'Read some more, Linda,' said Armie. 'It gets good.'

Linda read, 'Manky names. Bugger's Relief, The Inferno. Oh aye and you know, hen. See me, hen, I thought of a great one. I told him a great one, great name, Goudie's too thick to use....'

'No. No!' said Ronnie.

* * *

Arlene stood in front of her long mirror, Friday afternoon. Sandy ought to be home any minute. She'd like him to see her looking good; otherwise, she told herself, she didn't give a damn if he came home or not.

He'd humiliated her. Then CID had humiliated her. They'd let Debbie go the same day they'd lifted her. The slut had enjoyed her week with Liz and the boys, right under Arlene's nose. No doubt their visit had helped her shake off the trauma of being hauled in for questioning.

Arlene pulled on a smocked top and reached for her comb. She combed her hair straight up: it was too long now, it kept flopping. That hair gel we used to ladle on, she thought, it's pretty gross. But the kids use it. Maybe I'll get away with it too.

She tried a couple of dance steps. In fact they didn't belong to any dance: but sometimes anything goes.

Now there'd been another werewolf murder, poor Mikey's brother, a talented kid. But if only she'd waited a week. Then she'd have had two murders to blame Debbie for. The accusation didn't seem hard to swallow. Why couldn't the fuzz have used their tiny imaginations?

A discreet visit from Armistead had been the last straw. He knew, it seemed, that she'd sent that note. But out of the infinite kindness of his poxy little heart, he wasn't pressing charges.

Why not? But just then, the mirror told her why not. She simply looked fantastic.

'So you're going out,' Sandy said, gazing into the depths of his drink.

'Mmm.'

'The Spot?'

'Mm. Maybe,' Arlene said. 'Yes.'

'You sure now,' said Sandy.

'Why wouldn't I be sure?'

'Cause Gill Jamieson saw you dancing at the Inferno with that Goudie, and you told me that night you'd be at the Spot, that's why.'

'I was. What night did she say?'

'Tuesday.'

'Oh Tuesday,' said Arlene. 'That's right.'

Sandy tore his gaze away from the bubbles. 'That's right? But you weren't there, were you.'

'I was. I went over to Heaven later.'

'Oh so now it's Heaven.'

'That's what he's calling it,' Arlene said, 'wish I'd thought of that.'

She called in at the Spot and harassed her staff for half an hour, then made her way to Heaven. It was half past nine. She couldn't see Ronnie. The place was quiet; it didn't fill up till after eleven, even on Fridays.

Musicians were setting up: Rantin' Pipe and Tremblin' String. Astounding. Arlene didn't know if she should admire their guts or despise them for a shower of callous bastards, but she said to Vince Barnard, 'I'm so sorry about Gerry.'

'Aye, thanks,' said Vince. 'We all are. Gutted. Scuse me....' A boy in a rollneck sweater was helping Vince, crazily lugging a Fender combo almost as heavy as himself. 'Tommy, here, I'll take that, thanks. Sorry, I – My cousin,' he said to Arlene. 'Just helping so he gets in for free.'

'I don't suppose you've seen Ronnie,' Arlene said.

'Not yet,' said Vince.

But Ronnie made it by half past ten. Arlene was just leaving. He swept her into his arms in the small crowded foyer. 'Hello gorgeous,' he said. 'Going somewhere?'

'Where've you been?'

'Ah. That's a long story.' The band were playing and he waltzed her around, ricocheting off people. 'Come away with me. Let's go look at my etchings.' He led her downstairs, through the bar and into his office, and switched on the light. 'Want a drink?'

'Later. Did you get stuck in town?'

'Nnn....' Yes, he wanted to say, that was it. Stuck in Glasgow, absolutely. He hung up his coat; then he took hers and hung that up. He opened his private drinks cabinet, fiddled with glasses, finally turned to look at her. 'No. No, the polis. There's been a misunderstanding.'

'Oh Jesus,' she said, 'those bloody devious halfwits.'

Saints alive, Ronnie thought. 'I knew we were twin souls,' he said aloud. 'Too bad about cops, eh. The spirit is willing but the brains are shite.'

But the system's all right, he thought. At least I got bail.

sixteen

Between Cop and Wolf

THE MEN had gone. The little wolf had grown accustomed to the changes. The bitch's scent, the various oils and tars had faded; shrill voices, sharp loud bangs, insistent low-key throbbings, she'd almost forgotten. Still she kept away from the meadow, raiding instead the margins of the spruce-wood to the north.

But with the approach of winter her hunger grew. She stripped berries from brambles, gulped droppings and stuffed herself with dead things of all kinds. There was live food too: mice, voles, a limping roe brought down with a rush and lunge. There were rabbits.

Under the rising quarter-moon she made her way to the meadow. The pre-dawn twilight would see them emerge, little round twitching hummocks on the turf.

Armie tucked up his car beside the forest gate, got out and locked the doors. Even with the moon that hung beyond the spruces it was dark: but the dawn wasn't far off, and the sky was clear. It felt frosty.

He ducked under the bar. The track was soft here under the trees, frost or no. His shoes would get muddy. So be it. He wondered how long the walk would be, compared with driving.

Last night they'd all felt like celebrating, even though Ronnie had to be let loose again. At least they'd charged him, and the charges should stick. Armie had gone home so he and Susie could share a couple of extra cocktails before bed. Then he'd gone straight to sleep.

But at three in the morning, he'd suddenly snapped awake. He'd been dreaming he was in Horncross Forest, hopelessly lost: but all the same he was looking for something, that treasure of Ronnie's, or something in the tinkers' camp. Now he was hot and he couldn't sleep. He had too many ideas.

He sneaked out, leaving a paper trail of notes for Susie.

That treasure's long gone, he thought as he climbed through the wood. Vanessa Garden must've tapped into it; the tinks have got it and buggered off. But there's something amazing about their having actually found it. A metal detector's not enough, that queer old map wasn't enough. Do some folk have second sight? Probably. But they shouldn't.

He was getting warm. He wore a tweed jacket over a sweater, corduroy trousers and some clunky old shoes; he'd expected to be chilly, not hot. But the air was keen, and the light was growing. He stubbed his toes less often as time went by. Then he was through the spruce wood: he'd come to the pines, with their shaggy open glades. A small bird sang invisibly. It was almost day.

The meadow at last: brown after the long drought, soggy with dew, the travellers' ring of blackened stones still here. The vans had left scars, too, and the heaps of stuff, wheels and whatever, had stood long enough to smother the grass underneath. This was a point Armie wanted to pursue: how long the tinks had been here.

The junk was gone. All that remained was a lonely bucket lying on its side. Armie turned it upside down and sat on its bottom. He gazed across the meadow at the farther pines, beyond which, out of sight as yet, the sun was rising.

The trouble was, there were so many threads. Follow some of 'em, and they tangled, suggesting connexions that might be illusory. There was Willy, bringing his family here: how did that fit with the timing of the murders? He'd worked with Lamond, this was the thing. Who knew about that treasure?

Was the treasure so valuable? Was it valued in money or something more, in sentiment or pride? Was it really two thousand golden guineas, and who'd kill for that today? Imagine the weight.

But Lamond, this could've been something else. Could be drugs, Ronnie and drugs, Ronnie and Willy mixed up in drugs, Ian mixed up in something or knowing of something that Ronnie and Lamond were cooking up, or Willy. He'd be useful, hiding away up here. Drugs up here?

Imagine living up in this camp. The designated site in Whixton, so ugly…. but at least it has water laid on. Is there a spring here? Or have they to haul it up in jerry-cans?

You'd be horribly close to your in-laws. But Vanessa Garden, she's the only one who's not family.

Vanessa, trying to flog the treasure. And that first time up here, that was eerie. Who in hell did she remind me of?

But never mind tinks. Start at the beginning. Beames: Tracy and Beames. Fabe says – and he's sharp all right – don't forget Beames is a killer. So Beames goes for Tracy and Tracy fights him off with that bottle and slits his throat. So she's tasted blood. But she doesn't stop there! How about that? Fabe says. Makes as much sense as anything else.

Only it sounds like one of Guin's ideas. Guin would never pursue it of course. Guin and Fabe, how I hope they're OK.

And the other women. Wee Sonia McHardy had vanished. She wasn't at college; but then no one was, because of the tattie holidays. They'd be back Monday, she'd better show up. Linda was worried; he was too.

And how had Sonia got mixed up in this? Arlene Third, basically. What about her?

Arlene's alibis weren't great. She spent Wednesday nights at the Odd Spot, mostly doing the books: in other words she sat in her office and sometimes nobody saw her for ages. And what about Debbie? She'd lied doggedly about her affair with Sandy, while Arlene had coolly accused her of murder. A fine pair of wifies, then.

So... the woman at Souter Johnnie's. Those barmaids, he'd show them some photographs. But getting the pictures together was taking time. The longer it took the less they'd recall of the woman that Gerry was with, the woman wearing a butterfly clip in her not-so-long red hair.

The sun was up. On the grass-tips the dewdrops split the light, red, blue, purple, amber, green. Armie tilted his head this way and that to see the colours change, thinking, must look a bit mad, this. How silly I'd feel if I looked up and saw someone watching me with round yellow eyes at the edge of the forest just below where the sun's coming up.

Round yellow eyes, and those quizzical eyebrows made of softest fur.

She wasn't afraid. It was funny to see him rocking like that. She herself had discovered that if you acted foolish, some foolish creature would approach too close. But the man wasn't trying to catch prey. He was in that dream-state she welcomed at dawn, a waking, healing dream that preceded sleep.

Now there was something about the man. He smelled good. He carried the smell of her friend, the dog. It was old but strong. She snuffled it in, held it.

Armie sat still. The eyes weren't round now but elliptical, oblique. The creature settled; the sun rode up above the pines.

* * *

Ronnie thought he'd better sleep a little. Otherwise the days would get all mixed up. He had a few hours, he was his own boss after all.

He heard the door close below: Arlene was gone, hitting the trail to her house which was four minutes' walk from here, although of course she was driving. There went the car. A wonderful woman. He wished she'd love him, instead of just putting up with him for the sake of a good time.

But thinking about Arlene was nicer than thinking about Geordie and the MacBride affair. It was better too, if you must think about it, to concentrate on the happy chance that they couldn't pin MacBride's murder on him. True, they'd soon notice that Todd was his nephew, but how could they prove he'd conspired with Todd? MacBride hadn't known that, and surely Todd wouldn't tell them.

It's funny, he thought, but I don't mind so much if I'm done for the hit on MacBride. And they finally told me he'd died, by the way, after letting me sweat over it for hours. But Todd made a right old balls of things, letting the guy do all that talking.

But it's funny. I go cold all over, thinking of the little bank girl. I really did not want to go down for her, I'd be there yet, and things are so much better these days, in fact I think they've worked out for the best and this will blow over and I'll still be out here.

The little bank girl. No, not for the best. No, she just fell. It's so sudden, so sudden when it happens, this is the thing.

* * *

'Eliminate her,' said Fabe. He blew on his coffee; the steam dampened his lashes. 'Eliminate Tracy if it bothers you. You have to ask yourself, why would a woman do this.'

'Why would Tracy?' Armie said. He yawned. 'She's gone, OK, to meet Beames at his house. He makes a move on her. She suddenly realises, hey! He's going to kill me! Whack! Hack, slash, you know. Not bad, but why does she go and do it again?'

'There you have me,' said Fabe. 'You're the one who wanted to tie the murders together, not me.'

'I only want the truth,' Armie said. 'What does Guin know? She knows something.'

'What makes you think that?'

'She doesn't come to see me anymore.'

'Aww.'

'She normally would. So it's Tracy. Tracy's on her list. She can't talk about it. Does she talk to you about it?'

'You're imagining things,' said Fabe. 'No she does not. But....'

'But! Exactly – she knows something, told you so.'

On the morning of the second murder, Tracy had been alone. No one could vouch for her movements when Ian was killed.

She didn't like coppers, Ian had nicked her dearest friend – before she'd known him, but still, he had – and she lived across from his maisonette and seemingly spied on him.

So did she see something that moved her to kill him? Or had she stalked him, pried for his weak spot? She'd have found it soon enough.

But the third murder was baffling. By then, she'd had Frank living in. He'd swear she'd been home, even if she'd gone out. In fact, though, Tracy admitted going out. She hadn't noticed what time she got back, either; the moon had been well up, that's all she knew. But if she'd been out until three in the morning, hauled poor Gerry all the way to Horncross and left his van in Whixton... never mind the damned moon, she was lying, that's all.

But she hadn't been at Souter Johnnie's, surely. And why in the world would she stage the discovery of the corpse?

'The band members,' Fabe said. 'Gerry's pals. Did they not get a look at this woman of his?'

'Not really,' said Armie, 'the two of 'em kept drifting up to the bar.'

'Oh for God's sake. Was she tall, short?'

'Shorter than Gerry. He was six foot two. The barmaids' description's good though. And we do have a picture of Tracy to show them. I'm just waiting for portraits of some of the other ladies.'

'You have Sonia,' said Fabe.

'Linda's got that, I've ordered a copy. She's been asking folk if they've seen her... anyone, everyone....' Armie stepped to the window in time to see Linda's golden head vanish within the building. 'Well well, must be lunchtime. I'm not getting on today for some reason.' He yawned again.

In the afternoon Armie stopped by the Inferno: Heaven, rather. The door was locked. He pushed the bell, and waited.

'Geordie,' said a muffled voice. The door had a peephole, Armie saw. 'Christ, now what've I done?'

'You tell me.'

Ronnie let him in and locked up behind him. 'I probably would, too, just as you said. Especially today.... I feel sort of down. Have a dram.'

'No thanks, Ronnie. What's eating you? You seemed gey contented yesterday.'

'I wasn't. I don't fancy prison again. Been there, done that. You know? Besides....'

Armie watched in silence as Ronnie poured himself a shot of malt.

'Sure I can't tempt you? Course I can't... and besides – slainte.' Ronnie lifted his glass, then drank. 'I have this wonderful woman.'

'No kidding?'

'I think I may be in love, Geordie. I think I may actually be in love.'

How are the mighty fallen. 'You'd know if you were.'

'But I never fell in love before in my life.'

'Oh balls, man. You must have.'

'No.'

'Well,' Armie said, 'I have. Nothing wrong with it. It was fine.'

'You mean it is fine,' said Ronnie reproachfully, 'you've still got yours.'

'It gets different after a while. At first it's crazy. Like a roller-coaster. And then after a while... it's just gold.'

'But I've got gold, Geordie. That isn't the same.'

'You've got it?'

'As good as, aye. I can take it whenever I like. And stuff Willy. It's mine as much as his.'

'Well far be it from me, Ronnie. As long as nobody gets hurt – what's that look for?'

'What look?'

'No one gets hurt. Hear me? You're in a delicate position. Besides, you won't want to disappoint what's her name.'

Ronnie sighed. 'Ah now… she's using me, why would she care….'

'Hell's teeth, man. Don't upset yourself. I only came in to ask you if you've seen these women.' Armie produced two small photographs from his wallet. 'Either or both would help.'

'Well.' Ronnie stared at them glumly: wasn't that the wee terror from the forest, God forbid? 'I know the tom, never seen the other bint,' he said.

'The tom?'

'Sonia. Who's the other one?'

'Friend of a friend,' said Armie. 'Wondered if she ever goes to clubs.'

'Not to mine. Try the Bugger's, it's more for the young idea.'

'And Sonia. You seen her lately?'

'Not for weeks,' said Ronnie.

* * *

'So Guin, you're busy.' Armie glanced round the showroom. 'I'll come back another time.'

'Well if it's about the murders,' Guin said, 'it won't wait. These folk are just looking, you know.'

'All of 'em? How do you make any money?'

'With difficulty. I'd ask Dad to step in, but he's in the workshop. Frank and Tracy went out.'

'Dog walking?'

'Mmm, I suppose. With any luck they won't find another body….'

'Wrong moon,' Armie said. Guin was watching him. 'It's mostly about Tracy.'

'Oh aye.'

'You know when we met at Ian Barclay's place. You said you wanted to see inside her flat.'

'That's right.'

'Did you ever do it? Get a look inside?'

'I did, actually.'

'And the view from the window?'

'The bathroom window,' Guin said, 'it's the one. You look down at the back door. The other windows are no use.'

'You speak to her about it?'

'No… course not.'

'She's very wary with me, you know. Doesn't trust me.'

'She doesn't like the polis,' Guin said. 'I'm not about to question her, before you ask.'

'I wasn't…. Look,' Armie said. 'I'm trying to eliminate her, OK? Not incriminate. The view from her window….'

'Can only incriminate her. That's the only point.'

'No, no, no, not necessarily.' People were turning to look at them. 'Look, this isn't a good time. Tell you what, if you get any brain-waves just –'

'My brain is only so-so,' said Guin.

She thought after he'd gone, he'll find out. I can't stop him. I might as well hand them over.

But I won't. She's not guilty. She just did something stupid, it isn't a crime, it's embarrassing and it doesn't have to come out. He doesn't need it, it's not relevant.

But he wants it.

Why the hell would Tracy do that, anyway? She's not really crazy, is she?

* * *

So what do I make of it? Armie wondered. Damn it, if Guin thought the bloody woman had killed three people she'd hardly be sitting on it.

He drove out to Whixton. It was late, but not dusk yet: next week, after the clocks went back it'd be twilight round about now. He wondered where this year had gone.

He rolled into the travellers' designated site, and parked. There wasn't much room. Everyone seemed to be home. Vehicles stood at all angles, kids pulled bicycle stunts and dogs roved underfoot. There was even a spotted pony, tethered and with a hay-net handy.

Armie didn't see anyone he recognised. He knew which van was Willy's, though, so he wriggled through the crowd, and knocked.

Lee answered the door. 'Nobody home,' he said.

'I'm home,' Moira shouted from the depths of the van.

'Everyone else is out having fun,' Armie said. 'What's up with you two?'

Lee hesitated. His gaze slipped past Armie's shoulder. 'In, having fun,' he said. He shut the door.

'Keep your nose out of here,' said a grown-up voice: Vanessa. Armie got down from the step. She was heading his way. 'You've got no business.'

'Hello Mrs Garden. I have business with Willy Smith, actually. Is he here?'

'No.'

'Any idea where I –'

'No.'

'D'you think he might be –'

'No,' she said absently, looking down. There was little Squeeter the lurcher sniffing his trouser leg. Vanessa bent and gently took hold of one of its ears. 'Best dog in the world,' she said, and straightened up. 'Haven't you cleared off yet, you... Well! Seen a ghost, have we, Mr Plod?'

seventeen

Moonshine of Your Love

SYLVIE, SYLVIE. Come out.... come out. This is how it begins, she thought.

She's under the covers, he's teasing. He knows she's not going to come out. He's got to get in, she's teasing him.

I'm under the covers. I'm under the bed. I'm making myself as small as I can. I'm invisible.

175

Above the scrunch and boyng of the mattress I can hear her giggling. I can hear him pretending, grrr, grruff, he's a scary monster. Now I'm going to run.

I'm making myself invisible. I can see everything right through the sheets. I can't run away and I can't shut my eyes. But I must be invisible because here he is, sitting up, and Sylvie's almost sitting up, I can see their faces. I can see his face. I can see his hands, how big, scary, he can't see me though. He doesn't look up. He looks down. His eyes are wide, his face like a mask. His mouth smiles, it's open like a mask. His fingers close on her.

Oh good God. Thank God. Oh Jesus, that's too real. That is too real. Jesus, I can't be doing with this.

She lay still until she was sure no one else was in the bed and then she sat up. She rubbed her arms: the hairs still prickled, her heart raced. She shuddered and breathed deeply and grew warmer.

Beyond the curtains it seemed to be daylight. Someone's underpants covered the clock. She wondered what time it was.

* * *

'Some things it's better if you don't know,' Armie said.

Susie passed him a plate of buttered toast. 'I'm sure,' she said, 'but isn't that a bit like the thing about the tree?'

'What tree?'

'In the forest. If the tree falls in the forest where no one can hear it….'

'Oh right,' said Armie, 'is there a sound. Right.'

'It's like that. Isn't it? If no one knows things, they don't exist. For them. For the person who doesn't know them.'

'For everyone else they do,' Armie said.

'Aye but what I mean is, how can it be better for someone not to know something, if for that person, it doesn't exist?'

'You're losing me,' Armie said. 'Finished with that jam?'

'I mean how can the person feel better about something that…. I'm talking bollocks.'

'They can't feel better. No, I see what you're saying. But I was trying to be practical.'

176

'You mean you have something,' Susie said.

'I have something.'

'Keep quiet about it. If it doesn't matter....'

'It's just so amazing.'

'Well tell me then.'

'It's a long story. But still.' He poured more coffee. 'Once upon a time there lived a man, and this man had a wife....'

So he didn't get to the nick as early as on most Monday mornings. Fabe and Linda were there before him.

'What's so weird is,' Linda was saying, 'her written work's being handed in. One essay and a piece of short fiction. On the deadline, the lecturer says.'

'But he doesn't see her?' said Fabe. 'The lecturer?'

Armie hung his coat up. He heard Linda say, 'He doesn't see her cause she only has to put it in a box in the porter's office. No one's seen anything.'

'You mean little Sonia,' Armie said.

'I thought she was dead,' Linda said, 'until college went back. You know, they print their essays and things. So there's no telling who wrote them. But she signs her work. It looks like it's her.'

'What about that band? You know – Rantin'?'

'They haven't seen her either. Not for weeks and weeks.'

'But she's alive.' Armie sat down on his desk, and sighed. 'What if she's hiding because she knows something?'

'Or did something,' said Fabe.

'But you'll find her. For one thing she has to go in and get her papers back when they've been marked. So it's good,' said Armie. 'And now I move on... to the moon. Full moon.'

It'd be a few days yet; but he had plans. There was a pattern and they'd use it.

'We can't be everywhere,' Linda said. 'All the pubs in Hornbridge as well as the night clubs? And Whixton.'

'No,' said Fabe, 'but he doesn't mean all of them. Do you?'

'No no. We're finite,' said Armie, 'we'll circulate and perhaps we'll be lucky. Or at least be noticed. I'd rather think I'd prevented a murder, if nothing happened at all.'

'Do we hunt in couples?' said Linda. 'I mean, just to observe, or are the gentlemen meant to be bait?'

'I don't know,' said Armie, 'I'm open to suggestions. But I'm no use as bait. Nor is Wattie.... And I think our killer will recognise us. No, we have to observe, that's right.'

'Recognise us,' Fabe said. 'You think so?'

'Well it's possible, isn't it?'

* * *

Wednesday evening: Arlene paced the kitchen tiles, ran her fingers over the counter, turned, paced back again. What's wrong with me? she wondered. She fetched the cocktail glasses from their cupboard, and set them side by side on the marble counter-top.

He's getting too heavy, that's what it is. Possessive. And Sandy too: who do they think they are, these men? Sandy especially, he knows damn fine that I'm on to him. Stuff him.

He ought to be here now. In fact he was. His exhaust burbled up from the bottom of the lane. She took out the ice: a ghost of cold air chased her as she closed the compartment. Be the season for sherry soon, she thought, or rum.

'Hey babe,' said Sandy. 'You look great.'

'Save it – you get a drink anyway. Here.'

'Oh well. Just one.' He clinked his glass on hers. 'Here's to the girl of my dreams.'

'What's got into you?'

'Thought I'd go out. A midweek break,' said Sandy. 'Thought I'd try out some of these night clubs. You know, the Odd Spot, Heaven....'

'You're going to spy on me,' Arlene said. 'How grown-up.'

'Spy?' Sandy said. 'Why would I do that? Maybe I just hope I'll bump into you. Is it so wrong to dream?'

But she reached the Spot ahead of him, and had another cocktail before settling down to her spreadsheets.

'Down on last year,' she mused out loud. 'Hell, what's going on here? I ought to....' Someone knocked at the door. 'Yeep! Who is that!'

'Only me,' Ronnie said. 'If you don't want to see me....'

178

'Oh come in,' said Arlene. 'Don't go all pathetic. Look at this, I'm losing money. Well, not making it like I was. I know what it is too. I'm never here.'

'You are now.'

'Well I'm usually not. I'm at your place…. I suppose you're doing OK.'

'Not too bad, thanks for asking. You coming by later? You are, aren't you?'

'Ronnie,' Arlene said, 'don't get needy.'

'Me? Needy? I like that… I mean suit yourself…. You're a busy woman, and I was forgetting! A married woman. Your man's at the bar. Is he –'

'Bloody Nora.' She rose and got her coat. 'I need air. The knights are drawing in! Look Ronnie, I'll catch you later. Or not.'

Later, around half past ten, the woman who called herself Sylvie stepped into the ladies' at the Beggar's Belief. A couple of girls pushed out past her, and she was alone. She unclipped her hair and ran her fingers through it.

The mirror showed her a wild being, dressed in black, with huge eyes more black than blue. That was the poxy lighting in this place. It tinged her hair purple, not that she minded that at all. She combed the errant mop, then ruffled it up again and put the clip in her bag. She'd not need it tonight.

* * *

'If we do Friday as well,' Linda said, 'what about Sunday? I mean the moon's not really full till then.'

'Sunday too. Aye, I thought we would. Wattie, you have your paper this morning?' Wattie produced the Hornbridge *World*, and Armie shook it open across his desk. 'Entertainment, ah here we go. Rantin' are playing this weekend.'

'They always do,' said Fabe. 'Have we to go hear them? I want extra for that.'

'Nothing wrong with Rantin',' said Linda. ''Cept the name.'

'So tomorrow night then. Linda – Rantin' at Souter Johnnie's. And the Beggar's Belief have a Guy Fawkes disco.

Whatever next,' said Armie. 'Mira, you take the disco. Can you get Sam?'

'He'll be free on Friday,' said Mira, 'he's on call the other nights.'

'OK, and Wattie? Souter Johnnie's, all right? Saturday. If you get cheesed off, change over half way through. I'll speak to the rest of uniform later. But work it out between yourselves, you know? Get spread out, that's the thing.'

'And what will you do?' said Fabe.

'Me? I'll be everywhere. I'll be all around you. Start with Heaven I suppose. So Ronnie doesn't forget me.'

* * *

The moon waxed. Friday night came. Armie stayed at Heaven only long enough to hear Ronnie's views on women: or rather on Arlene.

'She doesn't know what love is, Geordie. Look at her, she's trampling all over me.'

'She's only dancing with her husband, man.'

'Aye right. So who does he think he is? Christ, just look at 'em would you.'

Wattie was keeping an eye on the place, so Armie set off for Whixton. Why Arlene, he wondered as he drove: who is Arlene, what is she? He left Hornbridge behind, speeding between bare hedges and winter fields.

The road was nearly deserted. Clouds covered the moon, but the night was bright; still two days from the full, thought Armie, I don't know what I'm fussed about. I don't know why I think it's to do with the moon.

Along the straight by the forestry office he slowed, watching the verges sidelong. Wolves in November were fine enough: not so fine when lambing time came. Well! sufficient unto the day.

He climbed from his car in front of the pub. He fancied he could feel the bass, even out here. Rantin' Pipe billed themselves as Celtic-rock fusion: so, he wondered, why 'Sunshine of your Love'?

He found the band in a small hall, an annexe to the pub.

'Evenin' all,' he said into Linda's ear. She jumped. 'Where's Grassy?'

'Gone to the bog. If you creep up on me like that again I'll stick one on you.'

'You should show more respect. Any action?'

'Can't see any.'

Grassy was edging through the crowd. Armie waved to him and said, 'Scuse me, think I'll move up to the stage.'

'You'll go deaf,' said Linda hopefully.

From the front, Armie could see girls with their hair in butterfly clips. But they were young girls, and every one of them plump. The woman the barmaids had seen was slim, and no youngster.

A damn shame about those barmaids. He'd pinned too many hopes on them. They'd looked at his photos of all those women, and recognised practically every one. But neither of them could tell him which, if any, was the woman who'd picked up Lamond.

He stood at the side of the stage for a while. The band had replaced their keyboard player, he saw; but you'd hardly have known. The poor sod banged away and nobody could hear him. There ought to be someone listening, setting the balance of sound: and there was. A bunch of cables snaked out to a mixing desk in the middle of the hall. Armie recognised Barnard, the big roadie, sitting at the mixer, sliding his knobs. The chap next to him in the rollneck sweater looked very young: skinny, with big eyes, doting on the band. The cousin.

The number finished. Several people applauded. Armie didn't want to look conspicuous but he clapped anyway. What the hell, he didn't get out much.

The roadie's cousin was gazing adoringly at the roadie. Armie noticed that the kid had a thin dark moustache: boot polish, probably. The band launched into a new number, the kid looked up at the stage and Armie saw who it was.

He went back through the hall. 'Look,' he said into Linda's ear, 'but don't stare.'

'What?'

'The roadie's helper, I said don't stare.'

'Oh my God,' said Linda. 'Bloody hell, Armie. What do I do, pick her up?'

'Let's not spook her. She'll stick with the guy, we don't want to lose the plot tonight.'

* * *

So help me God, thought Ronnie, if Third pulls that again I'll break both his ankles. Then let's see him dance.

But it wouldn't make Arlene care for me, would it. I'm knackered whatever I do.

He threw himself into his office chair. The night was over: wasted too. What had gone wrong? Let's face it, he thought, I'm out of my depth here.

In the bar the staff were clearing up, stacking chairs and tables, mopping the floor. They were used to seeing him swan out an hour or two before closing, with some local talent in tow, latterly Arlene. Now here he was hiding away. How were they meant to respect him?

He stared with distaste at the drinks cabinet. He'd had a lot, now he had a hangover and he didn't need more drink. What he needed was coffee: but no. He needed sleep. Or maybe it was simpler simply to be dead.

Geordie had no idea, actually. No clue. Yes, he had fallen in love once: that was the trouble, literally once. He'd fallen in love and she'd loved him back. He had no idea at all.

But he was solid, Geordie, he was straight. See me, he'd say, if I saw it I'd say it. If I didn't see it I can't say I did: and no one can make me. Sorry, lads.

* * *

In the small hours of Saturday morning Willy Smith lay awake. The travellers' site was noisy at night, but that didn't bother him. What bothered him was the certainty that he'd lost the gold.

He'd hidden it well. Not just well, *in* a well. Down the shaft, on top of the treasure, he'd stuffed armfuls of bark chips. Over the well-mouth he'd planted a great old stump with whiskery roots. It was heavy as lead, and awkward besides. But after all his backbreaking trouble Goudie had got the gold.

The bastard, thought Willy, he's as much a Blythe as I am. Otherwise I'd have beaten him.

I'll beat him yet. But I have to check it out. And how could he have found it? Maybe I'm cracking up.

Noiselessly he got out of bed, dressed, pulled on his high boots and slipped away in the moonlight.

eighteen

November

THE PHONE rang when Debbie was climbing into her waterproof trousers. It was seven-fifty, Saturday morning. She hopped back into the kitchen, muttering, and snatched the receiver from the wall.

'Debbie it's me.'

'Christ, Sandy. Where's Arlene?'

'She's sleeping. We were out all night. Listen, I have to see you.'

'What?' She hopped herself into the other trouser leg. 'Why now? I'm trying to get to work right now. You know that.'

'I'll meet you down on the road. I'll leave now.'

'Sandy....' But how could she stop him? She hung up, and leapt for the door.

Soon after the wreck of his Nissan Sandy had bought another one. He slid into it hastily now, started it up and set off down the lane. As he passed Debbie he realised he was driving in slippers. What an old fool he looked. Nae feels lik aul feels, his dad would've said.

He pulled up at the road end. Almost at once Debbie flapped to a stop beside him. She shook off her hood: her hair was still damp, combed back, but beginning to dry and fall softly forward. The fitful sunshine turned the dry bits gold. 'Let's get it off our chests, shall we?' she said. 'I'll be late otherwise.'

'I need you, Debbie. Arlene's been....' Breaking my balls, he'd been about to say: but it wasn't quite true. 'She hates me. Please say you care about me. Please?'

Debbie rolled her eyes skyward. 'Sandy. God almighty. I'll say this once, OK? I love you. See you later.' She put her feet back on the pedals, and made to move off.

'Is that true?' shouted Sandy.

'Of course it's true, why wouldn't it be true? Now go home to bed for God's sake. You've got eyes like pissholes in cement.'

* * *

The detectives' high room rang like a cocktail party with voices. You wouldn't think we had a serial killer on the loose, thought Armie, perched on his desk. But they'd all had such a good time last night: and tonight was yet to come.

He got down, and went to the whiteboard. The talk died away. 'Nothing concrete,' he said, 'from last night's binge. Well – we found Sonia McHardy, that's something at least. And no one's been murdered. That's something too. Now tonight's the same drill. I shuttle between venues, while you circulate at moderate speed....'

The moon wasn't full till Sunday. By then they'd be jaded.

'We don't mind if we don't catch a killer, remember. We don't mind if we're recognised. It all acts as prevention. The only way that things can go wrong is if the killer changes her – I say her, could be his – behaviour, and picks up a victim in the street... or Marchbank for a change, who knows.' He tapped the whiteboard, where clubs and pubs were listed with their locations. 'All up for grabs, folks, and if anyone likes Rantin' Pipe –'

The din drowned him out. All right then, he thought as he slipped to the window; let's have fun. But why shouldn't she pick up someone in the street? No, I feel like shit. Luckily it means nothing. I for one don't have second sight.

'I wish I could ask you to come,' he said later as he sat in Susie's office at the bank. 'Nearly everyone else has a date.'

'No big deal,' said Susie. 'It all sounds crazy to me.'

'I'll be late again, too.'

'No biggie. Maybe you'll catch this person. I tell you what though, be careful who you chat up.'

'Ha ha. Oh I wondered – no, you probably can't disclose that.'

'What?'

'Whether Ronnie Goudie has a safety deposit box.'

'He has,' said Susie. 'He uses it, too. I don't think he minds you knowing.'

* * *

'So will you come out?' Fabe said, ignoring the stares of Saturday afternoon tyre kickers.

Guin shrugged, trying to smile. 'I could.' She studied the toe of her boot. 'If you want me I mean.'

'But I always do. I hardly see you during a case.'

'What do we have to do?'

'Just be out. At various venues. You'd have liked it last night. Or at least I'd have thought you would.'

'Well I'm more of a pub person,' Guin said. 'Let's do the pubs. Come round to mine about eight – unless you're eating with me.'

They started with the Goat. It was seamy; but that was part of the point, they thought.

'Linda says early evening is the time for toms,' said Fabe. 'And she should know.'

'Frankie used to come in here a lot,' said Guin, 'but I think he's gone off it. Maybe Tracy doesn't like the place.'

'Oh they're at the stay-at-home stage,' said Fabe absently. 'These women all look like toms to me. Want another?'

'Well… but shouldn't we move on? Why just Hornbridge and Whixton anyway? What's happening in Marchbank?'

'The victims seem to have been picked up in Hornbridge or Whixton, that's all. And let's face it,' said Fabe, 'there's only the Crown in Marchbank and it's petrified.'

'There isn't only the Crown. There's the Oak. And the Strathdyre Arms.'

'No one goes in there.'

'My Dad might.'

'Well I think he'll be safe enough there,' Fabe said. 'Fancy this Souter Johnnie place, then?'

* * *

The Beggar's Belief was starting to fill up when the woman who called herself Sylvie walked in. She wore red silk, or at least it felt like it, a brocade that clung to her stomach and hips: a suit with flowing sleeves. She'd kept her hair black, short and tousled.

She sat at the bar and bought a small red rum. It seemed like the night for it.

There was a copper at a table nearby, the tall bony chap, she remembered him. He and his girlfriend were deep in talk. They wouldn't know her.

She'd run from Heaven, practically loped. She could always go back. It took five minutes, and that's where she wanted to be.

It was embarrassing to retreat but she'd had to. Someone risky had turned up. Such things would happen on nights like this when the world was out on the tiles. The whole world, the whole police force: there went another cop with a boyfriend in tow, boogying round the floor.

One policeman she hadn't seen was the Inspector. He'd probably be taking it easy though. He was meant to be the boss.

But she'd have spotted him in Heaven if she'd looked. He was walking in when she whizzed out past him, leaving him wondering if he'd missed something.

Armie had just come from Whixton by way of the Odd Spot. Now he sat at Heaven's bar, watching covertly, not meaning to stay; maybe he'd try the other clubs, come back in a while. Davie Howat was here with his cheery wife to shield him from temptation.

But here was a man to watch. Sandy Third stood in the doorway. In the mirror Armie watched him hovering there until someone pushed him aside. At that he came into the room, then paused, craning his neck around.

Ah, now he'd seen her. The office door by the bar half-opened, and Arlene peeped out. If she'd been thinking of ducking back in she was too late. Sandy was coming over. His jaw stuck out in front, like the prow of a tiny doomed ship.

Ronnie's voice came from behind the door. 'It's OK hen. Ignore the wee shite. This is my place.'

'Arlene,' said Sandy. 'It's time we had a talk.'

'She doesn't want to talk to you. Get lost.'

'I wasn't speaking to you, I was speaking to my –'

Ronnie pushed past Arlene, bunching up his fists. Armie abandoned his stool. 'Ronnie,' he said, 'don't spoil things for yourself. Look around you, man, everyone's happy.'

'You're right, Geordie man,' Ronnie said. 'Let's do this outside! Come on you wee jobbie! Let's see what you –'

'Ronnie,' said Armie, 'did you hear me?'

Arlene glared at her husband. She glared at Ronnie. She gave Armie an inscrutable look, and left.

'Arlene, where're you going?' Ronnie wailed in her wake.

'Far away from you,' Sandy said. Ronnie turned purple; Armie got between them. 'I have to talk to her,' said Sandy. 'She mustn't go.' He struggled off through the crowd. Arlene had disappeared.

The woman called Sylvie came back about twenty minutes later. The foyer was busy and she slipped through, down into the bar. She paused at the door to look: dancing, sitting, lounging, conspiring, folk everywhere, many that she knew. But nobody risky.

She stepped onto the dance floor. A little space spread around her and heads began to turn. Instinctively she tucked in her backside, squared her shoulders with a little wriggle. Now she stood straight in her red brocade. She could dance alone for as long as it took.

But there again, damn it, was someone. It was surely himself, with his balding dome. He stood with his back to her but the mirror behind the bar would show her up. In fact he was turning. She darted to the ladies', opened and closed the door. Screened by the bodies standing in front of it, she legged it for the foyer.

One risky person she hadn't seen was Armie.

Hell's teeth, he thought, it's her, it's her. She's gone to the loo. Why'd she run?

Maybe she'd seen him, recognised him. He hadn't been trying to hide.

'Hell's bloody fire,' he muttered, reaching the ladies' and fearing to go in. While he dithered a couple of girls came out, the wrong girls. He looked round for Mrs Howat: she'd help him.

But after another thirty seconds he knew he was too late.

Outside in the street there was no one. He phoned Fabe. 'Listen,' he said, 'I know who she is but I've lost her.'

'Eh? Speak up. I can't –'

'Then go outside, man. It's urgent. Get whoever else is there to…. Just get outdoors, OK? Hell's teeth.'

'You're so sure,' said Fabe a few moments later. Guin stood beside him on the pavement, stamping for warmth: no duffel coat tonight, it somehow didn't go with night clubs.

'I'm…. Aye. It's something I remembered about oilmen. Damn it, I knew. Bloody oilmen, we just don't get them round here.'

'So you want me to what? Don't just gibber down the phone.'

'I want you to look for Debbie Chalmers. But it's not Debbie Chalmers, it's a woman in red. Red suit, floppy sleeves, black hair. Sticky-uppy.'

'Black hair? Debbie Chalmers?'

'That's right. I have to find Ronnie,' said Armie. 'Listen, where are you?'

'The Buggers.'

'OK, get back in. See who's there. We need…. I don't think she left with anyone. But I've gone and lost Ronnie. I want to know right away if you see him. Or Arlene or…. Sandy's here. He's in here, it's OK. I'll get back to you Fabe, I'm ringing the station. Wattie can go over to Ronnie's. Good luck.'

As they pulled up at the cottage she hugged her knees, a big smile breaking across her face. He didn't see. Absorbed in his infidelity, he wasn't looking.

He switched off the engine. Moonlight glanced off the Toyota's sheen, splashed a black shadow on the cottage from the hollies by the door. He turned to her, stroked her thigh. Poor fellow. He was doing this by the book.

'Let's go in,' he said.

She'd tried keeping the knife in her hair-clip and it had worked fine. But that clip was known: she'd had to change tactics, holding the blade on her forearm with a couple of satin scrunchies under her sleeve.

She'd just leave her top on. It might be nicer. The moment was coming. His eyes in the moonlight were like dark fruits with silky skins.

The instant she'd found out about Arlene's lover she'd wanted to take him. It had meant waiting for days and days. But also it meant the moon was full; that would amuse the media and the police.

The bedroom curtains were open, the light streamed in. He hugged her awkwardly and turned to take off his jacket, his shoes, his trousers, getting tangled up, leaving his socks on.

The sleeves of the red silk top were loose, impractical looking, but perfect. She'd practised the move until she couldn't do it wrong. Now she moved close to him on the bed, kneeling beside him and kissing him on the lips. She didn't close her eyes. He didn't close his.

He didn't close them, and they weren't like fruits: they were wide awake, a hawk's eyes, daring her. She drove the knife up hard between his ribs and he groaned. He fell back on the pillows. His eyes closed, and a ribbon of blood rolled down his chin.

* * *

189

Wattie swung the police car through the last roundabout. The lights of Hornbridge sank behind him. The full moon should make it bright as day, he thought: instead it deceives, alters everything.

He'd been having fun but it couldn't go on forever. In any case this was better, racing off to the home of a known and fabulous villain in the night.

Black shadows under the trees, black shadows startled him. Ahead of him suddenly was a deeper blackness. Was there a....

Wattie's eyes opened. Did I pass out? Car's not moving. He rubbed his forehead. Urgency. Urgent, Armistead. Goudie. Oh damn, bugger, bugger. Goudie. I've done it now. And I will personally kill the bastard who parked this trailer here.

The car started, thank the Lord. It moved off, crumpled but indomitable. He switched on the siren.

* * *

Armie looked all over the club for Ronnie. The man had vanished, along with Debbie and Arlene.

'Mr Third,' he said. It was half past midnight; Sandy had given up his quest and was drinking himself silly. 'Sandy, man, what's your home number?'

'I forget.'

'No you don't.'

'Seven oh oh two three two. Marchbank.... I'm not in.'

No one was in. 'How about the Chalmerses?' Armie asked him. That one didn't answer either. How he wished he'd taken a note of Ronnie's home phone, or his mobile for that matter. But thank heavens, Wattie would be there by now.

His own mobile was ringing. He darted into Ronnie's office and shut the door.

nineteen

Death Outran Me

'GEORDIE. GEORDIE, that you.'

'Ronnie. Great, I was just –'

'Geordie man. Listen, she's done me.'

'What – she what? Who? Debbie Chalmers?'

'She's cut me, Geordie. I'm going. Listen.'

'Ronnie, where are you?' said Armie. 'Are you home?'

Armie heard him laugh, a gurgling laugh. Then came wheezing. 'Ahh! Jesus, Geordie. Jesus Christ I'm going. She's made a muck of it, Christ it's not good. It's not good.'

'Hold on. We're coming. I've a man on his way, are you at the cottage Ronnie? Where are you?'

'Listen, need to know,' said Ronnie. His breath crackled. 'You've needed, you need to.'

'Hell's bloody fire man. Tell me who did this.'

'The bank girl,' said Ronnie. 'Tell you now. Should've – aahhh bloody shitin' hell. Need to tell you.'

'Never mind that now, who's cut you? Tell me who cut you, man.'

Ronnie was sobbing, or else laughing. 'Should see the blood Geordie. You will see. I know you. The knife…. Aah Jesus, oh Geordie, this isn't good. I, you… the bank girl.' He whimpered. 'She just fell.'

'Christ, man, will you tell me who did this.'

'Oh Jesus God I hear, she is.' The hoarse voice was sinking. 'She's coming.'

'No,' said Armie, 'hold on.'

'No time. Listen Geordie. I never….'

'Ronnie, no.'

'So sudden,' he whispered.

'Hold on man.'

'No,' said Ronnie. 'No, she just fell.'

And I told him, Ronnie thought, smiling. And I told him and he's easy now.

Geordie Armistead. The best, the best.

I've been a fool, so I have.

* * *

He was still smiling when they found him. His throat was cut. By the cottage door, his car burned, not fiercely now but steadily. The bedroom light was low and the flames glowed on the walls, amber speckled with blue flashes from the vehicles outside.

'How'd she manage it?' Fabe wondered. 'To overpower this guy, she'd have.... Armie?'

Dr Greig said, 'Leave him. It'll all do later.' He put a hand on Armie's shoulder and tried to steer him out of the bedroom. Armie shook his head and turned back to the corpse.

He couldn't stop shaking. He wanted someone to explain but nobody would. Greig was being kind and wise as always and trying to distract him and he wanted someone to explain.

'I don't understand,' he said aloud. Fabe and Wattie and Greig all stared. I should shut up, he thought. Is this grief? 'OK, I do understand. We pick up Debbie Chalmers. Or go to her house, or something.'

Where was the knife? Ronnie had said knife. Armie blinked and set his teeth. He knew who, why bother asking, why can't we have that conversation again?

'Chalmers,' he said firmly. He blew his nose. 'Look Doctor, the throat. How long?'

'After death? No, it wasn't. He would've been alive.'

'He spoke to me. We were talking.'

'He could've been unconscious – dying. The chest wound, it's almost certainly got the lung.'

Armie's shivering speeded up. 'How long ago then?'

'Minutes.'

'She's here then.' He looked round. Fabe had gone, Wattie too. 'I should go,' he said, wishing he had more officers: where in God's name was Linda? 'Hell's teeth. I should go.'

'You should sit down and take a couple of these,' Greig said, proffering a small bottle. Armie waved vaguely at it. He sat on a plush hassock next the bed, but almost at once jumped up again.

'Calm down,' pleaded the doctor.

'I've never been calmer. I got pricked in the arse,' said Armie. He picked up the hassock and turned it over. 'The knife, he said knife. Look! It zips.' He tussled with the plush cover. 'Oh and look. There's blood.'

* * *

The great tree in which Willy Smith sat was a hardwood, an oak, he fancied, from the feel of its bark. Its leaves had mostly fallen. He felt exposed in the moonlight, and foolish for having climbed up here in the first place: he should've just run.

It was Goudie's fault he was in this mess. Goudie, ripping him off. The thought of Goudie lying dead on the bed cheered him, but only a little.

The crazy woman had done it. She'd come out of the cottage with no pants on, carrying a bundle. Willy had been flat behind the holly by the door. He'd seen her stuff something into the back seat and then take off her top and thrust that in. He'd watched her wrestle with the filler cap, then give it up and set light to the clothes on the back seat. They went like blazes: she'd doused them with something, he was sure.

After she'd run off he'd gone inside. Like the idiot he was, he'd even gone upstairs. He wished he hadn't.

Blue lights still flashed by the house. Coppers were charging about, arguing and bellowing and slamming doors. Torches bobbed in the garden – my footprints, Willy thought; and headlights bobbed, dancing up the lane where the madwoman had run. Good. Away from here, away from where I left the truck.

His boot-soles were slippery: he couldn't brace himself with his feet anymore. The branch he was sitting on bored into his groin. His hands were chilled and stiff. The climb down would be a treat all right, assuming he lived to try it.

* * *

Lovely hot shower. Trouble is, the police will be here. Oh, they've come.

She'd always improvised. She'd always been lucky. You can't win 'em all, she reminded herself. But she couldn't complain. Tonight had been wild, even though the end had fallen flat.

She wrapped a towel around her head and put on one of Geoff's tartan shirts by way of a bathrobe, and went downstairs to get the door.

* * *

'Questioning is one thing,' Bob Marshall said. He nodded towards the closed door of Interview Room One. 'But you'll have to find some evidence to detain her.'

'But I'll find some. I know I will,' said Armie. 'There must be traces.'

'You might've thought to find 'em first,' said Bob. 'As things stand, she's been arrested for being married to an oilman.'

'Two weeks on, two weeks off. I should've seen it as soon as she told me.'

'No you shouldn't, Armie. It doesn't even tally with the damn full moon. And this woman in red. Can you prove it's her? And what if it is?'

'The stuff in the back seat's very like burnt silk, Bob. Besides, I recognised her.'

'You say.'

'I did, man. And what's she up to, going about like that and then claiming she doesn't?'

'Settle down,' said Bob. 'You going back in?'

Shaking his head to say yes, Armie reached for the doorknob.

They'd pulled Debbie in right away in the hope of surprising her, of finding some evidence she hadn't had time to hide. It turned out to be a bad strategy. By the time they'd got Charlie Henderson in, they'd used up half the time allowed for detention and questioning.

They hadn't found evidence in her house, either. They were quite clear on what they wanted: hair colour, the theatrical sort, in little bottles or perhaps in tubes. All through the rubbish and the cupboards they hunted, but in vain. There was plenty of ordinary make-up on her dressing table, and a wide spectrum of nail varnishes: but then, she was no slob. She always turned herself out well.

At six-fifteen Armie and Fabe stood soberly at the window. Debbie had gone, driven home by Wattie in his battered patrol car.

'Quite a night,' Armie said. 'I don't even remember you taking Guin home.'

'I haven't.'

'You what? You don't mean she's still in your car.'

'Don't worry. I cracked the window.'

'God, Fabe, she'll leave you. You know, you'd deserve it. Get her up here at once or else take her home, you hear me?'

But there was Guin looking in at the door, rumpled, wearing Fabe's coat. She knocked and Armie waved her in. 'Coffee, Fabe, what are you waiting for?' he said.

'I have to speak to you, Armie,' said Guin. 'You. Bye Fabe.'

'What do you mean bye, Fabe? Oh hell. OK, I'm going.' Fabe pulled a face, and left.

'Speak to me?' said Armie, pulling out his chair. 'Sit down. What a night eh? What is it?'

'I had evidence,' she said. 'I've been sitting on it. You have to have it. It's back at my place.'

'What?' He sat down on his desk; a stack of papers collapsed and skittered off. 'No. I don't believe it. What evidence?'

'Tracy....' Guin glanced at the door. 'I haven't been able to talk to Fabe. I still can't. He, I don't know, I trust him but then I actually don't. About Tracy. I don't know what to do.'

'You do, hen,' said Armie. 'You're talking about it.'

195

'Tracy,' she said. 'She took pictures…. Look, it's just embarrassing. I didn't think it mattered, cause she didn't kill Barclay, I know she didn't. But she'd been taking pictures of him. Must've used a long lens. There were some on the roll – oh I might as well tell you.'

'Mmm,' said Armie, 'might as well.'

'That morning in St Margaret's Lane. She'd her camera with her. Before you got there she took out the film…. She slipped it into Frankie's pocket. I saw.'

'Oh well done.'

'Well it wasn't, was it. I thought she'd… I don't know, got something to hide, and I…. But they got developed. And I know – I think she had lots of pictures cause later on, lots of something got shredded. But this one roll didn't, she had it for some reason, tucked up in – damn it Armie. I'm sorry.' He passed her some tissues; she blew her nose. 'I'm sorry. I knew they were something, I snuck into her place and found them.'

'You beauty.'

'Well.' She sniffed. 'I looked at the first few. Ian Barclay's place, him with two women – oh not together – with different women. They're like coming out the door, down the path. OK, and a couple through the bedroom window…. I didn't look at 'em all, I got so depressed. Why'd she do it? It's so stupid.'

''Cause she hated his guts. Remember? He nicked your brother,' Armie said. 'She wanted to get him in trouble.'

'But it's pathetic, isn't it? And I didn't want to tell anyone. And especially Fabe. But then last night…. while I waited for him, I made myself look at the rest of 'em. It's…. Can we go get 'em? I couldn't bring 'em with me. No pockets in this get-up, see.'

* * *

As it was Sunday, most people didn't yet know about the fourth killing.

Vince Barnard's cousin Tom didn't know. Cousin Tom still slept, in fact, curled up next to Vince like a skinny little cat. Vince himself was only awake because he needed to pee. He stared at the ceiling, not wanting to move. Funny how soft drinks can do this to you, he thought: worse than lager.

Someone knocked. The flat was two floors up, they'd somehow got in from the street at this hour: Vince took a stealthy look at the clock. Nine-twenty. So, three hours and fifty minutes' sleep, thanks a lot, whoever you are. Sod off. They knocked again.

He sat up. Tom curled tighter. Vince pulled on his track pants and tiptoed through to the sitting-room. 'Just hold on,' he called softly through the letterbox. He padded into the bathroom.

They knocked again before he could stop. 'Will ya hold on,' he said through clenched teeth. Not a peep out of Tom though; just as well, the poor kid needed sleep.

Vince bounded to the door, opened it a crack and scowled through. There stood an incredibly beautiful blonde. His hopes rose, then plummeted. It was that copper again.

'Mr Barnard,' said Linda. 'Is your cousin here?'

The small figure snuggled next to Vince on the settee, swathed in an outsize sweater. 'I didn't do anything.'

'I never said you did, Sonia….'

'Tom.'

'She likes being Tom,' Vince said. 'Let her alone. She's fine.'

'Tom Hardy,' said Linda. 'English literature. I can't believe nobody got the joke.'

'Well they didn't,' said Sonia. 'The whole rest of the band think I'm Cousin Tom.' She giggled. 'I love it. I love being a man. You ought to try it. I'm not kidding.'

'I don't think Miss Ferris can be a man, Tom,' said Vince gently.

'Thanks,' said Linda. 'Tom, this is the thing. Where were you last night?'

'Where was I?' Sonia's eyes widened. 'I was with Vince, where else?'

'Where'd you go?'

'With the band, of course. We were playing at the Horny in Whixton.'

'Horncross Hotel,' said Vince.

'OK,' Linda said, 'I saw you. I was there myself till eleven. But I'm thinking afterward. When did you leave?'

Sonia looked up at Vince. 'Half past two?'

'Ish,' he said.

'And the rest of the guys, were they there right through?'

'Zack helped us load,' said Sonia. 'The drummer.'

'How in hell do you keep 'em all thinking you're a guy?'

Sonia snuggled down in her sweater and grinned. 'They don't look. Plus, dim light and a big woolly jumper.'

'Why are you asking all this?' said Vince. 'I don't like it.'

'A man's been murdered,' said Linda. 'And this will interest Tom. Ronnie Goudie.'

Sonia sat up in surprise. 'What about him?' The rolled collar slipped down, showing a fresh red gash across her neck. Hastily she sank back into the wool. 'You mean Goudie was killed? Or –'

'His throat was cut,' Linda said.

* * *

Guin's flat smelled faintly of petrol and dogs and fried chicken. It was almost welcoming, now that the heating had turned itself on. She filled the kettle. 'I'll get 'em OK? You make yourself at home.'

Armie had never been to Guin's place before. It was oddly spartan, as though she'd never intended to stop long. Her old hairy duffel coat hung on a chair, her helmet from a hook. There were a lot of paperbacks lying about; but the place was subtly neutral, undecorated.

He sat in the kitchen, at the formica table. He could hear her opening and closing a drawer in the next room. The kettle began to hiss. She brought the packet of photos, laid it before him, got mugs and a filter, kept moving.

'Thanks,' Armie said. 'May I look?'

'Mmm.'

The prints were dated 13-08-03: the day Beames was killed, assuming it happened after midnight. There were two all-black mistakes to begin with, then Ian and friend for snap after snap.

Coffee tinkled through a filter somewhere. Armie shuffled through the photos, wondered for the twentieth time why he hadn't seen Barclay's unhappiness while he lived.

He was into the last few shots now. The scene had changed. This was an interior: Beames's house. There was the tiled entry, then the staircase, the lower hallway with its pale striped paper and that gilt-framed painting. Gilt-framed, invisible behind reflective glass.

'Take sugar?' said Guin.

'No thanks. Black, no sug…. You seen this?'

She didn't answer. He turned to look up at her: she gazed over his shoulder, her face grave.

'You did see it,' he said, taking the coffee. He set it down and riffled eagerly through the snaps. 'I don't suppose there's any more of those.'

'We're both idiots,' he said a few minutes later.

'Speak for yourself. But I don't feel too clever.'

'I told Tracy off for concealing evidence. Just on principle. I had no idea what she was hiding.'

'She didn't either,' Guin said.

'We're all three of us idiots. Her, me and you.'

They finished their coffee in silence. Guin rose to make more.

'It has to be the killer, doesn't it,' she said.

'It does, aye.'

'There in the house with her.'

'In the front room, aye. So it seems,' said Armie.

Together they gazed at the picture some more. 'Who's it look like to you?' said Guin.

'The Scream, by Munch. No,' he said, 'I'm not sure yet. Technology will tell.'

'She can't have looked at these. If she had….'

'She'd have shown them to me. To prove she hadn't killed Beames.'

As she let Armie out she wondered why he'd called himself an idiot. He stopped at the foot of the steps, turned and waved the handful of snaps with a cheery grin. It wasn't the time to ask him.

She went back up to the flat. Should get some sleep, she thought. But instead of going to bed she sat by the window, looking out over the privet hedge at the bracken-brown ridge beyond the town.

Goudie and Gerry, if only she'd spoken, and perhaps even Ian, they'd still be alive. Why hadn't she? What was wrong with her?

Bad seed, or whatever made Frankie get in trouble. It's not just him though, it's all of us. Beginning with our Mum.

twenty

Hangovers

AFTER WATTIE dropped her at her door, Debbie let herself in and thought of sleep. But she was restless: she prowled the house and garden looking for signs of damage, for the cops had searched well. At least, she thought as she slammed shut all the cupboards in the kitchen, they were honest cops. The Glenfiddich she'd laid by for Geoff's homecoming was still here, tucked away at the back of the counter.

But honest or not, they'd been everywhere, inside and out. They'd even bothered to open and probe the half-used tins of paint in the garden shed.

She'd thought of those too. But she wasn't going to mess with paint tins when she didn't have to.

She took off her coat and Geoff's shirt, got a sweatshirt and leggings from the airing cupboard and stretched out on the settee. Upstairs was depressing, the guddle in the bedroom put her off going in. Make-up seemed to fascinate the officers on her case. Much good might it do them.

She slept.

Sylvie, Sylvie. Don't leave me.

You're leaving me. Don't go. Don't go. I love you, Sylvie, you're leaving me, don't.

It was terror, blind choking terror like falling from a high building. It woke her. She wasn't crying when she awoke, she couldn't cry, something was clutching her throat, her heart. She couldn't even scream. She struggled to focus outside herself, on the coffee-table or the cushions on the chairs, or the curtains closed against the day.

She sat up. The terror had abated. In its place, a terrible desolation grew. It filled her and made a lump in her throat. She swallowed; it hurt to swallow. She almost buried her head in her hands, but instead she lifted her chin and stared resolutely at the strip of light between the curtains.

A shadow crossed the light. At the outer door, someone knocked.

It was twenty years since Sandy'd had a hangover like this. He kept thinking he'd beat it, he'd stand up and not feel sick, and then it'd hit him worse than ever and down he'd go again. It was foul.

Arlene wasn't in bed with him but she must've brought him home. He couldn't remember. He didn't remember anything after his argument with Goudie. That guy was a bully and a total prick. In fact he was a criminal. Obviously Arlene didn't care, since that's where she must be right now, over at his place.

His memory suddenly did him a favour. Debbie! They'd made love yesterday. Yesterday evening, for the first time in ages and ages.

He dressed, sitting down at intervals. At length he picked himself up and tottered down to the kitchen. Water, liver-salts. Sugar.... Oh God, he couldn't keep anything down.

Debbie'd be home, it was Sunday.

At her door he knocked and clung to the handle for support. Presently it turned, and there she stood. She looked shaky too. There were purple smudges round her eyes and she was shockingly pale. 'You OK?' he said.

'You're a funny one to be asking,' she said. 'You're a wreck, Sandy.'

'I was bleezin last night.'

'No fooling.'

She let him in: what else would you do? He made a beeline for the kitchen, groaned, and fell into a chair. She started some coffee. 'What time is it?' Sandy said.

'Daytime. Did you go out? Or did you get blootered in the sanctity of your home?'

'Went out. I told you I might go out. I went and found Arlene. That bastard she's seeing… I showed him what's what.'

She smiled down at his balding head. 'Good for you, sweetie. Take sugar in this, it'll perk you up. Lovely dark sugar.' She sat down opposite.

'You're an angel, Deb…. You sure you're OK? There's some bug going about.'

'Well maybe I'm sickening for it.' She sipped her coffee. 'But I doubt it.'

But his hangover wasn't done with him yet. 'Sorry,' he said, putting down his mug. 'Gotta give Huey a shout.' He scuttled out and down the passage: the Chalmerses had a downstairs loo. Debbie shook her head and covered his coffee with a teacosy.

Throwing up was a complex process, he reflected, sniffling and blinking in the loo. You didn't just toss it, you got it up your nose, and sometimes you'd to clean round about. He blew his nose and looked around for a sponge.

The littlest room was strange today. Debbie was such a stickler for order. It was funny that she'd let things get so jumbled in the corner cupboard: scouring powder spilled, bleach on its side, sponge cloths jammed in the door. Now he noticed the wall-mounted cabinet gaping open, the bottles and tubes and tweezers and plasters inside in a terrible hooley.

He wetted a sponge cloth and wiped the floor, rinsed and wiped again and felt sick. He shut the lid of the toilet and sat down.

The top of the cistern was cockeyed. He turned, risking nausea, and set it straight. No, he didn't feel sick any more: but he had a headache coming on. He looked in the cabinet again: aspirins, paracetamol, something.

Aspirins. He shook the little plastic bottle. No sound, but it wasn't empty; it weighed a bit. He worked off the cap, and looked inside, frowning.

'Deb, have you any aspirins?' He slouched in the kitchen doorway. 'The ones in that cabinet have gone off or something.'

'How d'you mean gone....' Oh dear God, thought Debbie. Oh God no.

'They've turned into a sort of red gunge.'

'Oh those,' she said. 'Sorry bout that. I... I'll come and see if there's more shall I? I'll come look.'

'It's like a bomb dropped in there,' he said. He started back down the passage.

'Sandy,' she called.

He paused, his hand on the toilet door. 'Hmm?'

'Sandy, you know that I love you.'

'Do you, Debbie?' he said. 'You really do?'

'I really do. I always have. Don't you ever forget it.' She lifted the bottle of Glenfiddich from its nook, and hefted it by its neck. Then she hurried after him.

'Debbie,' said a voice behind her.

Arlene had found the front door unlocked. She hadn't knocked. This was the sort of thing you saw when you didn't knock: your husband romping with his lover, fuelled by the finest malt.

'Jesus, Debbie, this is no time. This is no bloody time!' she said. 'Sandy!'

He turned. There was Deb with a bottle in her hand. Arlene stood behind her, her arms folded: or rather she was hugging herself. Her eyes were wild.

'Arlene?' He felt giddy again. 'Why are you here? What's wrong? Where've you been?'

'I've come from Ronnie's. That's what's wrong, what the hell did you think? He's dead, Sandy.' Now he saw she was weeping.

* * *

'So not a shred,' Bob Marshall said as the detectives settled into chairs in his office.

'Well not quite,' Armie said. 'I mean that's not true, there's those footprints....'

'Man's footprints,' said Bob.

'And the knife....'

'Nothing at Chalmers's house, I meant.'

'No,' Armie said. 'Not nothing, no. We're getting a better picture of Debbie all the time. Aren't we?'

'Aye, I am,' said Linda. 'She's size seven feet.'

'And what size are the footprints at Goudie's?' said Bob.

'Tens,' said Fabe, consulting his notes. 'Man's tens. Smooth soles. Similar to Armie's but Armie's are smaller. Your prints are all over,' he reminded his boss, 'you went galloping up those stairs.'

'Did the size ten man go galloping up?' said Bob.

'So it seems.'

'But Debbie Chalmers did not.'

'Seems not,' said Fabe.

'But Debbie's feet aren't particularly small,' Linda went on, 'and that tallies with the hands the barmaids saw.'

'I've never heard anything so tenuous in my life,' said Bob.

'Her hands are nice. She wears gloves. She has gardening gloves and painting gloves. She uses her hands. We also found ladies' size seven wellies, you know? She has tools....'

'Her husband has two weeks' leave at a time,' Bob said, 'I should think he'd be the one using tools.'

'There's a light bow-saw in the shed, for instance,' said Linda. 'A hatchet.... They've one small wood-stove in the house and one open fire. Looks like she cuts the wood. Oh, there's a lightweight strimmer – electric – a Flymo and....'

'Where is this going, Linda?' said Bob.

'All I'm saying is she works with her hands. Her hands are very nice, but they're large. And her nails....'

'Her nails are fine too,' said Fabe. 'They're painted red.'

'So what?' said Bob. 'I'm sorry, but it seems to me that you haven't a shred. No hair colouring, no comb. No – aagh.' His phone rang. 'Marshall – Hah! Aye we are! That's.... Good man. Well done. Thanks Wattie. I'll tell him – You too. Later, bye.' He replaced the receiver. 'That was Wattie. And speak of the devil, the colouring and the comb to boot. At the Odd Spot – in the ladies' waste-bin, or at least that's what they think.'

'What they think?' said Armie. 'Don't they know?'

'No. The staff empty the bins each night – morning really. But the things are mixed up with the ladies' rubbish. It's some black stuff in a tube. They're sending it over.'

'The Odd Spot,' said Armie. 'Interesting.'

'Now that's got you worried,' Bob said.

* * *

'I didn't bring you,' Arlene said, wiping her eyes. 'I couldn't find you when I left Ronnie's club. I left, I went back to look for you and you'd vanished, God damn you. So I don't know.'

Debbie handed the coffee round in silence.

'I don't remember anything after you walked out,' said Sandy. 'Nothing that matters. Just drink.'

'I came home about three – even earlier. Earlier,' Arlene said. 'Cop cars and all sorts were swarming round Ronnie's.' She helped herself to a handful of Debbie's tissues and blew her nose. 'Fire engines. Well – fire anyway. And I stopped, obviously, and asked…. But this big girl in uniform waved me on…. I couldn't get anyone to tell me anything and I wasn't exactly sober, so I split and went to bed. You weren't there, Sandy. I didn't know where you were.'

'Did you care?' he said.

'I did, Sandy. But I had looked. You know, I had looked, you weren't anywhere…. And I woke up at ten and there you were in bed with me all alive-o. And yes, I was pleased. But then –'

'You were?'

She ignored him. 'I got up eventually. I went down to Ronnie's again and they finally told me, the cops. There was mobs of 'em there. And I gave 'em a statement, and I said you'd come home with me.'

'But I didn't.'

'But I told 'em you did. Give me some credit would you?' She blinked away tears. 'You lunatic, Sandy. We can't let 'em find out you're a killer.'

* * *

After Fabe and Linda had gone Armie said, 'I've something I'd like you to see.'

'Secret is it?' said Bob.

'Delicate, aye. I had it from Guin Catto. She'll no doubt tell him in her own time.' He passed Bob the snap of Beames's front hall. 'Whenever that's going to be.'

Bob studied the photo. He looked at the date on the back. 'I'll be buggered. But was it taken that day? And who....'

'Classified, Bob. But I think I can confirm it.'

'Classified bollocks,' said Bob. 'Confirm it and damn well put it on record.'

'I'm putting it through for analysis.' Armie took the snap back. 'If it isn't Rod Andrew, if the date checks out, he has to be released.'

'Don't tell me my job,' Bob growled. 'Just go and.... Oh shit, Armie. What next?'

'What next?' Armie considered a while. 'I tell you what. I think I'll go see Susie.'

'The pilgrim returns,' she called as he sneaked in at the back door. 'Want a drink?'

'Oh Suze, I'm sorry. It's been so.... Aye I do, but it's too damn early.'

She made him tea. 'You're not doing this again tonight are you? The moon....'

'No,' he said. 'It was last night.'

'No, it's – Oh. The killing was last night.'

'This morning. It was.... Hell's teeth.' He was choked up for some reason. He gulped some tea, sighed, shook his head, gulped some more tea and croaked, 'Hell's fire.'

'What on earth's wrong, Geordie?' said Susie. 'It wasn't another of yours.'

'No. No. It was Ronnie. Ronnie. I mean damn it, Suze.... bloody Ronnie Goudie even now.'

Later he said, 'I found out today that he'd slashed a girl's neck to intimidate her. With a Stanley knife. She went into hiding, so completely we thought she was dead.... I tried to put him away, Suze, but I.... And he – at the end all he wanted was me. To talk to me. And the killer was coming upstairs.'

'Coming back?'

'To finish him off. I think. I think he was left with the knife in his chest and whoever did it came back, pulled it out... cut his throat... he was helpless by then. And the knife was pulled out. So... that's how it was, unless there were two different people.' He shuddered. 'That'd be something else.'

'I think you should know he's been making deposits,' said Susie. 'In his box, every couple of days.'

'Big and heavy and awkward?' said Armie.

'Not especially. Why?'

'Do I get to see? I mean without fetching a warrant.'

'You might.' She looked into his eyes for a while. 'If it brightens you up.'

* * *

Armie got back to the station at six. There at his desk sat Fabe, with the contents of Ronnie's wallet spread out before him.

'That's my desk,' said Armie, 'if you please.'

'Mine's got things on it. Where'd you go, anyway?'

'Home.' He leaned over Fabe's shoulder. 'That Ronnie?'

'Who else?'

'See those funny wee diagrams,' Armie said.

'Is that what they are? Diagrams of what? They look queer.'

'Someday I'll tell you.'

'What do you mean someday you'll tell me? Tell me right now,' said Fabe.

But Armie kept quiet. He had plans for the gold. Or has it got plans for me? he wondered. Must ask Suze about that.

* * *

That Sunday morning, Willy had gone to church. He'd wanted to thank God for his escape the night before. He'd also needed to grieve for his treasure, and the service put him in the proper mood.

It turned out that God hadn't let him off the hook. At lunchtime on Monday, two detectives showed up at the Horncross spruce woods where he was helping the foresters.

The detectives sat down with him on a log and asked if he'd rather talk here or over at Hornbridge police station.

'What's it about?' he said, without answering their question.

'Where were you Sunday morning?' said the gangling cop who'd introduced himself as DS Finnie.

'In church.'

'Early Sunday morning,' said Fabe. 'Two o'clock, say.'

'Two o'clock? In bed,' Willy said, after seeming to ponder. 'In the van, at Whixton, in bed. That's right.'

'I fancy,' said the Inspector, 'that sitting on logs like this is bad for you. Look, this one's got ice on it.'

'Anyone else use your pickup, Willy?' said Fabe.

'No. No one. Why?'

'Don't you find those boots a bit slippery for the woods, Mr Smith?' Armie said. 'I mean look at the soles. And you should have steel toecaps to work with a chainsaw, surely.'

'What's that got to do with anything?' Willy said.

'It's this way,' said Fabe. 'Those boot soles look a lot like the prints we found on the stair carpet in Nellfield Cottage, Marchbank – where a man was murdered on Sunday morning. Your pickup looks a lot like one that was seen in a lay-by Sunday morning, four fields or so from the cottage as the crow flies.'

'My pickup wasn't there,' Willy said. 'And my boots weren't either.'

'The boots went out of the house again and climbed a tree,' Armie said. 'And we think that the boots went off across the fields. They might've been going to get in the truck. So naturally we want to speak to the owner of the boots. Cause he may have witnessed a murder.'

'I heard about the murder,' Willy said, putting one hand in his jacket pocket. 'I swear I'd tell you if I knew anything.'

'Mr Smith,' said Armie, 'you're crossing your fingers.'

'No I'm not.'

'You could come back to the station,' Fabe said.

'But I told you everything. I wasn't there. They're someone else's boots, aren't they.'

This was hellish. He wished he'd never come here. If only the sight hadn't shown him the gold, he'd be in Sussex right now. But it had been so clear.

Oscar was on his case as well, and Vanessa. They followed him about, relentless as the undead. It had taken them only minutes to deduce that he'd taken the gold to Fairyhill.

Grand. Let them think it was still up there, hidden somewhere in the clear-fell or the remaining trees. Let them sweat. He'd bet they'd never even find the well. And he'd be damned if he'd admit that Goudie had beaten him.

'He's lying,' said Fabe as they drove away. 'He was there.'

'I agree.'

'Why, though? I don't get the connexion. He hadn't gone there to steal, or he'd have turned the place over.'

'Not necessarily,' Armie said. 'He might've have been interrupted. More likely, the thing he was looking for isn't there.'

'And you know what it is, do you?'

'Correct.'

'So when are you telling me what it is? Or is it to remain forever --'

'Trust me, Fabe. Just trust me.'

'What do you mean just trust you? I can't. This could be vital. And you won't explain....'

'I will explain,' Armie said. 'Very soon. But first I have to be sure I'm right about the killer.'

* * *

Armie dropped Fabe at the station. They hadn't had lunch; he thought about calling on Susie, but didn't. He needed to get to work with Ronnie's cryptic maps.

Ronnie had once shown him old Blythe's map. But he'd worked from a tracing; the original was too frail to carry about. The tracing, a half-sheet of A4, was much re-folded and grimy. The second diagram was fresh and new.

He drove to Fairyhill. The lay-by was deserted now. The wood was felled; the log pile was its monument, gleaming with rime in the low sun, waiting to be hauled away. He sat for a moment. Let's get things straight, he thought. Was it here? It could've been here.

He took out the newer of the two maps, turned it round a few times, nodded to himself and climbed from the car.

The bare hill seemed alien, horribly scalped. He supposed they'd replant it with tiny trees. Then these trees would grow until the hill was again clad in deep shade, with green rides and deer-trod pathways. He wouldn't see it. Trees and man, he thought: we're out of step.

Ronnie's diagram had him looking for landmarks. Some of these had been trees: most unfortunate. Moreover he had no idea whether Ronnie had measured distances in paces or feet, or what; and if paces, how long? They couldn't have exactly the same stride, could they?

So, paces. That's what treasure maps normally use. His paces weren't so different from Ronnie's after all. They led him to the centre, the focus of the map: an enormous detached stump which Ronnie had indicated with X and a circle, labelled 'stump'.

It lay in a shallow gully that fell away southwards. There were stones underfoot, as though this had once been the bed of a stream. Could that be? The river lay far below, out of sight, dividing this woodland from the town.

He seized a couple of the roots and pulled, hitched the stump this way and that. It hanked on something, then gave way so abruptly that he almost sat down. He tugged some more, and peered over the top of the stump into the shaft of the stone-lined well.

Just as he recognised the objects at the bottom, his mobile began to ring.

'It's Dougie, Armie. I've done your picture. Thought you'd want to hear.'

'You've done it! Wonderful, Dougie. Who?'

'It's the wifie Chalmers. I've tried other folk, but she's the one. It's actually pretty clear really. I mean didn't you recognise her?'

'Aye I did, but I'm prejudiced. I'd see her in a patch of damp.'

'So you don't want me to pass this on.'

'Not yet, no. No, but I'll come back in and.... I'm coming in. Oh and Dougie, the glove. Can you get DNA from the inner.... You have? Oh Dougie man, you're a star.'

He put his phone away and gripped the roots again, working the monster stump back over the shaft.

Christ, he thought. What am I doing? There's a skeleton down there. I can't do this.

'Fairyhill,' he told Fabe when he got in. 'A body. We'll get up there now shall we? There's a few hours' light left.'

'But I don't get it,' said Fabe. 'How'd you know to go there in the first place? What has Fairyhill to do with anything?'

'Anonymous tip-off.'

'Oh don't bullshit me.'

'I didn't mean to, Fabe, I'm sorry. Of course it's BS. But it's official BS for the present time.'

'It was Ronnie,' said Fabe. 'Those diagrams of his. Am I right?'

'Absolutely. Look Fabe, I'm doing the best I can. Please believe me.'

'I don't believe!' Fabe snorted. 'I find out.'

'So you do. Want to come to Fairyhill now? We want SOCO... and Anya Ferencz. Better do it right.' Armie picked up the phone, and started to punch in a number.

'You'll push me too far someday,' said Fabe. 'You know that?'

twenty-one

Old Bones

WHEN TRACY awoke Tuesday morning she could feel that something had changed. But what? She took stock: Frank fast asleep, illuminated clock reading 5:02, low late moon looking in at the window. All much as always: must be me, then, she thought.

Then she remembered she'd landed a job with the Hornbridge *World* the day before. So that must be it. Fantastic. But at the same time it meant responsibility, time-keeping, chains. Start next Monday they'd said. Any loose ends, she'd better sort out right away.

Loose ends. She slipped out of bed and headed for the bathroom. The habit of sneaking a peek at Barclay's windows had died hard: now she looked out to confirm that the place was still dark and deserted. One set of ends was tied up anyway. Those damn photographs were history.

Cold mornings now. She tiptoed back to the bedroom and opened the wardrobe, finding clothes by touch. This room, she thought, now in November, really should have the curtains drawn. She always left them open: she liked the moonlight, the street lights, the morning light if she overslept. But Frank liked his little dark nest.

Come to think of it, there were some good curtains in the wardrobe, that she'd bought from the charity shop in Hornbridge the day....

Oh no.

No, she couldn't have left the damn photos in there, she couldn't have. It'd be too stupid. She lifted down one of the big carrier bags, and felt all through it: nothing but curtain. She lifted the other one down.

Nothing but curtain.

Still Frankie slept. He was a master-sleeper. Tracy lugged both bags into the kitchen and switched on the light. She was damned if she could remember where those pictures had ended up.

They weren't here.

Vaguely she recalled slipping the newly developed snaps down the side of the curtains as she lugged them along. Sure enough, the plastic was dimpled where the packet had been, but the packet simply wasn't here.

Dread crept into her guts. She'd never taken the packet out. She hadn't, had she.

Inspector Armistead had kept on and on at her, hadn't he. About Barclay.

She went back to the bedroom and sat down on Frank's side of the bed, and he woke up.

'What, lovey?' he said.

'My bloody photographs,' she said. 'The damn police.'

* * *

'There's a young lady to see you,' Wattie confided on the internal telephone.

It was five past eight. Armie was getting ready to go back out to Fairyhill and the freezing wind that the felling of the woods had unleashed there.

It was a cold case, cold as could be. On Monday, Dr Ferencz, the ex-Regional archaeologist, had joined the team on the hill. Anya Ferencz was an apple-cheeked little old lady who wore her hair in a bun; she was also a fine forensic scientist, especially if you happened to have been murdered long ago. She was sorry – for she loved ancient things best – to report that the deceased had lived as recently as the early eighteen-hundreds.

Anya didn't feel the cold. But then, Armie reflected, she spent her life squatting in the open air, digging holes in the rocks with dentists' tools.

'OK,' he said into the phone. Maybe he could stay in his nice warm office for awhile, after all. 'Thanks Wattie, send her up.'

He should've asked Wattie who the visitor was. Tracy startled him. She glared, and her face was pale.

'Miss Wiseman,' he said brightly. 'What brings you....'

'You bastard,' said Tracy, 'when did you do it?'

Why am I always on my own when this happens? Armie wondered. 'Take a seat,' he said. 'This one.' He tipped Fabe's collection of witness statements off one of the chairs. 'Let me tell you all about it. Coffee?'

'Go to hell.' She sat. 'When did you break into my flat?'

'I didn't,' said Armie.

'Someone did it for you, then. Don't get clever. You had someone go through my things without permission. Isn't that a crime? I'll bet it is.'

'Miss Wiseman.... It is a crime, yes. If I say I didn't do a thing it usually, I can't honestly say always, means I didn't do the thing.'

'Well someone did it.'

'And why me?'

'You were on and on at me about Barclay. Now something's gone missing.' She blushed scarlet. 'God. I thought you had them but you don't, do you.'

'Suppose I promise to tell you nothing but the truth,' Armie said, trying to look solemn. 'And you tell me what it is you're missing. Would that be fair?'

Tracy's blush hadn't faded. She was shivering slightly, he noticed: she'd got herself good and mad before coming to see him.

'Pictures of Barclay,' she said.

'Got 'em! How's that for truthful?'

'So you did break in!'

'No. No I didn't. None of my people did.'

'Then how....'

'Private eye,' said Armie.

She gasped and smacked her hands together. 'Not Guin!'

'Good guess.'

'I'll kill her!'

'Why?' said Armie. 'I mean obviously it was wrong. But if she hadn't done anything, that'd be wrong too.'

'Wrong?' said Tracy. 'It's terrible. It's a vile thing to do.'

'OK,' said Armie, 'but I know why she did it. Maybe you'd rather hear it from her....'

'Why did she?'

'She was concerned about you.'

'Concerned!'

'You keep shouting, Miss Wiseman. Would it be better....'

'You'd shout if people were sneaking your things. Leaping to conclusions....'

'And what conclusions should we leap to?' Armie said. 'What's the point of taking pictures of Barclay?'

Tracy made a face. Armie wasn't sure what it represented. 'Was it so clever of you to stalk Barclay?' he said. 'Was it an honourable thing to do? Did you hate him so much?'

'No,' Tracy said, 'I hate what he represented.'

Armie shook his head. 'Car crime. Not something you believe in, is it? Part of a creed or....'

'Yes. It's the whole thing, the whole idea. Being able to deprive someone of their freedom. Having the power.'

'That's true,' said Armie. 'That is obnoxious.'

'Not to you.'

'Who cares about me? We were speaking about Barclay. And the roll of film.... which you had developed the day you found Beames.'

She frowned. 'So?'

'You shot the last few frames in that house, Miss Wiseman.'

'I... yeah. I did.'

'Ever look at 'em? The shots from the house?'

It was twenty-five to nine. Fabe appeared beyond the glass door. Armie spotted him, waved him away.

'No,' said Tracy.

'Well let me show you something,' said Armie, opening a drawer of his desk.

* * *

Sandy stared at the surface of his coffee and went over the whole thing again in his head. He'd been doing this for nearly two days.

Debbie. She'd said she loved him. She'd said….

Never forget it, that's what she'd said. Why on earth?

And why the whisky? He'd just been asking for aspirin for his hangover. Whisky, for God's sake? It was bizarre.

He took a gulp of his coffee. It must be the booze, he thought. I can't think. My logic circuits are fried.

I love you Sandy. I always have. Don't you ever forget that, she'd said. Then Arlene….

Arlene thought he'd killed Ronnie Goudie. She actually did – that he'd slit Ronnie's throat. But she couldn't believe that. She did, though. How could she?

And she'd stormed straight in. There he was. There was Deb with a bottle of whisky.

A good malt whisky. Long, green, Glenfiddich, in that slinky triangular bottle. He closed his eyes and pictured her with it, grasping its neck as if it were some rot-gut blend. Swinging it, almost. As if….

He opened his eyes.

It couldn't be true. That could not be true.

Linda came later to ask him some questions. He was trying to work, barricaded in the office at his motor showroom: a peaceful place, heavy with the scent of new upholstery.

'I woke up in bed,' he told her. 'I had the mother and father of all hangovers. I had on my underwear and socks. She must've undressed me.'

'Your wife?' said Linda.

'Of course my wife. She brought me home.' I'm a coward, he thought: I've always been one.

'But you don't recollect it.'

'No… but she does.'

'It's funny she left on your socks,' Linda said. 'Are you positive….'

'Oh she always does that. Doesn't like touching 'em.'

Well I'm not going to argue, thought Linda. I wouldn't either. 'We'd be grateful if you'd come down in your own time and make a statement.' She got up to go. 'And if you should remember anything more –'

'Like what?' said Sandy.

'Like, anything, Mr Third. Anything at all.'

'It doesn't matter what Arlene says,' said Armie.

Dusk was falling. Linda switched on the lights in the detectives' base. She and Armie turned to the window, noticed how hideous their reflections looked and turned away again. 'How d'you mean?' said Linda.

'He was legless. I saw him. I lost track of him, but I promise you he was too far gone to hurt anyone but himself.'

'But how'd he get home?'

'Someone got him past us. It has to be the case. But what's interesting is that Arlene's lying.'

'She's afraid we'll suspect him,' said Linda.

'It'd be tempting if he hadn't been so drunk. You know,' said Armie, 'there's one man who knows. The man in the tree. Scuse me.' His desk phone was ringing: he lifted the receiver. 'Armistead. Hullo! Mr Third, what's to do?' He raised his eyebrows at Linda. 'You did? Mr Third, you weren't – You don't mean that, surely? I…. Mr Third, I really –' He stood up abruptly. 'Where are you just now? Oh no. No. No, don't do that…. He's rung off. Hell's teeth, Linda, he's away to kill himself.'

* * *

It hadn't taken him long to work out. There were the cars, there were their keys, and in the workshop there was tape and tubing. The only other thing he'd needed was guts; or maybe it wasn't so brave.

It had got dark and his staff had gone home. He'd just sat there, sat at his desk in the dark, unable to stir hand or foot. Arlene hadn't rung to ask where he was. If only she had.

Then he'd made his decision, phoned Armistead. It might give Debbie some sort of a chance. He'd hurry now, before Armistead came, before Arlene, but no, she thought he was a murderer. If she cared she'd have phoned him, it was late. She ought to have rung.

217

How he wished she'd have rung. She used to. His eyes were stinging.

The engine hummed, rumty-tumty-tum. Then the siren. Running footsteps, shouts, slamming doors. He opened his eyes: a blue light. So, it was ending.

Someone was shaking him. Armistead. His ears buzzed, his eyes wouldn't focus. Armistead vanished. Some fat bloke appeared in his place, thrusting a plastic thingy at him: an oxygen mask, he realised as he began to breathe freely, deeply.

'You can't question him now,' said the fat bloke.

'Mr Third,' came Armistead's voice, 'do you remember saying –'

'I said you can't question him now, Inspector. Inspector....'

In the ambulance he woke up again. There was Armistead. Maybe it was real.

'Do you remember confessing to the murder of Goudie, Mr Third?'

He nodded.

'Why did you do that? Is it true?'

He nodded again.

'How can it be true? You were terribly drunk that night. You could barely stand up.'

'I killed him,' Sandy whispered. 'Me.'

'No you didn't.'

'Ask Arlene. She'll tell you....' He began to weep. 'I killed the others. I did it. Me.'

'Not you,' said Armie. 'Don't give up hope, Sandy. Don't give up. I've rung your wife. She's meeting us at the hospital.'

* * *

It took until Thursday, mid-morning, to get everything from the well. Scraps of fabric, a pinchbeck necklace, the halves of a broken whetstone – the weapon, they thought: these things and more they tenderly bore away, as well as the bones.

The bones had excited Anya Ferencz. They appealed to her sense of romance: within the skeleton were the barest remnants of another, a tiny one.

All the time Armie was on the hill he felt somebody watching. He kept looking around, but the well was in a fold of the ground that hid it from the near distance. From time to time he climbed out of the hollow and looked about, and once he thought he saw a vehicle pulling in behind the log pile. It was a shooting brake of some kind. His attention was drawn away before he could identify it. But even when no vehicle was there, he felt eyes.

The foresters hadn't felled the whole plantation. They'd left the old, tangled trees that grew on the plunging slope above the river. From the bare hill, Armie could see the upper branches of these trees; if there were hidden watchers that's where they were. Was that thought rational? He couldn't tell.

At half past eleven he thanked Dr Ferencz and the SOC team, and drove away towards Horncross.

'Everyone's going,' Oscar said. He turned the binoculars carefully round, and wiped the eyepieces with Vanessa's hat.

Vanessa shifted her weight gingerly on the branch below. 'The old bat too?'

'She's packing up. God, I wish we'd thought to bring a flask.'

'And the curly little bobby, he still there?'

'Heading down to the cars. Christ,' said Oscar, 'they've screwed us properly.'

'I don't think they got it,' Vanessa said.

'Of course they bloody got it.'

'No, *he* got it. They didn't, not the proper police. They don't even know about it. Why else wouldn't it be in the papers? Even that local rag just says a skeleton was discovered. Not gold.'

'If it's not out here,' Oscar groaned, 'why are we? I'm freezing. My arse isn't half sore and you know what? I'm bursting. Besides, we've a trailer to finish.'

'I still say that little cop's got it,' said Vanessa. 'He snuck off with it and then called in the rest of 'em.'

'Look queen, you could be right,' said Oscar. 'I mean probably you are. But I don't see why you're so sure.'

'He's been running round like a blue-arsed fly since Monday night.'

'Who hasn't?'

'No one up here Sunday. Not a soul. But when I come by Monday, he's turned up mob-handed. Blokes in white suits, that old dear with the shovels.'

'She's a rare one. Maybe she got there first.'

'Oh no. He's been nosing round. He's a copper, Oscar. That's what they do. He probably smelled the gold.'

* * *

Armie motored along to Horncross thinking, poor little wolf. How she must hate those guys working there, with their zip-zip-zip and thundering up and down. But Horncross is big: there's the pine wood, the steeps of the southern boundary, the river. It's wild on the south side. Must get out some maps later.

On the forest's northern edge he pulled up on the verge. How do I know she's a she? he thought. From her size? Or is it just a feeling?

Willy's pickup was parked up ahead. The thinning operation had moved westward since Monday. Armie walked through the ride, making for the noise, hampered by fresh cuttings. It was probably too late to look at Willy's boots. How stupid not to have done it straightaway. Ah well.

'Inspector,' said Willy suddenly from behind a tree. Armie jumped six inches. 'Oh sorry,' said Willy, cracking half a smile.

'Mr Smith,' said Armie. 'I've been thinking about your boots. Have you any idea how rare it is to find smooth soled boots these days? Everybody's going about in commandoes.'

'You're not.'

'No, but cops never think ahead. I tell you what, let's have a loan of yours a minute. See if there's any tree bark sticking in the buckles.'

'Tree bark?' said Willy. 'Well obviously. Look around you, mush.'

Armie looked. 'No oak trees.'

'Oak trees?'

'Tell you what. See if your mates have got a spare pair for you. And I'll just borrow these, OK?'

'Just a minute,' said Willy. 'Can you do that, mush?'

'I don't know do I, mush? I could try. We could DNA test this bark in the stitching. Plants have DNA, too, you know.'

They picked their way slowly along the ride. 'I don't know,' Willy said. 'I didn't think to check the time. And a lot of cars must've gone up.'

'Did any come back? I mean, back down the lane and away.'

'I don't know…. I mean I'm sorry, but I really wasn't interested in cars.'

'You went up those stairs, Mr Smith,' Armie said. 'You stood in that room.'

'He was dead,' said Willy. 'I swear it.'

You're not crossing fingers this time, Armie thought. 'He rang me,' he said. 'Ronnie Goudie did. He was dying. He said someone was coming, coming to finish him. Was it you?'

'No.'

'This is off the record, Mr Smith, did I tell you? No Sergeant Finnie hiding in a tree.'

'Goudie was dead when I got there. And I didn't go to kill him, did I? I went to look for the gold.'

'Ah! The gold.'

'When I saw him I just knew I had to get out. His throat was cut, there was blood….'

'See a weapon?'

'I don't remember.'

'You know it was very strange,' Armie said. They'd stopped, within sight of the foresters; but there was a lull in the racket from the saws. 'Like he died almost as we were speaking. Minutes later, there I was, looking down at his body. We went back a long way, you know?'

Willy shrugged. He glanced over at the other guys, but, Armie thought, he was listening all right. 'Aye we did – a long way.' He watched Willy's face. 'And he was an absolute bastard but… I have to say I was shocked…. My knees folded up, I just sat down on this wee sort of hassock next the bed.'

Not a flicker, not a fraction of a smile. Well, he might not find it funny, thought Armie. 'So,' he said, 'you see anybody? Alive?'

221

'I.... you'll never believe it, will you? This woman.'

'What sort of –'

'Naked woman. Not naked but nearly. Believe me, or not?'

'Why shouldn't I?' said Armie. 'You see her face?'

'I wasn't looking at her face,' said Willy.

* * *

On Friday night Geoff Chalmers came home to find that his wife had been arrested for murder.

She'd left him a note. 'Dearest G, been arrested for murder. Keeps happening but it's OK. Hornbridge CID. Home soon, don't worry. Love, love, love, D.' He thought he'd go nuts. He was knackered after the tour and the flight and the drive home. Now he felt wounded, as if some part of himself had been torn away.

'Why do you suspect my wife?' he demanded over the phone. 'Can I speak to her? I have to see her.'

'By all means, come down,' Armie said. 'She left you a note didn't she? That says she'll be back?'

'How'd you know that?'

'I was there when she wrote it, Mr Chalmers, and I think she will be back. Most folk get bail. But come down by all means.'

'What the hell does she mean, this keeps happening? Have you –'

'We'll explain everything when you get here,' said Armie.

'We can't question her about Ian again,' Fabe said.

'Well we might.' They leaned against the wall in the corridor, expecting Geoff any minute. 'When Dougie's finished with that glove, we might. But not now... not about Ronnie either. And forget Gerry Lamond, there isn't a bit of evidence.'

'So it's Beames.'

'It's Beames. Look Fabe,' said Armie. 'There's something I have to tell you.'

'Funny time for it.'

'But it's good news.'

'So let's have it, what are you waiting for?'

'I've waited till now because.... Oh.' Mira walked briskly towards them with a man, a fine angry specimen in a stormproof jacket. 'This must be Mr Chalmers.' Armie held out a hand. 'DI Armistead.'

Geoff ignored his hand and snapped, 'Where's my wife? I have to see her. Now. Where's Charlie?'

Armie nipped back into Interview Room One. 'Charlie, Mrs Chalmers, Mr Chalmers is here. I'll need you both back in fifteen minutes.'

'Spit it out,' Fabe said when they were alone in the room.

'You know Fabe,' said Armie, sitting down on the table, 'when you get to be an Inspector, I hope folk will show you respect. Ronnie used to talk about respect, you know. He fair craved it.'

'And look where it got him,' said Fabe.

'True. But when you say spit it out like that, it means you think I've been keeping things from you just cause I'm wilful, and that's not true. I had to be sure of my ground.'

'What is it you're trying to say?'

'That I have a photograph that shows the reflection of Debbie Chalmers's face in a glass in Beames's house on the morning of his murder.'

'You what? What do you mean you have a –'

'It's off a film that came into my possession quite recently. I had the image checked out – Dougie did it – and it's certainly Debbie. And it's certainly that morning as well.'

'But why not tell me, for God's sake? Are you crazy?'

'I don't know, Fabe. See you, you're sharp as a razor. You would want to see the rest of the roll. And the rest of the roll compromises young Tracy, whom you suspect of I don't know what.'

'Tracy shot it? What, in Beames's house? Christ, Armie, I – what do I suspect her of? I never said I did.'

'You did say you did.'

'Why – aye, but so did you,' said Fabe. 'You questioned her.'

'So did you.'

'But what made her give you the pictures? I mean, if they're.... Why do they compromise her? Wait a minute.'

'It's complicated, Fabe,' Armie said. 'She didn't give me the pictures. You're sharp. I can't keep things from you…. She's given me permission to use them. It. The one with Debbie in it. The others are some of Ian.'

'Of course.'

They heard voices beyond the door. 'They're back,' Armie said. 'You ready?'

'You're a piece of work,' Fabe said. 'How'd you get 'em? You tell me. Or I won't show you any respect. Not ever.'

'You already don't.'

'That's just not true.'

The door opened. 'Tell you when we're done here,' said Armie. 'Mrs Chalmers. Everything OK?'

'What do you think?' said Debbie.

She couldn't concentrate after seeing Geoff in such pain, after holding him, wanting to go home with him. He wasn't supposed to be part of this. She could handle it as long as he didn't know.

He'd promised to ring her sister Liz. That would help. He'd do anything he could, she knew that. It'd help him to have things to do.

'Aahh… no,' she said, in answer to Fabe's last question. 'I don't think I did notice him especially. Most folk just go through the checkout and pay and go out and the next one comes along.'

'You don't remember thinking when you read of his murder in the papers….'

'I don't think I did read about it,' said Debbie. 'I heard on the radio, that's how I heard.'

'Wasn't he all over the front page of the *World*?' Armie said. 'And you sell newspapers, pass them over your counter.'

'Well,' she said, 'if he was all over the front I didn't recognise him. I didn't remember him as a customer.' God, she thought, you do ask the weirdest questions, get it over.

'OK,' Armie said. 'Well it can be a shock. Folk that you know getting killed like that. It brings it home…. Come to that, these other victims must've shopped at Safeways.'

'We're not speaking about those,' Charlie said, 'we're speaking about Beames.'

'Beames was a serial killer,' said Fabe. 'Did you know, Debbie?'

'Well I had heard, yes.'

'And this latest guy was a villain, the worst villain for a hundred miles. Ronnie Goudie.'

'He doesn't come into it,' Charlie said. 'Please stick to the point, Mr Finnie.'

'He was a friend of mine,' Armie said.

'Poor you,' said Debbie. 'Let's leave him in peace. Like Charlie says, eh?'

'I'd never thought of him as a friend,' said Armie. 'An enemy, that's how I thought of him. Not a friend. But he was a friend, cause he actually liked me. It's crazy, isn't it?'

'I couldn't agree with you more.'

'Inspector,' said Charlie, 'you have to stick to Beames, you're not questioning Mrs Chalmers about Goudie.'

'No I'm not,' Armie said. 'I wasn't. It's stupid, I know, I just have trouble forgetting it. Him. How I suddenly realised he'd been my friend, but too late, cause there he was dead. Imagine.'

'My husband's waiting for me,' said Debbie.

'Throat cut. Just been speaking with him. I went all wobbly. Sat down plump on a wee sort of hassock next the bed.'

Whoa there. 'Will you please leave off about Goudie?' She'd spoken too quickly: they were watching her. Were they? No change in Finnie's hatchet features, none in Armistead's.

'OK,' said Armie.

* * *

'OK,' said Fabe when the others had gone. 'The photo.'

'Just a minute,' said Armie, 'just wait a minute. What did you think? When I told her about sitting down.'

Fabe scowled. 'She didn't laugh, did she.'

'But it got her.'

'It might've got her.'

'No,' said Armie, 'it definitely did. It's not funny, is it, from her point of view. It's dead serious.'

'Right,' Fabe said, 'it is, she reacted. I'm with you. Better try it on Willy though, before we jump to any conclusions.'

'I have tried it on Willy.'

'And?'

'Nothing, not a sausage. It's her all the way.'

Fabe shrugged elaborately. 'OK, and the photo? You promised.'

'Guin gave me the film,' Armie said. 'She sneaked it from Tracy's while she had their bunch of keys.'

'She gave it to you? Why the hell did she give it to you? What's wrong with me? Why couldn't she just give 'em to me?'

'I don't know, maybe she's shielding Tracy?'

'From what?' Fabe roamed round the interview room, frustrated by the lack of anything to fiddle with. 'From me? I don't get it, why shield anybody from me?'

'I don't know,' Armie said, 'maybe we're just devious. See me, I've got secrets, remember? And Tracy's a bit of an anarchist. She took all those pictures of Ian, didn't she. And Guin really likes her…. Oh Fabe, settle down. It's not what you think. They're women, they're bound to stick together.'

'But Guin,' Fabe said. 'She's…. I, I mean, it's not like that.'

'That's true. It's not like that. You're right.' Armie rose from the table and opened the door to the corridor. 'I'm a bad influence and she was misled. Everything will be fine….' They stepped out into the corridor, looked up and down. The place was dead silent, even though it was only eight-fifteen. 'Everything will be fine,' he said, 'when you've had a chance to talk.'

twenty-two

Once Upon a Time

MEN WERE coming. She heard their breath, rapid breath, and now and again a vocal sound. The smell was strong. One was female. The other she'd smelled before.

She'd taken to sleeping in a bramble thicket, up above the place where men came with engines during the day. Sometimes a dog would pinpoint her hiding-place as it went past, and fuss round the margins for a time; but none had ever come in to her. She waited there for the dog she'd once played with. It was one of his places. A trace of his scent clung to the stones.

The man on the steep rocky path below smelled faintly of her big dog. She lay open-eyed, her nose twitching. The dog wasn't with them. Not this time. But she could wait.

'This is a better way,' Armie gasped as he breasted the top. 'Lots quicker.'

'You'll give yourself a heart attack,' said Susie.

'Well the damn stuff's heavy, isn't it. That's sort of the point of it.' He staggered to a halt. 'Got to put this down a minute. Bloody strap's killing me.'

Susie stood with her own rucksack dangling to the ground, taking some of the weight. 'So where did you see the wolf?'

'Where we're going. Sort of open clearing. Where the tinks used to be, their camp.'

'Are you sweating?' said Susie. 'I bet your tee shirt's wet. Do your jacket up.'

He pulled up the zip. They set off along the plateau. The little wolf tucked her nose beneath her tail and closed her eyes.

'So when I was here last time I looked for the spring,' Armie said as they tramped. 'It's on the map, look.' He produced a folded Ordnance map from a pocket. 'But the time before I didn't.... Here, it's over the fold. I didn't like to poke around cause the beastie would've been frightened.'

'Wolves don't scare.'

'But they should. Everyone's hand is against them.'

'Your hand isn't against them,' Susie said, scanning the map. 'I see what you mean, the spring and the little burn.'

'By there, in the rocks, there's this perfect wee hole. Now I shouldn't talk, should I. Somebody's been watching me, did I tell you? All the time at the other place.'

'If anyone's watching you here,' said Susie, 'it's the wolf.'

* * *

The lady standing at reception said, 'I'm Liz Webster. My sister's been charged with murder....'

'Oh Mrs Webster, that's right,' Wattie said. 'DI Armistead said you might call. Trouble is he seems to have taken it into his head to have Sunday off. I'll give him a ring. He'll come in if I can reach him.'

'I don't want to be a nuisance,' said Liz, 'but I have to get back tonight, my kids....'

'Tell me about it,' said Wattie.

Armie answered from the roundabout on the edge of town. 'It's not clever to drive and talk on the phone,' he remarked, swinging left without signalling. 'See you in a bit.'

He found Liz having tea with Mira at reception. 'Good of you to come, Mrs Webster,' he said. 'Bring it along, we'll go upstairs.' He seized the biscuits in passing.

In the detectives' room he gave Liz a chair, sat down on Fabe's desk and waited while she got herself settled.

'So Mrs Webster,' he said. 'You're her younger sister.'

'Two years younger,' she said. 'A little less actually.'

'You don't look much like her.'

'No,' said Liz, 'naturally enough cause we're both adopted, that's sort of what I wanted to say.'

228

'You're just not related at all.'

'No. No… we're sisters though. We've always been together. That's what makes people sisters, I think.'

'You were adopted young then?'

'Well I know I was. I was seventeen months old. So she'd have had to be, let's see. Two years seventeen months when I came along, and… or a little less. Oh well, I mean you can see she was young.'

'How far back can you remember her?'

'All my life. But I'm glad…. I came from an abusive home, you know? Got knocked about. They say.'

'When you were wee?' said Armie. 'Good God.'

'It happens.'

'That's true, but I can't work out why. I see these things, obviously.'

'Well,' said Liz, 'the thing is, our parents, our adoptive parents, were super, great parents. They're wonderful, wonderful people.'

'You were happy kids,' said Armie.

'I was a happy kid, yes. But Debbie…. The thing is, I think our mum and dad had a thing for abused children. Like you said you wished it wouldn't happen? They'd made up their minds to help make it better. So, Debbie was from a tragic home. I found out. She doesn't know I know, and I've never told a soul, you know, but I have to tell you.' Liz put her teacup down and looked up at Armie, her brown eyes troubled and not at all like Debbie's.

'Tragic?' he said.

'I found out about five years ago actually. Her father killed her mother. He murdered her. I don't know if this has any bearing on this case. I don't know if my sister's guilty…. I don't see how she could possibly cut the throats of all these men. It doesn't seem possible. But….'

'Murdered,' said Armie. 'How old was Debbie then?'

'She was two and a bit. He was her father, not like me. It wasn't my real father who duffed me up. But this was her natural father. His name was Stevens.'

'This is extremely helpful, Mrs Webster. I'd like to look into it.'

'Well she doesn't know about it herself,' said Liz. 'As far as I know. She doesn't remember. So –'

'You don't want me dropping bombshells on her. Poor woman, she's on a serious charge.'

'Did she do it?'

'At this point,' said Armie gently, 'I'd say that it's likely. But I may be mistaken. Time will tell.'

'I can't imagine it, any of it. Debbie.... I know she's been an unhappy person....'

'Has she? She seemed happy with her life, her marriage....'

'Oh yes, lately.' Liz puckered her brows. 'Geoff adores her, oh I can't believe this has happened. They're so.... Scuse me.' Armie handed over the tissue box. 'And she's sweet to my kids. Oh hell. It wasn't always plain sailing....'

'Can you tell me about her? Take your time.'

'We were at the same school,' said Liz, wiping her eyes. 'Mixed school. She was about fourteen, I think, when I noticed she had a lot of boys – she had boyfriend after boyfriend, people had started to talk. And I thought it was weird cause she hadn't, you know, somehow the personality for it. She'd always seemed, I don't know, not shy, but sort of, not humble, either, but... she just didn't make much of herself. And now I know more about people than I did when I was twelve.... I think she suffered from the sort of low self-esteem that's supposed to make you promiscuous. To compensate. Or whatever it is.' She blew her nose. 'Damn it.'

'You studied psychology, Mrs Webster? You're a guidance teacher, am I right?'

'I know, I did, but that's all so open-and-shut.... But I think in her case these patterns might fit. Like, when we weren't quite in our teens, she went through this phase when she had terrible posture. The teacher who took us for games would moan and go on – look at your little sister! she'd say, stands as straight as a wand.... Oh, I didn't, not me! But Debbie.... And she'd slouch along, and then suddenly straighten up. It put inches on her. It's hard to describe.'

'She tucks in her backside and wriggles her shoulders,' Armie said.

'Oh OK, so it's not hard to describe. When you put it that way. It's funny she decided to be a PE teacher herself.'

Sunday afternoon. It seemed ages since they'd had one, the two of them.

'Hell, Guin, I'm sorry. I had to ask. I don't understand….'

'She made a mistake. That's all.'

'I miss you. I miss the way things were. I want you to come and live with me, and I want you back. I mean it.'

'Live with you?' said Guin. 'In the garage?'

'Of course in the garage. Listen, why didn't you trust me? I don't give a damn about Tracy. But you – if you asked me to hush up anything I… almost anything… no, anything. I care about you.'

'Don't you like this flat?' said Guin.

'Oh hell. I'd like a hole in the ground if that was where I could be with you. But since you ask, it's a poxy flat, OK?'

'It sort of sucks,' she said. 'I know what you mean.'

'I want you back,' said Fabe.

'What do you mean you want me back? I was never away. I'm sorry I got you so upset. I hate not telling you things.'

* * *

'The knife, Mrs Chalmers,' Armie said. 'The knife is the same. It's a knife you could buy at the Safeways. You've got some similar.'

He nodded towards the counter by the stove. There were some knives in a block there; when Linda and Fabe had searched the house, they'd found more in a drawer. But none of those could have made the wounds in Beames and Barclay.

'Anyone could've bought it,' said Debbie. But why do I bother? she thought. It went to the seaside. He'll find out. He's let me out on bail and still he hangs around, building a case I suppose it's called. And he'll do it.

'I see Sandy's come home,' she said. 'Is it true that you saved him?'

'I hadn't thought of it in quite that way,' said Armie.

'Why'd he do it?'

'He told me he'd killed Goudie. But he'd have had to do it blind drunk, of course.'

'He said he killed Goudie?'

'That's right.'

'But surely he couldn't.'

'No, he couldn't, you're right.'

'So much for Arlene and her alibi,' Debbie said. 'I mean his alibi. She actually accused him, you know? Of killing Goudie. I heard her. She did. And she gave him this phony alibi. She lied for him. It's amazing.'

'Is it?' said Armie.

'Well it's perjury, isn't it? I thought she'd gone mad.'

'Maybe she had. Cause that's love, isn't it? Kind of crazy. Sandy lied for you.'

'Sandy?'

'When he said he'd killed Goudie.'

'Don't try to trick me, Inspector. I'm not –'

'It isn't a trick. It's the truth,' said Armie. 'The thing is, he's convinced you're the killer.'

'Me?' said Debbie. 'He thinks it was me? No, you're lying. Why would he ever think that?'

'Well he does, Mrs Chalmers. But because he loves you.... You were lovers, weren't you.'

'Poor Sandy.' She covered her face with her hands momentarily. 'Poor Sandy. Poor love. Yes we were.'

'You still care for him?'

'Oh of course I do. I can't help caring for him. He's so – so appealing... those big brown eyes. But I've been trying for months to shake him loose.'

I've got brown eyes myself, Armie thought. 'I wish you'd help me here,' he said. 'Were there other men?'

'Does it matter?'

'In the circumstances I should think it does, Mrs Chalmers.'

Geoff had gone out, left them alone: he'd gone to the shops, where she should be right now passing groceries over the bar-code reader. She sighed. He was fetching a feast for her, making the most of the time they had.

'Geoff is a wonderful man,' she said. 'It's me. I used to think I was having fun and fulfilling my natural appetites. And how could it hurt to do that, and isn't it wrong to bottle things

232

up? But now I think I might've just been lonely. I mean,' she shook her head sharply, 'not now, but when I was a teenager and at college. I mean I definitely was quite wild. Not after I married though. Not at first.'

'Your marriage has been a success,' said Armie.

'It's been heaven. But Geoff goes offshore every month. I used to go clubbing or just out to pubs, pick guys up, one-night stands, no strings. The thing with Sandy is different, totally. That's why I thought we should end it....'

'Were you living a double life? I mean, going out as somebody else?'

'Not then. Sometimes I'd even pick guys up from the store – that's risky. But I didn't look the same going out, hardly anyone would recognise me. People don't very often, even in the street. You have to be wearing your overall.'

'That's true,' Armie said. 'They have to see you in context.'

'Right. So yes, lately there's been other men. It's stupid. It's so stupid. I thought he'd just never find out.'

'But Mrs Chalmers. Some men have been killed. We can link you to these murders, you know. I didn't charge you just to show off. Please tell me the whole story. I know you can.'

'I wanted to tell Liz,' she said. 'Liz was here. But the words wouldn't come.'

She stared past him at the little leaded window, where just now the low morning sun tracked perceptibly across frame after frame. Outside there was ivy; it hung heavy, twinkling with last night's rain.

'I thought of her boys, and I somehow....'

He waited.

'It was Beames,' she said. 'The serial killer. I picked him up at a pub, the Crown. It's in Marchbank.... I think he was trying it out cause he hadn't been living in Marchbank long, and he said it struck him as a town with no pubs. But then he was used to Edinburgh. Anyway... we went on to Hornbridge. Made a night of it. Got a meal, went on to a club. And we walked... got a taxi back into Marchbank and walked all the way from the Cross to St Margaret's Lane. We were going to bed....'

She wasn't seeing the window now. 'We went to bed, obviously. I was.... There was nothing different about him. Nothing. If the room had been dark.... He was going to kill me, you know how I knew? I looked up and saw it. His eyes. His mouth… his *mouth!*'

Armie almost jumped. Debbie shuddered; she turned to him. 'And I saw he'd kill me, there in the bed. I hit him. I hit him with a bottle. It was next to the bed. I'd noticed it when I was taking off my clothes.'

He nodded: that's right, a bottle; it's what you do, go on, go on. 'It broke,' she said. 'His head was back. Like he was out. So I stuck it in him, the glass. He bled….'

As you do, Armie thought.

'And he bled and he bled. And I felt this… I felt this… lightness.'

Time hadn't stopped. The tick of the clock was loud. 'Light. Something lifted. Rose up, let go… came out with the blood. And it washed away.'

She'd stopped speaking. The clock ticked; they looked into one another's eyes and he said, 'It was the moment.'

'It was,' she said.

* * *

Fabe hadn't forgotten that promise of Armie's, to tell him about the well.

'How'd you know?' he asked, Tuesday morning. 'You were going to tell me.'

'Ronnie's diagrams,' said Armie, 'plus Willy. Willy worked up there. It's a matter of buried treasure.'

Fabe's ink-blue eyes betrayed disbelief and longing. 'Oh right, aye, buried treasure.'

'Ronnie was descended from gypsies,' said Armie. 'They have a tradition. There's meant to be buried treasure that one of them hid near here. Now, Willy has second sight, so you'd think he'd have found it. But Ronnie, he'd inherited a map.'

'Oh come on,' said Fabe. 'Six paces from ye olde blasted oak?'

'Worse, really. But you see, Ronnie told me all this. And Willy didn't deny it.'

'So he did go to Ronnie's that night! He was there!'

'He doesn't deny that either. But Fabe, I know he didn't cut Ronnie's throat. I've proved it.'

Fabe snorted. 'Buried treasure. Pieces of eight! A haar, Jim lad! Good God. I don't mind the gypsy – I don't think gypsies live in the real world anyway. But Ronnie?'

Later, Armie got Vanessa's phone call. He wasn't sure where she'd picked up his number; in any case, she wanted to meet.

'It won't work,' Oscar had warned her.

'It will work. Why won't it work? He can't have me telling the world he's taken the treasure.'

'You're mad, queen. I'll come, just don't ask me to…. Where are you meeting him?'

'Where d'you think?' she'd said. 'By the well.'

Half past two. The Shogun was there. Armie walked from the log pile onto the clear-fell, noticed that he was holding his breath: he was listening, that's what it was. His footsteps crunched. A buzzard cried over what was left of the wood.

Vanessa stood in the hollow; Oscar sat nearby on the stump. 'Inspector,' Vanessa said. 'Punctual as the day.'

'What's to do, Mrs Garden?' said Armie.

He saw now that they'd pulled the stump aside, exposing the shaft. 'We've been having a look,' she said. 'Not much point though. I know where the gold is.'

'Good,' said Armie. 'You'll be a bit richer now.'

Oscar rolled his eyes heavenward. Vanessa said, 'You're meant to say what gold. *What* gold, he said innocently. You know?'

'Well,' said Armie, 'I know what gold. So, what's to do?'

'I want it,' she said.

'But you've got it. You said you knew where it was….'

'So I do. I know you've got it.'

Armie blinked. 'No I have not.'

'Then you know where it is. And you've kept it. You told the other police that you'd found a dead body. You took the gold first and hid it for yourself. You tell me where it is, and I'll keep quiet.'

'That the deal?' said Armie.

'You heard. You tell me. Otherwise, you're in deep deep shit, my friend.'

'Oooh,' Armie said, 'I see what you're saying. OK, here's the deal, Mrs Garden. I'll tell you where it is, no problem.'

Vanessa's face lit up. 'Tell me,' she said, 'and make it fast. It's parky out here.'

'It was your idea to come out here,' Armie said. 'Here's our deal. *I'll* tell you the place after *you* go and tell your daughter you're sorry.'

She went chalk-white. 'I don't have a daughter.'

'You do. And a son.'

'I do not have a son. I have no son.'

Oscar was on his feet. 'Here, you,' he said. 'What did you say, what are you saying? You stop it now.'

'Tell her you're sorry you left her to bring up your children, a child of twelve. You go to the showroom on the Hornway, right where it always was. She's there.'

'Vanessa,' said Oscar. 'Your kids, Vanessa.'

'A lot you ever cared!' she shouted.

'And if you'll do that,' Armie said, 'I'll take you to the gold myself.'

She quivered all over, and her face was red. 'He's fine, the boy. He'd be fine, she'd look after him. And Teena, everyone worships Teena.'

'She was murdered,' said Armie.

'Liar!' She grabbed for him suddenly, both hands clutching. But this was routine; he stepped out of range. 'You lying bastard, you liar!' She swung a punch and he ducked.

'Let her alone.' Oscar picked up a branch, landed a blow to his head that made him stagger. 'We're not frightened of you.' But Armie recovered, moved in crouching, brought up his elbow in Oscar's throat. Oscar grunted and flailed. Armie dodged, and his foot went into the well.

As he went over backwards he felt something deep in his thigh let go. Oscar came down on top of him and he stabbed his fingers up at his eyes. He heard a scream, lots of screams.

Fabe had followed him simply because he hadn't said where he was going. It was too much, all this sneaking around. It was ironic when you thought of it. Armie had had that crazy idea that people were shadowing him, and no one was. But now, thought Fabe, it's time. This has to stop.

He tailed him to the lay-by, and slipped past. That brake there, the Shogun, he didn't know, but clearly Armie had gone to a meet. Fabe drove on a while and turned and went back. He set out across the snags of the clear-fell. It must be the well, he thought. Then he heard shouting. He picked up his feet, bounded towards the noise.

He kept catching his toes in the branches and turning his ankles on stones. Once he fell, got up, his hands and knees stinging. When he saw Vanessa he leapt on her and flung her aside and landed a clout on Oscar's ear that brought blood. Then he landed another. Vanessa was kicking him, and he slapped her so hard she sat down on some vicious old brushwood and stayed there.

'God, Armie, are you all right. Oh God, I left it too long.' Fabe panted, bent over, hands on his knees. His knuckles were bleeding.

Oscar stood rubbing his ears. 'You evil sod,' he muttered. His eye looked bad, with a blood-spot coming. 'You can't do this to people.'

'Fabe,' said Armie. 'Fabe man, you're knackered. I'm OK, I've kind of a gammy leg.' He held up a hand. Fabe hauled him to his feet but he groaned and sank back to earth. 'So Mrs G,' he said faintly. 'We don't have a deal?'

* * *

The snow fell. In the mornings small birds hunted among the leaves that lay half-covered, white above, dark beneath. The blackbirds scratched the leaves aside and busily picked up whatever life lurked there.

Tracy listened to the robin whose song was now the only one she heard: a tinkle like ice breaking, curiously sweet. She was walking with Martok in the park by the river, where Guin used to take him each morning before opening up. Since Guin was living over at Fabe's she didn't get in so early. She could have done; but she didn't need to, now.

The snow fell and melted on Tracy's nose. It speckled Martok's fur with white, landed in his ears and made him

237

shake them. He left huge footprints. Tracy thought of the wolf, lying up in the forest with its tail over its nose. A wolf would be happy in snow, if it could find food.

The snow fell and the meadow grew pale, the grasses nodded with caps of white. The little wolf drank at the spring and shook the wet flakes from her coat. She looked out from the shadows. A rabbit hopped and stopped, black against the snow.

Not now. Now it's day. It's time to sleep. It's time to go to the bramble nest. There may be somebody coming today, my big dog might be here today. The days are short. They grow shorter.

She trotted among the cold tree-stems. Snow stifled the forest; but a robin sang with a tinkle like the river, the river of the fishes. From the forest's edge a pheasant shouted. A field-mouse shrilled.

I'm not hungry now. I had deer liver. I want my big dog. I feel him coming.

Snow on her nose, melting. Her tongue lapped across it. She trotted into the morning.

About Liz Laighton

American by birth, Liz Laighton relocated to the British Isles at age 17, and has lived there ever since. She and her husband, a blacksmith turned IT analyst, have lived in England, in Wales, and on a 25 foot boat in the Irish Sea, finally settling in Aberdeenshire, where they reside in a crofter's cottage, with various dogs, cats, and lizards.

Liz Laighton is the author of two previous Marchbank mysteries, as well as numerous short stories and plays. She holds a PhD from Aberdeen University in zoology/animal behavior.